Main Street Merchant

J. C. Penney

MAIN STREET MERCHANT

The Story of the J. C. Penney Company

by NORMAN BEASLEY

Whittlesey House

McGRAW-HILL BOOK COMPANY, INC.

New York · Toronto

MAIN STREET MERCHANT

Copyright, 1948, by NORMAN BEASLEY

SECOND PRINTING

PUBLISHED BY WHITTLESEY HOUSE
A division of the McGraw-Hill Book Company, Inc.
PRINTED IN THE UNITED STATES OF AMERICA

Contents

Introduction

THE STORY between these covers began not so long ago in years but a long time ago in changes of thought and living. In material ways we have come very far indeed since 1902, the year of the opening of the first Penney store in Kemmerer, Wyoming. At the beginning of the century, on this side of the Atlantic, at least, the thought of war troubled no one and yet, since then, we have lived and fought through two. Under their impact we have grown unbelievably great in production and in industry. We have become "greatest" in many things!

It is doubtful, however, if our spiritual growth has kept pace with our material development, for there is abroad in the land a notion that society, or government, should do for us what, individually, we lack the moral stamina to do for ourselves. It is for this reason, chiefly, that I believe the story of the J. C. Penney Company is worth telling and I feel that here it is well told.

In the nearly half century which "Main Street Merchant" covers, America, actually, has not changed much. Individual success stories are as frequent today as when I found and used my opportunity. There is, however, this difference:

More frequently today than a half century ago success comes as the result of group endeavor rather than from the dynamic achievement of a single individual. In that respect I believe that the Penney company was a pioneer. From the very beginning we stressed, and emphasized, as we do today, that the individual can grow, develop and be rewarded only to the degree that he contributes to the growth and development of his fellow workers and of the community in which he lives and has his being.

What is needed today, as always, is an ideal strongly believed in and pursued with single mind.

What is needed today, as always, is the ability and the will to work hard toward the achievement of a goal, any goal, which is right and clean and decent and worthwhile.

In essence, those are the things that built the Penney company. Those same things keep it alive, today.

I hope that young men and women reading this story will be strengthened and encouraged to challenge the cynicism which is the fashionable attitude of the times—strengthened and encouraged to put to the test this formula for successful living: Respect yourself; respect others; work hard and continuously at some worthwhile thing.

This simple formula served me well in the early days and it has continued to serve those thousands of devoted men and women who have followed me in the building of the J. C. Penney Company. It has been their respect for themselves, their respect for others and their singleness of purpose, continuously worked at, that has built this great and growing business.

Building well for themselves they have built well for others.

They have not drained this business dry!

They have left in it more than they have received.

The opportunities which lie ahead for those who are now young in the J. C. Penney Company, or who have yet to join it, are greater by far than at any other time in our history.

Main Street Merchant

ONE

Corn-Country Boy

NOT LONG before he died, the minister went to see the merchant about his son.

"Mr. Hale," said James Cash Penney, the minister, "my boy, Jim, wants to be a storekeeper, so I came over thinking I could talk with you about him."

J. M. Hale, senior partner in the firm of J. M. Hale & Brother, dry goods merchants in Hamilton, Missouri, did not answer the implied question. Instead, he stared at the minister, protesting, "Mr. Penney, whatever brought you out on a day like this? I heard you were sick in bed."

"I have been, Mr. Hale. But last night I got to thinking about my family. I had the children come into the bedroom, and Jim and I talked quite a while. This morning I figured the best thing to do was to see if you would give Jim a job and teach him the business."

Hale hesitated, pursed his lips, then said, "I don't exactly need a new hand, Mr. Penney. February is a dull month— still, I guess if Jimmy wants to come in here, make himself useful, and learn the business, we can find something for him to do. But I can't pay him much, not more than $25 for the rest of the year."

"Jimmy won't mind that, Mr. Hale. I think he will make you a good hand."

"I kind of think he will too, Mr. Penney," said the merchant.

"Thanks, Mr. Hale. I feel better already. When do you want Jim to start?"

"I'll put him on the pay roll starting tomorrow. Let's see, that will be the fourth of February. Have him come in tomorrow morning."

As hard and economically thankless as the lot of country preachers often is, James Cash Penney's lot was even harder and more thankless than most. He was a minister among the Primitive Baptists, a sect which had a rule prohibiting the payment of any money to its preachers.

To support himself and his family, the minister relied on his 390-acre farm, about two and one-half miles outside of Hamilton, Missouri. He bought cattle, grazed them, and sent them to market. He worked hard, for work also was a part of his faith. Money was almost a rarity: debt was a constant guest. A small bituminous coal mine on his property, which he leased out at five-cents-a-ton royalty, did no more than blunt the edge of his persistent fear of privation for his family.

A Kentuckian, James Cash Penney had brought to Missouri an almost passionate fondness for bluegrass. He was so proud of his rolling pastures that when he was out walking he always carried a pocketknife to dig up any weed his eye caught defacing the carpet. He refused to plow any bluegrass for planting, which meant that, while he could graze cattle, he had to buy corn to fatten his stock for market. It was an uneconomical operation, but Penney's love for the waving grass was his only extravagance.

It was on this farm that the boy who chose to become a merchant was born. The day was September 16. The year was 1875.

In that same year the James brothers, Jesse and Frank, were

thieves and killers. . . . These were hard times: a general railroad strike in which freight shipments were suspended on nearly every railroad, locomotives and freight cars destroyed, militia kept under arms in St. Louis, and gunfire in which strikers and soldiers were killed. . . .

With the panic years of the early seventies ended, there was a resurgence of business in the state, and corporations were multiplying so rapidly that there was much resentment against them; and the Governor felt called upon to sound a warning that "all persons, natural or artificial, should have equal privileges before the law." There was talk that department stores, making their appearance in this period, would drive the individual merchant out of business. . . .

Wife beating, woman suffrage, the liquor question—all were persistent subjects claiming public attention. . . . There was a plague of rats, and in 1879 two Missouri counties went bankrupt paying bounties. . . . Rather than get stuck in the mud, Missourians did little traveling in the late fall and early spring; the faculty of Central College at Fayette petitioned against Christmas holidays because of the uncertainty of the students' return. . . . There was a good deal of barter trade. . . .

"Woe be to the preacher in the country or small town who made somebody mad," wrote Frederic Arthur Culmer, Missouri historian, "and woe be to the teacher who got the school community het up over something." Culmer went on to tell how "gangs of young men [would] tramp loudly into a country church during the sermon, sit down for a few minutes, and go out only to repeat the performance."

Horse trading was more than a pastime. "At one funeral I attended," wrote Culmer, "two horse trades were completed outside the church while the service was in progress." . . . And in the smaller communities, such as Hamilton, "There were the house raisings for the young people just starting out in life or for the older people whose houses had burned, corn-shucking contests, contests of all kinds, horse racing, barbecues, moonlights with dancing and all kinds of games in which usually the penalties were kisses. Life was simple and sincere among these Missourians."

This was Missouri when Jim Penney was born. Named after his father, Jim Penney was the seventh of twelve children, six of whom grew to adulthood. The minister wanted his children to have high-school educations; and while Jim was four years old, he placed a heavy mortgage on his farm and made a payment on a house in Hamilton. Now there were two mortgages: one on the farm and one on a little white house under a stand of maple trees in a farming town of about a thousand inhabitants.

Here Jim Penney, eight years old, sat one night trying to study—his thoughts a boy's thoughts, not of school or of lessons, but of recess that day and a jay's nest with four eggs in a cottonwood tree by the creek. His mother's voice broke into his dreaming, reminding him to "quit dawdling" and hurry along with his work before it became so dark that they would have to light the lamp and waste coal oil.

The eight-year-old had just closed his books when his father called, "Jim, come into the study."

The boy got up apprehensively and went in to where his father was waiting. Sitting in his heavy chair by the desk where he wrote his sermons, the minister motioned his son into a chair at his side.

"Jim, you're eight years old now, going on nine."

"Yes, sir."

In the firm but quiet voice he used when he talked about serious things with grownups, his father said, "Jim, from now on you will have to buy your own clothes."

Automatically the boy said, "Yes, sir." Then it occurred to him what his father had decided. His eyes fell on his shoes, on his black cotton stockings, his breeches, his shirt . . . back to his shoes, his only pair and each with a hole in the sole.

Noting the boy's anxiety, the minister inquired, "What is it, Jim?"

"But—but—"

The minister waited.

"But—but—" Then the words rushed out: "But, Pa, these shoes have holes in them, both of them—won't you buy me just one more pair?"

"No, Jim," said his father quietly. "I'm sorry, but you will have to begin now to earn those things for yourself."

Jim Penney had $2.50 he had earned working in the hay field on the farm. With that, he thought, he could buy a pair of shoes. Shoes should last a long time. Before they were worn out, something might turn up so he would have money to buy another pair of breeches besides his Sunday ones and a couple more shirts.

In bed that night he wondered how many errands he would have to run to earn a pair of shoes. "After all," he thought, "I am eight years old, going on nine, and people ought to be willing to pay me to run errands, as much as 2¢ for a long errand, even 5¢, maybe." But 5¢, just for running an errand, was remote; and he went to sleep thinking more about the jay's nest with four eggs. In school the next day he did some arithmetic on his slate and decided that he probably could never find enough errands to run.

He considered gathering scrap and rags and bones for the junkman, but he had tried that before and had got only a few pennies for whatever he was able to find. Just when the whole future seemed pretty hopeless, he remembered how his father bought animals, fattened them, and sent them to market.

He speculated what $2.50 would buy. He knew it would not buy a cow or even a calf, and he did not like chickens. Then, suddenly, he thought about pigs.

"That's it!" he exclaimed. "A pig!"

How to feed it? He would go to the neighbors, gather their garbage, and in return would clean the pails or boxes in which the table leavings were kept. He visited the neighbors, found them glad to accept his proposition, and bought a pig. It cost him exactly $2.50.

The pig grew fat in the pen he built. He sold it at a profit and bought more pigs, and still more pigs until the pen in the backyard held a dozen shoats. He widened his area for the collection of garbage and got additional feed by gleaning the corn rows after the huskers on neighboring farms.

Needing more green stuff for the pigs, he opened a livery stable filled with "stick horses." He painted them red and blue, dappled and gray, brown and white, striped and two-toned, and boyishly gave a name to each. Daily the children of the neighborhood straddled their stick horses and, with one end dragging the ground and tearing up the sod, had thrilling races in a neighboring field. The prizes were pins. Jim Penney's take was the grass and weeds torn up by the galloping hoofs of the "fastest horses in the county." The grass and the weeds he fed to the pigs.

Things were going very well when one night two years later his father again called him into the study.

"Jim, you've got to sell those pigs."

"They're not ready to sell," protested the boy. "They're not fat enough—besides, I was figuring on the money to get some new shoes and new clothes. These I have are pretty seedy. The shoes are falling apart, I've put so many half soles on them."

"Nevertheless, Jim, you've got to sell those pigs tomorrow.

The neighbors have complained to me. I don't know that I blame them. The pigs smell pretty bad."

The next day he sold the pigs for $60, one-half of what he had been anticipating. He was now ten years old, going on eleven.

On his return from the market his father inquired, "What did you do with the money?"

"I put it in the banks."

"Banks?"

"Yes, sir. I put half in one bank and half in the other, so if something happens to one of them, I have money for my clothes and shoes in the other."

Repressing a smile, the minister asked, "Jim, what have you learned out of selling those pigs?"

"I learned that I lost half of what I could have made by selling them ahead of time," the boy answered instantly, great injury in his voice.

James Cash Penney shook his head. "No," he said, "that is not the lesson you should have learned. Think about it again."

"About putting money in two banks?"

"No."

"About having to work for my clothes?"

"No, Jim, no. The pigs smelled bad. The neighbors complained. What does that mean to you?"

"I didn't think they smelled bad."

"Perhaps they didn't, to you. That was because you were making money out of them."

"I would have made more—"

"Just a moment, Jim," interrupted his father. "I am trying to show you that you have to think about your neighbors and about other people in the things you do."

"I did think about the neighbors," argued the boy. "I collected their swill and cleaned their pails and saved them from doing the work."

"You collected their swill and you cleaned pails because you wanted to make money out of your pigs," corrected the minister. "At first, when you only had one or two pigs, that was all right; but when you got a dozen, that made the bargain all one-sided. Don't you see that?"

"You mean I should have given some of the money to the neighbors?"

"No. You worked for the money. It belongs to you. I mean that you have no right to make money if you are taking advantage of other people. Consideration for others is the lesson I want you to learn from having those pigs. Do you see now what I mean?"

Thinking carefully over what his father had said, the boy finally nodded his head, saying, "Yes, Pa, I think I do."

The next day he bought a new suit and a new pair of shoes. He still had money left in Hamilton's two banks.

In the autumn, at wood-buying time, his father looked across the supper table one night and asked, "Jim, how would you like to try your hand at buying the winter's wood?"

"Me?"

"Yes."

"That—that would be fun," stammered the boy, thrilled with the responsibility.

Early the following morning Jim Penney was at the market, looking over farmers' wagons stacked high with cordwood. Having had the chore of sawing and splitting the winter's supply since he was eight years old, he knew a load of straight wood was a better buy than a load of crooked cordwood. Not only was it easier to saw and a lot easier to split, but there was more wood to the cord. He went from wagon to wagon, carefully appraising each load, getting prices, and finally picked out one that seemed to him the best. Hopping up on the wagon seat beside the farmer, he told him where to make the delivery. With the wood unloaded he carefully counted out the money and deposited it in the farmer's outstretched hand.

That evening he was in his front yard when down the street, creaking under a heavy load of cordwood, came a wagon drawn by a team of horses. Jim examined the wood with critical eyes, saw it was straight, and smiled smugly because some of the wood he had bought that morning was already sawed and split and neatly stacked in the woodshed.

As he smiled to himself he heard a voice, "Hey, sonny, suppose your folks want to buy a load of wood?"

"No, sir."

"Very cheap," invited the farmer, quoting a price that startled the boy. "Sure your folks don't want to buy?"

"No," Jim gulped. "I bought some this morning—see, it's back there in the yard."

The farmer clucked at his horses, but before they started he heard an anxious voice, "Why is your wood so cheap, mister?"

"Because, sonny, it's near suppertime, and I want to get home—so does my team."

The boy turned away to hide the tears in his eyes. He knew the difference in price was money his father could ill spare; and, too, he had lost a measure of his boyish conceit. He went inside, found his father, and felt better when, after hearing his confession, his father patted him on the head and said, "Sometimes it takes grownups longer to find out how to buy wood than it has taken you."

Encouraged by his father's words, Jim broached a subject that had been in his mind almost continuously since he had sold his pigs.

"I've still got some money in the bank," he said, "and I

think, Pa, that maybe if you'd sell me one of your horses, I'd pay you cash for it."

"And if I did, what would you do with the horse?" asked his father.

"I'd sell it to someone else."

With serious business like this to discuss, they went outside and sat on the back steps.

"So, you want me to sell you a horse, so you can make a profit on it?"

"Yes, Pa, but I'd keep the horse for a while before I sold it."

"I see," mused his father before adding: "Well, Jim, I'll sell you a horse, but I want you to understand that horse selling, or horse trading, is a game of pretty strict rules. According to the rules, if I'm to sell you a horse, or trade horses with you, I've got to try and beat you. I want you to know that. Do you still want to buy a horse from me?"

"You'd beat me!" gasped Jim, wide-eyed.

"Yes, you or anybody else. I'd give you a horse—no, I wouldn't give you a horse; but if I were to give you a horse, or give a horse to anyone else, I'd tell you, or I'd tell him, all about the animal. But, don't expect me to tell you anything about it if you're trying to trade, or buy, from me. That's the rule, Jim. If there are any blemishes, or if a horse has the heaves, or anything is wrong with it, it's up to you if you're buying or trading to find out those things."

"Maybe I'd better not buy one from you," concluded Jim after several minutes of thought.

"No, I don't think you should. I'd sting you, sure."

"If I see a horse I'd like to buy, will you go with me?"

"No."

"But you know more about horses than I do."

"Yes, I do. But if I went along that wouldn't make you self-reliant. Besides, if you got stung, I wouldn't want to be stung with you."

"I don't think I'll buy a horse," said Jim, doubt in his voice but knowing, even with his doubts, that was what he was going to do.

He bought a mare that walked very prettily and very quietly behind him as he led her down the street, in past the white house under the stand of maple trees, into the barn behind the house, and into a stall. He had no sooner tied her up than she started to kick. She kept kicking for days until he sold her for half of what he had paid. He retired from the horse business.

TWO

Penney's First Job;
Salary: $2.27 a Month

Every Sunday for twenty years James Cash Penney had rid-
den horseback, if the roads were bad, and driven a single-
seated buggy, if the roads were good, from the farm or from
Hamilton to Log Creek church, a distance of fourteen miles.

The white frame church, half hidden in a grove of oak trees,
seated perhaps seventy-five persons. Here his own father had
once preached, and here on this Sunday, James Cash Penney
had driven with his wife and their son, now fourteen years old.
Morning services were ended, dinner supplied by the parish-
ioners had been eaten, and afternoon services were in progress
when the minister again brought up subjects he had mentioned
many times before. Preachers should have special schooling;
it was wrong to choose them from the laity; every church
should have a Sunday school for children; preachers should be
paid.

The same thing happened as at all previous discussions;
some sided with the minister; some with John Thompson,
James Cash Penney's nephew. On this Sunday, Thompson was
especially vehement; he labored to the effect that "If the
church, without those things, was good enough for James Cash
Penney's father, who was my grandfather—and before him, my
great grandfather, who was also a minister of the word of God
according to the Primitive Baptists—it should be good enough
for James Cash Penney."

As the afternoon wore along, tired voices grew bitter, with

Thompson finally getting to his feet and demanding that "my uncle be excommunicated by this congregation until he changes his heretical views."

Before anyone else could answer, James Cash Penney was on his feet. "I have stated my views," he said. "I will not compromise them. Rather than cause any division in this congregation, I will leave now."

As he turned to leave, his wife was beside him, saying to the congregation, "I believe as Jimmy does. You can put me out, too."

Taking her son by the hand, she followed her husband down the aisle and out of the church.

All the fourteen miles back to town, there was silence in the buggy until the minister said simply, "Thank you, Mary Frances, for standing by me." He looked into his wife's eyes and smiled. "We won't go back because it would only start the rumpus all over again. We will go to church in town."

When he was seventeen Jim Penney was graduated from high school. In the previous spring, as a graduating present, his father offered him the use of four acres of land.

"Can I grow anything I want?" inquired the youth.

"Yes."

"And sell it?"

"Yes, and keep whatever money you get."

Jim thought about different crops, decided his best chance was with watermelons and, knowing his father was expert at growing them, began asking questions as to seed, planting, cultivation, spraying, and harvesting.

His father shook his head to all questions. "Jim, I'm willing to answer your questions," he said, "but only on condition that you pay me."

"Pay you?"

"Yes. You will have to pay for what I know because, if you

didn't, you would be getting for nothing what has cost me time and money to learn."

"But I don't know anything about raising watermelons."

"I have given you good ground."

"Yes, but—"

"You want to raise watermelons, don't you?"

"Yes, sir."

"Then go and do it."

The seventeen-year-old went it alone. He was fortunate: the season was good and his crop was good. So were the watermelon crops of other growers. As the season reached its height, average melons sold for a nickel each; the largest and best ones brought a dime apiece.

Jim hired a horse and wagon and peddled his melons around the town. Going from house to house one Saturday morning, he got an idea. This was the big day of the county fair. He headed his horse for the fair grounds and parked as near to the entrance as he could get. He was soon busy handing out melons and taking in money.

"Here they are, folks! Fine big watermelons! Sound and sweet! Watermelons, folks! Big ones for ten cents, good ones for half a dime!"

Shouting and making change at the same time, he saw his father coming along the crowded sidewalk. Jim grinned, waved a greeting, and raised his voice: *Here they are, folks! Fine, big watermelons! Sound. . . .*

His sales talk was interrupted by a hand on his shoulder, spinning him around. He heard a quiet voice: "Better go home, son. Go on—now!"

A deep flush spreading over his face, Jim Penney put down the melon, got back on the wagon seat, slapped the reins against the horse's flanks, and drove off. As the horse jogged down the street, he writhed with embarrassment and resentment; he was particularly hurt that his father should do what he did "before all those people."

The minister came home immediately to find the wagon with its half load of watermelons pulled up in front of the house. Jim was slumped on the seat.

Going up to his son, the minister asked, "Do you know why I sent you home?"

"No, sir."

"The fair is supported by concessions. Does that mean anything to you?"

Jim shook his head.

"So I thought. Well, since the fair is supported by concessions, everyone who sells anything inside the grounds has to pay a fee."

"But I wasn't selling inside the grounds."

"That's just it. Without paying anything toward the support of the fair, you were taking advantage of those who did. Everyone is entitled to earn a living, you and everyone else, but never by taking advantage of others. I spoke of that a long time ago—when you had those pigs. Remember?"

The youth did not answer.

"Do you remember?" asked the minister, sharply.

"Yes, sir."

"All right. Now go along and sell your melons in the proper way."

Jim Penney's parents were strict, particularly his father; but when he was eight and his father told him he would have to earn his clothes, that was not an uncommon practice in the little Missouri community. Frugality and hard work were requirements for parents and children alike. Moreover, the boy only had to earn ten or twelve dollars a year to buy what he needed.

From the time he was tall enough to stand by the churn, Jim

made the family butter; before he was eight he had the twice-daily chore of milking the family cow. Before he was twelve he had learned to plow, the cool, moist earth feeling good under his bare feet. He knew the back-breaking work of manure spreading and the little less racking job of corn gathering, the fun of haying, and the dust of harvesting. Boys and women had to eat last at the harvesters' dinner, and sometimes he got pretty weak waiting, but the weakness always passed when he filled up on chicken and potatoes, pie and cake, and cold milk fresh from the springhouse.

For the most part the Penneys, like other Missouri families, lived off the land, canning its fruit and vegetables, buying flour but making its own bread, slaughtering its own meat, smoking it, and storing it against the winter months.

Practically the only cash that was spent by the household was for clothes—and the clothes were always cut down to the last wearing, then to be sewn into patchwork quilts that became genealogical rewards of the growth and times of the Penney family.

Both James Cash Penney and Mary Frances Penney felt that moral principles were dependent upon religion and that educational discipline was dependent upon schools. There were daily prayers, bringing a spiritual security that more than compensated, as James Cash Penney often said, for the material insecurity that plagued the household. This was hard for Jim Penney to understand; but, boyishly, at the age of twelve, he thought of his father's words as meaning split cordwood stacked high and neat—and what a filled woodshed meant in warmth, indoors on cold winter nights.

His father drilled into him neatness in his work. In the fall, the leaves had to be raked daily from the front lawn; in the summer and spring, the grass had to be cut regularly, the weeds rooted out, and the corners near the fence trimmed with exactness. On the farm, furrows had to be plowed straight, as though a plumb line hung over them. Inside the home, his mother was just as meticulous. Shoes had to be scraped clean of mud before anyone was permitted to enter; pots and pans had to be in place; the beds had to be made early in the morning; and clothes had to be hung on hooks.

Kentuckian by birth and Missourian by adoption, it was in James Cash Penney's blood to follow, without deviation, the rules of horse trading—but that was as far as tampering with his conscience went. As a preacher he abhorred gambling; and one day when he was rummaging through the barn, he found a homemade set of rings, canes, and a plank in which holes had been bored for placement of the canes.

He wasted no time in summoning his twelve-year-old son.

"Do these things belong to you?" he demanded, pointing at his discovery.

"Yes, sir."

"Looks like one of those cane gambling devices I saw at the fair last year. Did you make these things?"

"Yes, sir."

"The canes, the rope rings—everything?"

"Yes, sir."

"What do you do with them?"

"We play with them on rainy days."

"Do you charge the other boys and girls to play with them?"

"Yes, sir. I charge them pins."

"Pins? Who gets the pins?"

"I give them to Ma."

James Cash Penney smashed the rack, broke the canes over his knee, bent his son over the same knee, and delivered a verbal lesson on the evils of gambling, while administering a few hard whacks on the seat of patched breeches.

Yet, although he seemed stern, the minister was proud of his family. He taught his children to magnify every job they did; taught them to make everything they did count for something; taught them that no work is menial; and reminded them of the words of Emerson, "that though the wide universe is full of good, no kernel of nourishing corn can come to him but through his toil bestowed on that plot of ground which is given him to till."

Particularly did he drill these things into his son; for now that Jim was seventeen and a high-school graduate, James Cash Penney was tying knots in the thread of principles he had sewn in a boy's mind.

A preacher and a farmer, he talked to the youth about the Bible and about the soil. He told him, "Everything is in the Book for your spiritual seeking and everything is in the soil for your material seeking. God wants you to be self-reliant. Don't wear out His patience by running to other people with your troubles. Work them out yourself."

"As I remember, that's about what my father said to me," recalled Penney more than fifty years afterward. "He told me that when he let me have those four acres for watermelons he wanted me to see them for what they really were."

"It is land, Jim," he said; "and if you are going to get anything from it, you will have to work. You will have to dig. You will have to plant. You will have to cultivate and you will have to stay up nights watching your melons so boys of the neighborhood will not run off with the best ones. When the melons are ready for market, you will have to gather them and sell them.

"You learned to do those things for yourself. You saved the money you would have had to pay me for showing you. Now you are ahead on both—experience and money. Always remember, Jim, that God will allow for your mistakes and will balance them out of the great goodness of His inexhaustible supply; and all He requires of you is that you meet His minimum terms. Those minimum terms are in a contract called the Golden Rule."

After his expulsion from the ministry James Cash Penney entered politics, becoming a candidate for Congress. He was defeated in 1890 and defeated again in 1892, the year Jim was seventeen. With the votes scarcely counted, the elder Penney announced he would run again in 1894. He was defeated for a third time in 1894.

After the elections he became ill. This was a sickness from which he was sure he would not recover—the sickness during which he called his children to his bedside, one by one, and Jim told him, "I am not cut out to be a farmer; I want to be a storekeeper."

The minister died six weeks after he had talked with J. M. Hale, of J. M. Hale & Brother. He said to his wife on the night before his passing, "Jim will make it. I like the way he has started out."

Had he known how his son was starting out, the minister might not have been so confident.

When he reported for work on the morning of February 4, 1895, Jim Penney was the seventh in a crew of clerks employed by J. M. Hale & Brother. The store was well established. The six other clerks had been in their jobs for years, and, as often happened in those days, the new clerk was subjected to vigorous hazing. Fun was made of his clothes; his salary was ridiculed; he was nicknamed "Mose." The other clerks refused to tell him about the merchandise, refused to help him sell; and when he did have a customer, he was usually called aside and told, "Mr. Hale wants me to handle this customer. He is afraid you will lose the sale, seeing as how you know so little about the store."

After a few weeks of hazing and customer stealing, Penney stopped trying to make sales. To keep busy he began sweeping the floors, cleaning and dusting the stock, filling in the shelves, straightening out the piles of clothing and dry goods. The neatness that his parents had drilled into him over his boyish objections was now a part of his nature; he even carried that neatness to the point of sweeping off the sidewalk outside the store, three and four times a day; and all the time he was doing these things he was studying the merchandise, getting to know it by feel, getting to know where every item in stock was kept.

Occasionally Hale spoke to him, but not often; and Jim began constantly worrying that he would be sacked—until the day came, after nearly two months in the role of chore boy, when he took stock of himself.

"Jim Penney," he told himself, "one of these nights Mr. Hale is going to say to you that you're not worth even the money you're getting, and you're going to be sacked. You're just making a fool of yourself acting this way. Now, be a clerk —or quit."

His head spinning with the resolution, he went to the front of the store, met a customer coming in, waited on her, and became a clerk. At the end of the year, even with his late start, he ranked third in sales.

At the start of the second year, Hale called Jim aside. "Jim, I want to tell you how much pleased I am with your work. At first, I didn't think you were going to make it. You have, and I can tell almost to the day when it happened. It happened one day when you were in the back of the store and you suddenly decided to assert yourself and be a clerk. I had been watching to see if you'd quit, or fight. I am glad you didn't quit. Your salary this coming year will be $200."

Hale began taking a real interest in his new clerk, began teaching him to understand merchandise, to study customers. He often talked to him of the value of good will, that all merchandise should be exactly as represented to the customer; that there was a best way to do everything, whether it was opening a box, sweeping a floor, washing a window, or taking care of the stock. "And, by the way," asked Hale one night, "why do you, even now, go outside and sweep the sidewalk three or four times a day?"

"I guess it's because it makes us look a little tidier," answered Penney.

The third year Hale began paying him on the basis of $300 for the twelve months. He was not yet a senior clerk but he worked long hours and drove himself so hard that before the year was half gone he went to see a doctor.

When he completed an examination, the physician said, "I haven't very good news for you. You've got to quit your job at Hale's."

"I can't—"

"You can, and you've got to. You have to get out in the fresh air. You've got to get out of this climate."

"You mean I have—consumption?" asked Penney, blurting out the dread word.

"Not yet," assured the physician, and repeated, "Not yet, you haven't got it—but you will have it unless you quit working indoors and get out of this Missouri climate."

With his mother and three younger brothers and sisters at home, and with himself as head of the family, so to speak, Penney protested that it was impossible. It did no good.

"My advice to you is to go to Denver. Right away," insisted the doctor. "That will be my advice to your mother, too."

Mother and son talked things over. The farm was doing well. Before he died in the spring of 1894, the family had persuaded James Cash Penney to plow up 225 acres of his bluegrass pastures and plant them to corn. The yield was 18,000 bushels. It was corn that sold for 25¢ a bushel, and most of the money was used to pay on the two mortgages.

During the intervening years, crops had been good. The mortgages had been further reduced. With his mother assuring him that "everything will be all right" and promising, "I will let you know the minute anything goes wrong," Penney went to Hale the next morning, told him of the doctor's findings, and resigned.

A day or two later he was on a train headed west, leaving behind in his mother's care his savings of $300.

THREE

Losing Out in the Meat Business

IT WAS June, 1897. Leaning forward in the red plush seat, Jim Penney looked out of the train window. As far as he could see there were acres of Kansas wheat ripening in the sun. It was his first train ride, and on the seat beside him was a box containing sandwiches, fruit, bread, a whole roast chicken, cake, and other things his mother had prepared for his journey. At one end of the wooden coach there was a round container filled with tepid drinking water.

After hours of wheat fields, the train began crossing the plains, where a dry, hot wind blew almost continuously. As it rattled over bridges spanning dry riverbeds, the temperature within the coach was well over 100 degrees. Except for the fruit his food was unpalatable, as unpalatable as the drinking water. There was one day and one night of constant heat and coal smoke swirling from the engine through the open coach windows before the air began to turn cool and sharp. Finally, from his car window he could see in the distance the peaks of the Rockies.

When he got off the train in Denver, he was captivated by the rugged grandeur of the mountains and stimulated by the thin, clear air. Lugging a heavy grip, he ignored the hacks at the station and started walking toward the business section of the town in search of a dry goods store. He thought of the doctor's admonition to find work outdoors, but the air felt so bracing that he decided to risk it at least temporarily. He called on several stores, ending up at the Joslin Dry Goods Company.

There, as in the other stores, he told of his experience in Hamilton and, as in two of the others, he was offered a job. However, this was his best offer—$6 a week. He took it, then found a home where he could get room and board at $4.50 a week. The next morning he reported for work.

In his new job a few weeks, he was showing a customer some eiderdown when the senior clerk stepped alongside, saying, "I'll wait on the lady."

After the sale was completed and the customer was out of the store, Penney went to the senior clerk: "That was my sale you took."

"What if it was?" laughed his senior.

"Just this," threatened Penney. "Don't ever do that again. If you do I'll thrash you."

Looking down at Penney's 5 feet 8 inches in height and surveying his 135 pounds, the senior clerk laughed loudly and walked away. He did not interfere with any more sales but led the other clerks in intensifying the hazing. In a few weeks Penney began looking for another job, found it, and quit the Joslin Dry Goods Company.

He was in his new job but a few days when, in looking over the stock, he noticed there were two different selling prices on some items. The particular item he was examining was a pair of men's hose.

Taking the socks to the proprietor, he observed, "It looks to me as though there is a mistake on the price marks on these socks."

The proprietor waited.

"One mark says to sell them at one pair for a quarter and the other mark says to sell them at two pairs for a quarter?"

"Your job is to sell socks, not price them," snapped the proprietor. "That price tag means, if you can't get a quarter for a pair, sell them at two pairs for a quarter."

"But that isn't honest!" protested Penney.

"You do as you're told to do."

Putting the socks back in stock, Penney went to the rear of the store, got his hat, and again presented himself to the proprietor. "I want my wages up to now," he demanded, and got them.

While he was looking for another job, he heard of a butchershop for sale in Longmont, a small town about forty miles north of Denver. Having had two bad experiences in the city and not liking Denver because it was too large, he decided that owning a butchershop would be ideal. On the farm in Missouri he had learned a great deal about cattle; and although he knew little about butchering, he thought he could hire a meatcutter so that he could stay out in the open air, buying the livestock.

He went to Longmont, liked the town, looked at the butchershop, and agreed to buy. He wrote his mother telling her of the opportunity and asked her to send his $300 savings he had left behind.

When he received the money, he was in business for himself. The first thing he did was to hire the meatcutter, and the second thing was to paint in his name "J. C. PENNEY" on the front window below the bull's head.

He was doing quite well for a couple of weeks when one day his meatcutter said, "The cook over to the hotel is pretty mad at you."

"Why?" he asked, surprised.

"Because he isn't getting his whisky."

"What whisky?"

"He's supposed to get a bottle of bourbon every week."

"What for?"

"For giving you his trade; and he told me this morning, when I delivered the meat, that unless he gets a bottle this week you will get no more hotel business."

Penney bought the whisky.

Having delivered it, he sat down to reflect on the whole situation. In Kentucky tradition, his grandfather and his great grandfather, although preachers, had each kept a barrel of bourbon in the cellar. His father had broken with that tradition; and the more Penney thought of his father's action, the more determined he became against furnishing whisky to the hotel cook.

The next week he sought out the cook, told him there would be no more whisky, and promptly lost the hotel business. Shortly afterward, he lost the butcher shop and practically all his savings.

In Longmont there was a dry goods and clothing store, owned by T. M. Callahan, which was quite similar to Hale's, in Hamilton. Penney went to Callahan and asked for a job.

"Aren't you the fellow who ran the butchershop?" asked the puzzled Callahan.

"Yes, sir."

"But this is a dry goods store—we don't need a butcher."

"I *was* a butcher," answered Penney, and explained how he got into that business. "I guess," he added ruefully, "that proves I'm not a butcher, but a dry goods man."

Callahan was not too hopeful. "I don't need a steady man," he said, "but one of my clerks is sick. It doesn't look as if he will be back for the holidays; so if you want to come in until he does come back, I can put you on."

The holiday season was over and inventory was being taken when the clerk who had been sick returned to the store. Expecting to be let out, Penney was surprised when Callahan called him into his office and asked, "Jim, how would you like to go over to Wyoming and help my partner in his Evanston store?"

"I'd like that fine," enthused Penney, "if you haven't got anything for me here."

Callahan admitted he would like to keep Penney but explained that he had no need for another clerk in Longmont and added, "But, Guy Johnson needs a man, and I told him I thought you would fill the bill."

During the conversation that followed, Callahan told Penney that Johnson had started working for him as a clerk in the Longmont store, and "he was such a good man that I bought a store in Evanston and put him in there as my partner." Continuing, Callahan confided in Penney his plan of having dry goods stores in different towns in Colorado and Wyoming. It was the first time Penney had ever heard of chain stores. He showed so much interest and asked so many questions that Callahan finally half promised, "You make good with Johnson and maybe some day you will have a store of your own, and we will be your partners."

Penney was so excited over the possibilities that he forgot to ask about salary, nor did he think about it until that night when he was walking home with Berta Hess. He told her of Callahan's half promise and strongly hinted that he was getting toward the age (he was twenty-four) when a man should be thinking about settling down and getting married.

When he arrived in Evanston on March 29, 1899, he learned that his salary would be $50 a month. It was the most money he had ever earned. He figured it was enough on which to marry. He wrote Berta Hess asking her to set the date. On August 24, 1899, they were married in Cheyenne.

The following summer, while Johnson was away buying merchandise, the mayor of Evanston dropped into the store with a proposition. He wanted Penney to open and manage a store in a near-by town. "I'll pay you $100 a month," he offered.

Penney was tempted but told the mayor, "I can't answer you now. Mr. Johnson is away, but when he comes back I will talk with him and let you know."

When Johnson returned and was told of Penney's offer, he said, "I hope you don't take it, Jim, but that decision is up to you. You know that Callahan and myself are thinking about branching out. We are getting closer to it all the time, and if we do it we will need good men to open and manage the stores. I'm not promising anything, but those are our plans. I'd like to have you stay with us but, again, I can't promise you anything right now."

Penney thought it over. He liked Callahan; he liked Johnson. He talked it over with his wife. She advised him to stay. He considered her advice good and went to the mayor with his decision.

Some time afterward, Johnson called Penney into his office. "Jim," he said, "do you remember our talk of a while ago when the mayor wanted to hire you?"

"Yes."

"Callahan and I are opening a new store next spring. We want you to manage it, be a partner in it."

"Thanks, Mr. Johnson, thanks," Penney stammered before he thought of the $10,000 Callahan and Johnston had invested in shoes alone in the Evanston store. Wondering how he would be able to swing such a partnership, he asked, "You mean another store like this one?"

"No, a larger store, in a larger place."

"Where?"

"In Ogden."

"Ogden is pretty big," observed Penney doubtfully.

"You're like Callahan. That's what he said. I told him it was time we were planning big things and to plan big things we have to go to the cities. Ogden is a good spot. It has more than thirty-five thousand people. We should do a rip-roaring business there."

Johnson and Penney went to Ogden, choosing the busiest day, Saturday, for their visit. They patrolled the streets, counted the horses and buggies drawn up to the curbs, studied the people, the store windows, went into the stores, and studied their handling of customers and their stocks. They made many inquiries, learned there were twelve churches in Ogden, eleven hotels, an opera house seating 2,000 persons, five banks, a public library, a brewery, three parks, telephones, electricity, and many schools.

The more enthusiastic Johnson became, the more doubtful Penney acted. Finally in a burst of annoyance Johnson turned to Penney. "Jim, what is the matter with you? You keep throwing cold water on everything I say."

"I don't want to come here, Mr. Johnson."

"Why?" he exclaimed.

"It's too big."

"The bigger the city, the bigger the business," argued Johnson.

"I still don't want to come here."

"Where do you want to go?"

"I'd like to go to Diamondville."

"Have you ever been there?"

"No."

"Then why do you want to go there?"

Penney explained that he had waited on people from Diamondville who traded at the Evanston store. "They're the kind of people I like," he said. "They're ranchers and miners. I feel I know them. These big-city people seem like strangers to me. They come into the store, buy something, go out, and most likely you never see them again. I like to know my customers."

All the way back on the train and again in Evanston, Johnson tried to persuade Penney to change his mind. When Callahan arrived the following week, Johnson told his partner of Penney's objections.

They made a trip to Diamondville and investigated its possibilities. On their return Callahan called Penney aside, "Jim, the woods up there are full of people, but Diamondville is not the place for you. Kemmerer is."

"Kemmerer?" repeated Penney. "Where is Kemmerer? What kind of a place is it?"

"It's a mining town between Diamondville and Frontier. It's a lively little town. Suppose you run up there and look at it."

Later that day Penney told Callahan and Johnson he would take their word for the possibilities of Kemmerer without looking at the town. He did not tell them he wanted to save the fifteen dollars it would have cost to make the trip. In his two or three years in Evanston, his salary had been raised to $90 a month. He had saved $500. It was this fact—the fact that he had only $500—that had prevented him from displaying enthusiasm for a store in Ogden. He knew he would have needed more capital. He did not want to go that far into debt.

In their discussions that day, Penney had the backing of Callahan in choosing Kemmerer; but before returning to Longmont the following day, Callahan had changed his mind.

"I'm not going to send young Penney to Kemmerer," he told Johnson. "It's no place for a young man to start a business, especially for the first time. A merchant friend of mine here in Evanston told me this morning that his three boys had each tried it and all had failed. 'They're just as bright and as willing as Penney,' he told me, 'and they couldn't make the grade.' "

The Evanston merchant's story of his three sons had reminded Callahan that he himself had once sent a young man into a town "like Kemmerer," where he had been an utter failure because of drink and gambling. "Let's drop this Kemmerer idea," he said.

Johnson told Penney of Callahan's concern, but Penney was not impressed. He insisted on Kemmerer and succeeded in winning Johnson to his point of view. Together, they tried to convince Callahan; but Callahan went to Berta Penney with the same objections he had first made to Johnson and then both to Johnson and Penney. Berta Penney listened and said, "If Jim wants to go to Kemmerer or to the top of the mountains, I will go with him."

With his wife's confidence backing him, Penney sat down with the two older merchants to figure out how much capital would be needed to start the new store. Johnson estimated, "six thousand dollars will handle it nicely," and when Penney disclosed he had only $500, the partners told him not to worry. "We will lend you the fifteen hundred dollars you need," they told him.

"At what interest" asked Penney.

"The going rate—8 per cent."

Penney talked with his wife and decided he might do better if he borrowed the money from one of the two banks in Hamilton. He wrote to one, detailed the opportunity, the history of the stores owned by Callahan and Johnson, and his own steadily increasing wages. He pointed out that he had saved $500, was investing it, and was cutting his own salary to $75 a month but would get a third of the profits. He left out no item of information, however small, and posted the letter.

"Did you write to both the banks?" asked his wife.

"No. Just to one. If it turns me down, I'll find out why before I go back at the other bank."

The Hamilton bank did not turn him down. It answered his letter, offering to lend him $1,500 at 6 per cent interest.

When he told Johnson where he had borrowed the money, the merchant inquired, "Why did you go to all that bother?"

"To save 2 per cent," Penney promptly answered. "All it cost me was a postage stamp, and I saved thirty dollars."

FOUR

The Merchant of Kemmerer

Without hesitation Penney decided upon arrival that Kemmerer was his "kind of town."

Lying in the southwest corner of Wyoming, Kemmerer was closer to Utah economically than to Wyoming. Running north and east of the town, the Continental Divide separated it from the remainder of the state, with Salt Lake City, a hundred and fifty-odd miles to the Southwest, being the nearest large community. Kemmerer was in a coal-mining and sheep-raising area. It was also a railroad town, being a refueling station for the tough grind of the high country between the Uinta Mountains and the Rockies where the railroad followed the covered-wagon route of the Oregon trail.

As soon as he got off the train, Penney visited the hardware store. Years before, he had learned that hardware stores were good barometers of community prosperity. Customers of hardware stores were the town builders, the family people, the permanent people in town. Having identified himself to the hardware merchant and explained his visit, Penney soon learned that the town had about one thousand inhabitants but drew business from a wide surrounding territory.

He introduced himself to the blacksmith, talked with him awhile; visited the grocery stores, the drug-store; buttonholed miners and ranchers on the streets, talked with them, and talked most with one miner whom he had served in the Evanston store. From this miner and his son he obtained a promise of the names of 500 other miners. He avoided going to the company store but visited the one bank in town, the First National Bank of Kemmerer.

When he told the bank cashier what he was planning to do, the banker was not optimistic.

"A cash store won't do any business here in Kemmerer," bluntly said the cashier, a man named Frank Pfeiffer.

"Why?"

The cashier hesitated, then said, "Well, Mr. Penney, while I don't like to say what I honestly think, I am going to tell you anyway. You are a young man and I do not want to discourage you, but I honestly think you won't be able to do business here. I don't think you, or anyone else, can do a cash business in Kemmerer. Most of our people are miners. They are paid once a month. Most of them are clean out of money before the month is half over, and some of them seldom ever see any money."

The cashier explained that the mining companies used a coupon system. In large measure these coupons formed the currency of the town, with the stores extending credit against them and turning in the coupons to the companies each month for redemption.

"Even the saloons accept the coupons," Pfeiffer told Penney; "so you can figure from that there ain't much money around to support a cash business. If you want to extend credit and take coupons—well, I guess you can do some business. Otherwise, much as the bank would like to have you for a customer, I'm afraid I can't advise you to open up."

"I have already rented a store," said Penney, quietly.

"Where?"

"That vacant building on Pine street, beyond the triangle."

The cashier was incredulous. "That's no location for a store," he cried.

"I believe, Mr. Pfeiffer," said Penney, "you will be surprised at the amount of business we will do."

"I hope you are right, Mr. Penney. I hope so. I hope so." Pfeiffer drummed his fingers on his desk, then opened a drawer, took out a new bank book, and asked, "What is the name of your firm, Mr. Penney?"

"Johnson, Callahan and Penney. It will be known as 'The Golden Rule Store.'"

Carefully the banker wrote the name in the book, accepted the deposit, and handed the bank book to his new customer.

The store Penney had rented was a jerry-built, wooden building, one and one-half stories in height. The business section of Kemmerer surrounded a triangle; although the townspeople called it a square. Surrounding the triangle, too, was a wooden rail which served as an almost continuous hitching post. Like other western towns in the early nineteen hundreds, cement had replaced the wooden sidewalks in the business section, but the far end of the street, where Penney was located, still had wooden sidewalks. For the most part the business blocks consisted of one-story, one-story-and-a-half, and two-story buildings, generally of wood construction.

The first Penney store consisted of one room on the street level and an attic, with the joists and rafters standing exposed. One small window served as a source of light, while an outside stairway led to the ground. There was no water on the premises. Water, Penney was told, could be obtained from a Chinese restaurant a few doors down the main street. As for the store itself, it was as bare as the attic. Nothing but four walls and a floor. No fixtures, no plumbing—but Penney imagined the store already crowded with customers and saw the attic as a home for his wife, himself, and for a baby one year old. The rent was forty-five dollars a month.

Within the week boxes of merchandise began coming in.

Penney carefully drew out the nails, made counters and shelves out of the boxes, and put out the merchandise—dress goods, clothing, thread, needles, neckties, socks, shoes, overcoats, overalls, something of almost everything in dry goods. He left some of the merchandise inside the opened boxes because there wasn't room on the shelves.

From the empty crates he carefully selected three, one a dry goods box and the others, shoe boxes.

These he took upstairs, upending them—the dry goods box to serve as a table, the shoe boxes as chairs. He had already bought a small, pot-bellied stove to do the double duty of cooking and heating. The stove and one new bed were the extent of his purchases as furnishings for the attic, while to the small window he fastened a rope for pulling up a pail of water borrowed from the restaurant each morning.

Before opening day he had the names of the 500 miners, and as the day approached he mailed fliers to each name on the list, telling the recipients about the new store and the savings they could make by trading there. The day before the opening he distributed handbills all over town—handbills that confirmed the savings, at *cash* prices, he had promised the 500 miners.

At sunrise on Monday, April 14, 1902, in Kemmerer, Wyoming, Penney opened for business.

It was nearly midnight of the same day when the last customer departed. Penney locked the front door and helped his wife, who had been his only clerk, up the outside stairs; he unlocked the attic door, went inside, locked the door again behind him, and lighted a lamp. With his wife sitting on one upended shoe box while he sat on the other, he used the dry goods box for a counting table. Spilling out the pennies, nickels, dimes, quarters, half dollars, silver dollars, and a few paper bills from a paper bag, he sat counting while his wife checked the piles of coins and thumbed through the paper money.

The first day's sales amounted to $466.59.

As he snuffed out the kerosene lamp and got into bed, his wife heard him chuckling, "I wonder what Mr. Pfeiffer down at the bank will say when he sees all this cash money."

The store opened at seven o'clock instead of sunrise on the second day, and seven remained the opening time seven days a week except Sunday, when as a concession to late Saturday night hours the opening time was eight o'clock.

Closing time was whenever the street became deserted. Penney checked every night by going out front and carefully looking up and down the street, each way. If there were no pedestrians, no carriages, and no people on horseback in sight, and if the hour was reasonable for such inactivity—say ten o'clock on any night but Saturday—he blew out the lamps, locked the front door, and climbed the outside stairs.

Obedient to the urge within him to make a success, he considered it a sin if anyone came into the store without being waited on; he considered it a greater sin if anyone went out without making a purchase.

A man named Steele who was a dispatcher for the railroad in Kemmerer came into the store one day in search of medium-weight woolen underwear. Although Penney had none light enough to suit his prospective customer, he was not discouraged. Taking Steele to another counter, he held up some light-weight woolen underwear, saying, "This is just the right weight—of course, it's women's underwear, but who is going to know that when you have it on, except yourself?"

It took Penney twenty minutes to sell Steele the idea of buying the substitute; twenty years later the train dispatcher saw Penney in another town. Walking up to the merchant, he held out his hand and said, "I have always wanted to meet you again, Mr. Penney. After I got home that day and looked at what I had bought, I decided to put it in my trunk as a reminder that a man will buy anything if he listens long enough and the salesman is good enough. Some time later I married. I had quite a job explaining the presence of women's underwear in my trunk."

While not typical, that sale illustrates why Penney was so successful. He kept his store open Sunday because, with the mines working six days a week and the sheep ranchers only able to get into town occasionally, Sunday—next to Saturday —was his busiest day. But, as the son of an old-school Baptist minister, he justified himself by taking refuge in the Biblical injunction about the lawfulness of doing well on the Sabbath.

Penney refused to hire anyone who smoked cigarettes. Liquor was out completely. He hired many clerks that first year in Kemmerer and fired most of them. He soon earned the reputation of being hard on his help. He expected everyone to work as hard as he did. He demanded, when they were not waiting on customers, that they keep busy, cleaning the shelves, dusting the stock, arranging it in place, sweeping the floor inside and the sidewalk outside. "You must keep busy," he told his clerks. "I'm paying you to work, not to be idle."

In his first year in Kemmerer he did a cash business totaling $28,898.11. Because of quick turnover and low operating costs, the profits were gratifying. When the year was ended, he paid his $1,500 loan at the Hamilton bank, had his interest in the store free and clear, had money in the bank, and owed no one.

In that year he proved the confidence Johnson had in him; as for Callahan, Penney had accomplished the impossible. Callahan was so pleased that he told Penney of plans to have fifty stores and offered Penney full management of them. Penney declined, saying he was not ready for such a responsibility.

Penney kept his sales records in a small paper-bound red book that served him not only in that first year in Kemmerer but through the three succeeding years. The book may have cost him 5¢, not any more, and in it he ruled three columns into each page: for the month and day, for shoe sales, and for total sales. He used a code of his own devising to conceal from prying eyes the daily business.

In the book he noted weather conditions and their effect on sales. For illustration, in November, 1904, the weather "all this month and also previous month like summer. No heavy stuff moved, scarcely speaking. No overshoes sold. No snow at all."

In November of the following year: "Quite blustery all month. Miners worked good. Sold quite a few overshoes"; December, it was "very cold. 20° below. Not much snow although ground was covered. Moved lots of overshoes."

As for prices, here is how Penney was advertising in 1903:

Men's sox as cheap as . . . .   2¢ pair
Men's bundle sox from . . . .   5¢ pair up
Men's black or tan 15¢ sellers . . . .   10¢ pair
Men's black or tan 20¢ sellers . . . .   2 pair for 25¢
Men's black or tan 25¢ sellers . . . .   15¢ pair
Men's fancy hose . . . .   15¢ pair

Children's hosiery . . . .   5¢ pair
Children's hosiery regular 15¢ seller . . . .   10¢
Children's hosiery . . . .   2 pair for 25¢
Children's hosiery 25¢ bicycle hose . . . . . .   18¢ pair
Children's hosiery Buster Brown in fine
    rib, coarse rib, any old rib . . . .   18¢ pair
Infants' white and black lace hose . . . . . .   15¢ pair up

Ladies' hose . . . .   up from 4¢
Ladies' hose . . . .   4 pairs for 25¢
Ladies' hose . . . .   3 pairs for 35¢
Ladies' hose . . . .   10¢ pair
Ladies' hose . . . .   2 pairs for 25¢
Ladies' hose . . . .   25¢ pair
Ladies' hose . . . .   35¢ fine gauge im-
                                                                                        ported

We push all the time. Rust never gathers on a sword that is in use. We are not satisfied. We are after more business. We are making prices that will get it.

Men's suspenders	5¢ up
A good suspender	10¢, 18¢, 25¢
50¢ President suspender	35¢
Men's summer underwear	15¢ up
A good garment	25¢
The regular 50¢ kind	37½¢
The 75¢ quality	49¢
Good weight ribbed garment	19¢
Good weight fleeced garment	29¢
Men's cotton flannel drawers	25¢
Men's black and white stripe shirts	19¢
Men's black and white drill stripe shirts	25¢
Men's black and white stripe double front and back worth 50¢	39¢
Men's 75¢ work shirts	49¢
Men's fast colors, reversible collar shirt	25¢
75¢ line of dress shirts, silk fronts, etc., most complete line you ever saw	49¢
Our line of $1 stiff bosom shirts	49¢
$1.25 & $1.50 dress shirts, fancy bosom	98¢
Ladies' sleeveless vests	4¢
Regular 10¢ sellers	7¢
Ladies' long sleeve vests	10¢
Misses' and children's vests and pants	3¢ up
Ladies' muslin pants, tucked	15¢ pair

The biggest and best line you ever saw, 50 per cent cheaper than anyone else.

Ladies' 75¢ muslin gown	49¢
Men's linen collars	5¢ up
Men's celluloid collars	4¢ up
Ladies' sateen petticoats as low as	29¢
Dotted Swiss up from 10¢ per yard	
Plain white dress linen	12½¢ yard up
Ladies' handkerchiefs .... 1¢ each—others, 2 for 5¢, and up to 15¢	
Ladies' china silk waists worth $2	$1.49
Children's headgear	5¢
Boy's Brownie overalls	25¢

Men's waist overalls .... 35¢
Men's Stetson hats $2.75

Notions:
Scissors .... 2¢ and up
Buggy whips .... 5¢ up
Clothesline .... 50 ft, 18¢
Clothespins .... 2¢ per doz
Shaving brushes .... 1¢ and up
Trunks as cheap as $1.98
Telescopes and grips .... 9¢ up
Infants' long slips .... 9¢ up
Men's shoes start at 69¢ and 98¢—$1.49 is a very good shoe, all solid
Miners' heavy shoes .... 98¢ up
White bedspreads .... 49¢ to $1.23
Lace and embroidery .... 2 yds for 1¢ and up

Men's suits from $2.49 up
Boys' suits from 49¢ up
Ladies' dress skirts .... 69¢ up
Men's light balbriggan underwear .... 15¢, 24¢ and 49¢

The average daily wage in Kemmerer in 1903 was about $1.50 a day. Penney and his clerks had to work hard to take in as much as $100 a day, and on their trips to Kemmerer, Callahan and Johnson often heard of Penney's demands on his people. Just as often as they mentioned it, Penney excused his methods by comparing them to "the ruthlessness of nature when a new life is born."

It was true Penney wanted to make money. He was only twenty-seven and had been given no opportunity to forget his boyhood. But, though he wanted to make money, a larger scheme was forming in his mind.

Since Callahan had taken Penney's imagination into the hills with his talk of a whole chain of dry good stores, Penney had thought of little else each night as he took the daily receipts upstairs and counted them on the table that had replaced the upturned dry goods box. (They had chairs in place of the upended shoe boxes; his wife had made and hung curtains for the small window. There were some pictures on the walls to hide the bareness of the joists. A carpet covered the floor.)

Often at night he talked with his wife about his growing reputation of being "money-mad" and stoutly defended his treatment of his clerks by saying, "Money is a by-product of building men as partners. Some day, I am going to have a chain of dry goods stores that will cover these mountain states. The men I hire will have to fit my pattern. They must be anxious to learn and willing to work if they are to qualify as my partners."

"Having a chain of dry goods stores that will cover these mountain states" was an expansive prediction, and Penney recognized it as such the few times he said it. Privately, he confined his thinking to having an interest with Callahan and Johnson in three or four stores, at most half a dozen, and even a half a dozen stores he thought to be far beyond his reach. He was aware of the amount of money needed to satisfy such an ambition—$75,000, he estimated, and told his wife, "That is shooting at the moon." She told him he could do it. He found great encouragement in her words.

With the idea fixed in his mind that the men he hired had to fit his pattern, or get out, Penney expected far more of them than any employer who only wanted to make money. His formula for partnership required that those he hired had to be able, and willing, to do all the things he did as well as he did them, even to sweeping a floor or a sidewalk.

Often he picked up a broom and swept the floor, or the sidewalk, again to prove that the job had not been done well enough. Occasionally he was not able to find any dust; the one who had done the sweeping before him was marked for further attention. If a clerk cut short his lunchtime by a few minutes to hurry back to work, he watched to see if it was a habit. If a clerk's sales showed steady increases, he noted that clerk as a possibility for partnership.

He watched everything, but instead of making things easier for clerks who attracted his favor, he made things more difficult. Working for him was much like running in an obstacle race, with the obstacles becoming progressively harder as the finish line was approached.

In other words, he was a perfectionist. He was intolerant of any effort but the best. The best he rewarded with partnerships. In later life he often repeated what he had told his wife when he began building with men of his own choosing:

"I want men carefully selected and trained, men capable of assuming responsibility, men with indestructible loyalty rooted in confidence in one another, men always prepared to place the interest of a common enterprise above their individual interests. . . . I intend to place such men in charge of tryout stores before taking them into partnership, never to place them under bond, but to trust them completely once they have been chosen, never to permit any difference of opinion or conflict in judgment to prevail over the integrity of the business."

When Penney spoke of "integrity of the business" he meant exactly that. He made it an inflexible rule when he started his store in Kemmerer (and it remains an inflexible rule in the company) that the merchandise offered for sale had to be the best possible value, and had to be sold for less money.

While still in Kemmerer, he went on a buying trip to St. Louis. One of the items on his list was women's cotton stockings. The two top grades were shown to him. They looked alike; they felt the same; but the difference in price was ten cents per dozen pairs. He bought the higher-priced stockings.

"Why, if there was no difference your experienced eyes and fingers could detect, did you buy the more expensive stockings?" he was asked.

Astonishment showed in his face before he answered, "How could I tell a customer the stocking was the best I could buy if I knew otherwise?"

"Would the customer know the difference?"

"I don't think so, but I would. That—the fact that I knew —was the difference."

This was one of the things Penney meant by his use of the word "integrity." The merchandise, whether it was a pair of stockings, a pair of shoes, a blanket, a suit of clothes, a necktie, or anything else, had to be the best in the price range.

That was his pattern. From his employees, nothing was acceptable but their best efforts; for his customers, nothing was acceptable unless it was the best in merchandise. Personally, he did everything he could to see that everything he bought was the best.

His "ledger" was a combination inventory and buying guide. It, too, was a small book, one he could carry in an inside coat pocket. It may have cost him ten cents because, unlike his sales book, it was clothbound and the pages were ruled.

He took it with him on buying trips, and it was an inventory of his stock. Turning the pages, one finds items listed such as these:

Fancy vests: Have none. Need good line.

Toilet soap: Have 19 boxes Cuticura. 5 boxes Pears. Have 3 doz. cakes Cashmere B. Have good stock of toilet soap to sell at 15¢ box. Buy 9¢ and 25¢ boxes.

Bustles and hip forms: Have nothing.

Sleeve protectors: Have only a few. Get something better than 15¢.

Cuff holders: Don't buy any.

Embroidery: Buy a small assortment of embroidery mostly 5, 6, 8⅓, 10 and 12½. Have no insertion at all. Don't buy any corset cover embroidery. Buy a line of Swiss embroidery with insertion. Buy some beading.

Men's silk handkerchiefs: Have good stock of 25¢ silk. Have 6 doz. colored borders 49¢. Have fair assortment 49¢ initials. Need some plain white and black to sell 49¢–69¢ and better.

Men's suits: Buy [sizes indicated] for from $5.90 to $18.50 each.

Arm bands: Have ½ gross sell 10¢, 2 doz. sell plain 24¢. Need everything else. Have no fancy at 25¢.

Men's dress gloves: Have nothing. Buy something in nice dress kid to sell $1.49 or better. Also buy all other kinds.

Miner's caps and *miner's lamps:* Have fair stock.

Playing cards: Don't buy any Bicycle. Need 10¢ kind.

Perfumes: Need everything from 5¢ up to 39¢. Have enough 49¢.

Ladies belts: Have big stock of all kinds and sizes. Might buy some fancy ones to liven up stock.

Fortunately Penney did not have to do too much fretting over the fickleness of styles. His customers did not thumb through the fashion magazines, and the names of Paris dressmakers were not household words in the small Western towns. Cotton dresses, shirtwaists, and suits in light, medium, and dark blue, black, white, and brown, with an occasional plaid, were for purposes of dressing up; kimonos and wrappers were sufficient the rest of the time.

Penney made no attempt to attract the so-called better trade. "My kind of people," he told his clerks and his partners, "are the people who work with their hands." He understood such people whether they were farmers or laborers, anticipated their needs, and supplied them. One day he wrote from his Kemmerer store to a wholesaler, ordering a quantity of women's dresses, and carefully stipulated that he wanted all the dresses made four to six inches longer in front than in back.

Knowing Penney, the wholesaler followed instructions, ordered the dresses from a manufacturer, but queried Penney regarding the unusual request. Promptly the wholesaler received a reply:

"I have a good many customers who are the wives of sheepherders and miners. Frequently these women are pregnant. Now a woman who is pregnant wants to be neat, the same as do women who are not pregnant. She wants a dress to hang even, and that is why I want you to send those dresses according to the specifications I have given you."

In Kemmerer the miners and sheepherders were people to whom the saving of a few cents meant a great deal. To save a few cents for them, Penney first had to save for himself. No piece of wrapping paper was wasted in his store; no length of string, however short, was thrown away. No boxes were thrown away; no nails were tossed aside. Everything possible was saved because he saw small savings not only as the difference between profit and loss in his store but as the seed for other stores. A farmer's son, he thought of dimes and nickels and pennies as he thought of corn and oats and watermelon seeds. To harvest what he was beginning to have in mind, he had to plant, he had to cultivate, and he had to watch.

Dreams he had in that one-room attic, with its pot-bellied stove and its outside stairway, so that, in the following year when Callahan and Johnson came to talk to him about another store, he had worked out a good many things in his own mind.

At about the same time that Penney had gone to Kemmerer, Callahan and Johnson sent another clerk to Rock Springs to operate a similar store.

This clerk was a musician and soon after his arrival in Rock

Springs he joined the town band. It was not long before he was concerning himself more with the band than he was with the store. Unhappy over the situation, Callahan and Johnson asked Penney to become a partner in the Rock Springs venture and supervise its management.

For a time, Penney put up with the musician's habit of absenting himself from the store so that he might attend rehearsals, or closing the store early so that he might play in the band concerts at five dollars a performance. Then he changed managers, putting in one of his own choosing. Soon the store was out of the red and making a reasonable profit.

This was in 1903. The next year, Penney proposed to Callahan and Johnson that they open a third store—in Cumberland. Cumberland was a mining town owned by a coal company which operated its own general store. Hearing what Callahan, Johnson, and Penney were planning, the company informed them they would not be permitted to open a store in the town. They opened one anyway, locating in a building just outside the town limits. The store was an immediate success.

However, prior to this transaction Penney had moved out of the attic into a cottage across the street. With three stores to manage he was away much of the time and was so busy that he saw little of Callahan and Johnson, although always in close touch with them by mail. It was with surprise and concern that he learned in early 1907 they had decided to dissolve their partnership.

They wanted to sell their interest in the Kemmerer, Rock Springs, and Cumberland stores. The price they set was $30,-000. Penney bought them out, giving his note for one year, carrying 8 per cent interest, for the full amount.

"You will have to accept my name on this note as your only guarantee of payment," he told them, as he prepared to sign the paper. "I will not give you a lien on the stock in any of the stores because you know, as well as I do, that to do that would hurt my credit."

Callahan and Johnson accepted those terms. At the age of thirty-two, J. C. Penney, as he now started to sign himself, really was in business for himself.

FIVE

Penney Finds a Partner

WHAT NOW concerned Penney more than anything—even the fact that he owed $30,000—was finding "men capable of assuming responsibility, men with indestructible loyalty rooted in confidence in one another." He was convinced Callahan and Johnson were right to train their clerks to become partners in new stores. He was equally convinced Callahan and Johnson were wrong to award partnerships before fully satisfying themselves as to the capabilities of the men selected, and he thought the former manager of the Rock Springs store illustrated their negligence.

As Penney saw it, a partnership was a two-way opportunity —an opportunity for the one who offered it, an opportunity for the one who received it. He felt, rather than knew, that the worst thing that could happen was to promote men before they were ready; for when this was done, it meant defeat for both the giver and the receiver.

It was this feeling that was behind his determination "to place men in charge of stores before taking them into partnership." He wanted to be sure the load would not be too heavy to carry. He wanted to be sure he was not impairing the integrity of the business. He wanted to be sure he was not taking a bad risk with his own money. He was always in search of the ideal employee who would become the ideal partner.

Unexpectedly, one day in 1907, he found such a man.

In Simpson, Kansas, Earl Corder Sams was restless. Like

Penney, he was a farmer's son who preferred storekeeping to following furrows and harvesting. Leaving high school after two years, Sams had tried storekeeping, bookkeeping, and was back to storekeeping. Now married, and not being satisfied with his job, he wrote the Businessmen's Clearing House Company, an employment agency in Denver.

In his letter Sams told the agency he wanted to locate in the West and inquired if it knew of any openings in any dry goods or men's clothing stores. In reply, the agency stated it had heard of "an opening for a dry goods man with the firm of Johnson, Callahan and Penney, in Kemmerer, Wyoming.

"This store," the agency informed Sams, "is one of a chain of about eight or ten stores through Wyoming and Idaho which is known as the Golden Rule Syndicate. We understand that the opportunities for advancement with them are particularly good, inasmuch as they frequently open up new stores and put some of their salesmen in the position of managers. If you make them a satisfactory man, you would undoubtedly be in line for one of these positions as manager. We have today sent the firm an outline of your experience and qualifications, together with your present address."

The information regarding the chain of stores was wrong although, with Callahan's and Johnson's permission, Penney had continued to call his the "Golden Rule stores"; but, right or wrong, Sams was not impressed. While making up his mind about getting in touch with the firm of "Johnson, Callahan and Penney," he received a letter from Penney.

In this letter Penney first explained that the Golden Rule Syndicate was no longer in operation, and went on to say:

"We are looking for a man who is experienced in all lines of general dry goods, shoes, clothing, hats. He must be a hustler, and not afraid to work. We open at seven, and never get closed till nine or ten o'clock, work half day Sunday. We have a good future for a man who is capable and not afraid of work. You might write us fully regarding your experience, giving us full particulars, also inclose references from those for whom you have worked—your recent employer and those before. We would also ask that you give us letters of reference from the banks in your town. Let us hear from you at once—as it is necessary we secure a good man at once, and as we have other men in view."

In reply Sams answered Penney's questions regarding experience and expressed interest but only if the job Penney had in mind for him had possibilities. Penney wrote again, this time in detail:

"Now, Mr. Sams, we would judge from the tone of your letter that you are an energetic, aspiring young man—looking for a future. There is not a doubt but what there are capable young men in the country who are worthy of better positions than they enjoy and who would make us a good proficient help if we only knew where to find them. Such men as we want are hard to find, we will admit.

"We are not particularly 'cranks' but we have certain principles of business, established lines, or methods we want carried out and we want men who are willing to adapt themselves to our principles, which we know are successful—for they have been proven so. . . . Now if you are the man you should be, in the five years with your present employer, you would have been associated with us in business. I think I wrote you, we didn't believe in hiring men as managers. Since we get capable men and interest them financially, we get better results. These men who are now associated with us are men who worked hard, were interested in our welfare when on wages, men who are not afraid of work, long hours, Sundays, holidays, or anything else.

"I think I wrote you concerning a man we had come from

Junction City, Kansas. We wrote him frankly, as we did you. Yes, he could fill our bill, was an all-around man, had good letters, thought himself capable of earning his $85 a month. But we could not use this man at all. We have a man at $55 a month who is a better man for *us*. He might have been a good man for some people, but we can't imagine who. He couldn't get a move on him—was not active and did not know the first thing about dry goods.

"This is not said in any way of fault finding—merely to show you what is considered a good man for some people may not be any good for other people. This country is a barren country, very little vegetation, and unless a man and his wife as well are strictly business, they might not like it. We want a man who can *wade right* into it—*not timid, a hustler,* one who can push, *show stuff* continually. We haven't any time in our store to read papers, talk, visit, etc., all *business.*

"We want to be satisfied as to a man's integrity, for the man we want must be capable of assuming some responsibility. As for wages, that is a secondary matter with us. We want a man who is a *man;* we realize they are scarce.

"If we get what we want, I would sooner pay you $85 than $75 if you can make it for me.

"I will reiterate what I think I said to you in a previous letter, for I nearly always do to an applicant whom I think is a favorable one, that 'you can have all the rope you want' if you are competent. As for your wife, no doubt if she is competent and experienced, we could use her part and perhaps all the time; that we could see about later, for it's the man we want particularly.

"The young man [who is] in charge of my affairs when I am absent—I am going to start in a store next year. I am satisfied as to his trustworthiness and he is capable of pushing a business. We don't expect a man to know it all. And we don't want a man who thinks he does. This young man is very modest, unassuming, a man we think will improve every day. It doesn't take long for a man to prove himself capable—and soon as he does, we are anxious to put him in business; for he can then make more money than he can working for us.

"I think I have made everything clear. I have tried to be brief as I could, to be candid—making no overdrawn statements which we never do. I could go ahead and 'paint some pictures' for you. I could tell you of the success of the other men with us, but that is useless and unnecessary.

"It's simply a chance for you or anyone else to make good, if you are competent. Willingness is an exceptional requisite. I am sorry distance prevents a personal interview, which might be more satisfactory.

"Now I do not wish to be considered any other way but frank in my correspondence with you. I believe in telling a man the whole thing and not keeping anything from him. I only hope you are the man we are looking for. If you are, you are just as anxious to identify yourself with people of the right sort."

In a postscript, Penney added:

"I want to give you plenty of time to consider this, and I would like to find out all about you I can. Nothing like being open and frank about it. In your next letter, kindly enumerate the nature of your duties, what you are best adapted to, size of stock, am't business done, whether you have complete charge or not."

Having heard from Sams, Penney again wrote:

"Am very anxious to get a man as quickly as possible—I would rather wait a while and get a man that suits me than to get one who does not. I received a very nice letter from the Bush Hat Company, also the Beloit people concerning you, and I only reiterate that if you are the man we are looking for, a man who can *produce results,* this would be the place for you.

We want no man who is not competent and ambitious. In other words, we want 'a live wire.'

"With your experience, and if you have the ability these people say you have—you certainly would climb just as fast as you like—the faster you climb, the better it suits me. One very pleasant thing concerning our methods. there are no restrictions against an ambitious man.

"In some places where I have worked there was 'jealousy' toward me, for I was bound to succeed. But as soon as I studied these people's methods [Johnson and Callahan] and knew that I would be unhampered regarding my advancement, I made a special effort to connect myself with them. Even though I was offered more in other places, I chose this for I knew partly what I was getting into. I am proud to say even my fondest hopes have been more than realized and I wish I was in a position to tell you just what I and others have done. But it is unnecessary and to you might have the appearance of a *boast*.

"I am very glad you are willing to come and see us, for I consider a personal interview far more satisfactory.

"I want a competent man for a permanent place and we wouldn't want you to come out, not knowing what you were coming into, any more than you would want to. You will then see just what is what. I would like for you to make your arrangements to be here not before August 10, as I may not get home before then.

"I am corresponding with another seemingly capable man. I have given you preference. This other party does not like Sunday work. We are looking for a man who is anxious to work any time of day—nights, Sundays, holidays, or any other day. One who *knows* no hours, and not particular about how much work he does. Only this kind of men I consider make rapid advancements. My theory is to make 'hay while the sun shines.' I am young and am anxious to fix myself so in my advanced years I will *have enough* to keep me comfortable and also to provide amply for my wife and children in case of accident to myself. I would be pleased to hear from you again, so I will know what to expect from you."

Sams went to Kemmerer. Arriving on a morning train, he visited the store and was told Penney was not expected until the afternoon. Identifying himself to the clerks, he stayed around the store for an hour, sizing it up. Afterward he said, "It was a pretty junky place, but the stock was well kept. It was clean. The method of display did not impress me, but I wasn't disappointed. Oddly enough, I expected to find just this sort of store."

Having looked over the store and the type of customers, Sams went to the First National Bank of Kemmerer, introduced himself to Pfeiffer, told the cashier of his correspondence with Penney, and requested, "Tell me frankly, Mr. Pfeiffer, what do you think about Mr. Penney?"

The cashier did not answer immediately but under Sams's questioning finally said, "Penney is scrupulously honest, but he is a pretty hard man to work for. He demands long hours, seven days a week, is very exacting in things he requires of his employees, but demands just as much, if not more, from himself."

"Do you think I would get along with him?" inquired Sams.

"I'll answer that question my own way," returned Pfeiffer. "If you are the type of man for Mr. Penney, perhaps you would like to talk to another merchant here in town."

"What do you mean?"

"I mean you might want to consider some other proposition which would be just as good, if not better for you."

Pfeiffer introduced Sams to the merchant he had in mind. Sams was offered the management of a store at a salary of $100 a month. He told the merchant he was interested but could not commit himself without talking with Penney.

Penney returned to Kemmerer in the late afternoon to find Sams in the store, waiting. Repeating what he had said in his correspondence about hard work, long hours, strict attention to business, and making hay while the sun shines, Penney made no promises except to pay Sams $75 a month if he wanted a job, as a clerk.

"Before I can decide about the job, Mr. Penney," said Sams, "I want to recall something you said in one of your letters. You told me I could 'have all the rope I wanted' if I proved myself."

"The more rope you take, Mr. Sams, the better I am going to like it," instantly responded Penney, "but first you have to prove you know what to do with the rope. Do that and you can go as far as you want."

Without mentioning the job at $100 a month that had been offered him that same day, Sams told Penney he would be in Kemmerer a month hence ready for work.

Returning to Simpson, Sams told his employer he had decided to "go with a man named Penney in Kemmerer, Wyoming" and had agreed to be there ready to start work on the first of October. His employer prophesied, "You will not like it," and supported his prophecy by assuring Sams: "Your job will be waiting for you when you come back."

A cold, crisp October-first morning in 1907 found Penney walking up and down on the station platform at Kemmerer. A heavy frost covered the platform, and in it Penney noticed his own impatient footprints—up and down, down and up, up and down, waiting for a train that was late.

Since Sams's visit Penney had thought a great deal about his new employee and was satisfied he had found the man for whom he had been looking since opening his store in 1902. Finally, in the distance he saw a black smudge, heard a long whistle, and stopped his pacing to wait as the train came in. Looking down the train's length, he saw a familiar figure getting down the steps with something in his arms, helping his wife down, and leaning over to release a fox terrier.

Hurrying down the platform Penney came to almost a full stop in a sudden thought, "Have I made a mistake in hiring Sams? Has a man who carries small dogs around with him the stuff in him to make good?"

Doubt, instead of impatience, was in his legs as he advanced to meet Sams, Mrs. Sams, and the fox terrier. The doubt remained throughout Tuesday, the day of Sams's arrival, throughout Wednesday, Thursday, Friday, and Saturday, to disappear Sunday morning when Penney came to the store to find Sams had been waiting since seven o'clock.

Apologizing for having forgotten to tell Sams about the later opening time on Sunday, Penney almost decided there and then to make Sams his "first man." A couple of weeks later, when getting ready for his next trip, Penney did decide to tell Sams about the promotion and added, "When we had our second child, Mrs. Penney wanted to be sure of the milk, so I bought a cow. While I am away, as my first man your job is not only to run the store but to milk the cow. You can milk, can't you?"

"Certainly," chuckled Sams, "unless I have forgotten how."

Before the winter was over, Penney had made up his mind to send out Sams as manager of the store in Cumberland. In telling Sams of his second promotion, Penney made it clear he still was not convinced as to "your ability to carry responsibility alone, but I can't find out until I let you try."

With his wife and fox terrier, Sams went to Cumberland. The store was about the same size as the Kemmerer store, but it lacked an attic. The Samses lived in two rooms in back. Like

Kemmerer it had no conveniences, and they got water from a mountain stream about half a mile away.

Sams and his wife both worked in the store. Their combined salaries amounted to $1,500 a year. Their ambition was to save $1,000. They fell short by $40. At the end of the year Penney invited Sams to become a partner in a store in Eureka, Utah.

With Sams doing well in Eureka, self-government in business, in the vastly important personal and moral sense, was asserting itself more and more in Penney's mind. More than ever he wanted only the best people because the business he visualized could only be run by laws written in the heart and character of the persons he trained and chose for partners. There was a close tie-up in his mind between economics and ethics. To him a just economic environment required a moral bond that was far stronger than any bond supported by money.

A strong moral bond was what brought Penney and Sams close together. Although with Penney only a little longer than a year, Sams was in all his calculations; and Penney was beginning to think, not dream, in terms of twenty-five or more stores and men to manage them and to be his partners.

He worked out a new plan. Briefly, it enabled a store manager who had accumulated sufficient capital out of earnings to finance a one-third ownership in a new store in order to get into business for himself, provided he had trained a new man capable of opening and managing the new link in the chain.

He submitted the plan to Sams, pointing out that they would always have their own trainees as partners, that sending out the head man to operate the new unit meant dividing the two principal people in each store—the manager and the chief clerk, or head man as he was called—into halves so that each half became not only a complete entity in itself but the nucleus of more stores.

Completing his explanation, Penney said, "If you want to

come in with me on it, Mr. Sams, you or I can put up the remaining two-thirds of the money needed to start each new
store. Or, if you don't want to do it singly, we can do it together."

Sams was getting all the rope he wanted.

The Greatest Asset—Men

IN 1906, there were two stores,* with gross sales of $127,-128.36; in 1908, there were four stores, with gross sales of $218,432.35; in 1910, there were fourteen stores, with gross sales of $662,331.16; in 1911, there were twenty-two stores, with gross sales of more than $1,000,000.

All this came about for two specific reasons. In the first place, there was the system itself; it was a system of enlightened selfishness. Each man chosen to be a manager, or a tryout manager, felt himself an owner because he managed without interference; but, to become a partner, he had to help others to succeed.

The second reason was that Penney believed he had no right to be in business unless his customers were able to save money on everything they bought. He had no fancy fixtures; he refrained from expensive locations; aisles were narrow, shelves were crowded, and merchandise consisted of articles for which there was a common demand and one price to all. Paying cash and carrying their purchases represented savings for his customers. In addition, his customers knew that if they were not satisfied they could return the merchandise and get back their money. Important, too, was the fact that he confined his efforts to the smaller communities.

Managers helped the customers feel at home in the unpretentious surroundings. They were men who had been brought

* 1902—Kemmerer, Wyoming. 1904—Cumberland, Wyoming.

up on farms or in small towns. They understood the customers and the customers understood them. That was why Penney was never afraid of the competition of a company-owned store or company coupons. He knew that most of the people in whatever town he chose to enter were interested in the same thing that interested him—saving money.

Returning to the first reason for his success, Penney also realized that, since none of the men he chose for partners was put under bond, any one, or all, could break away from the chain. He was confident none would. Before selecting men for partnership, he tested them until he found in each something that was less precise but more compelling than a surety bond.

"Men of character never break moral bonds," he said to Sams at the time. "I intend to have, as partners, only men of character. That is one of my reasons for working them so hard when they are in the tryout stage, as clerks or as managers. I want to know all about them."

Years afterwards Penney amplified that statement:

"This partnership idea that I learned from Callahan and Johnson appears to be unique in the history of merchandising. Many people find it difficult to grasp, largely, I think, because they find it difficult to believe that hardheaded businessmen would ever let such valuable properties get out of their complete control.

"They do not adequately realize that in a business such as ours the asset which towers above all other assets is not money, not buildings, not land, but *men*. Men inspired by confidence in one another. Men who see their own success in the success of their business associates. Men who are not working for one another but with one another.

"Men who in their relation to their customers and to the public generally are guided by the knowledge that their sins as well as their good deeds will be visited on every other man in the organization."

Penney found two more such men, John I. H. Herbert and George H. Bushnell, but it cost him money.

In 1909, it was customary for each manager of the six stores to go on buying trips twice a year, to New York and to St. Louis. Penney decided he would save time and money by being his own wholesaler and having a warehouse where goods would be available for member stores and from which the merchandise could be shipped on short notice.

He realized that it would be more efficient and economical to have one buyer for all stores and to pass along savings to the customers. Later, he defined the theory in these words: "One of the great economic advantages of the chain store form of business organization is the fact that the chain store makes it possible for one highly trained man to serve as buyer and bookkeeper for twenty stores, and thus cut down overhead costs."

Penney took his idea to his partners. They would have nothing to do with it. They told him they knew their customers and preferred to do their own buying. They were positive no buyer sitting in a central office could understand customer needs in different communities. Penney argued with them, offering them participation. They argued with him, and declined participation. They were independent; they felt so and said so.

Penney decided to go ahead on his own account. In the spring of 1909 he gave up personal management of the Kemmerer store and moved his headquarters to Salt Lake City. There he found a man of good reputation as a general dry goods buyer and set him up in business. Not wanting his partners to feel they were under any obligation, Penney supplied all the capital, established a wholesale business in the name of the buyer, and kept his investment a secret.

However, he did introduce the buyer to his partners and he did ask his partners to cooperate whenever possible. Soon the warehouse he had rented was filled with merchandise, but little moved out into the individual stores. With cooperation between the Golden Rule stores and the warehouse at a minimum, Penney confided his financial interest to Herbert, whom he had hired a year or so previously to do all the auditing for stores in which he had invested. Unwilling to share his problem with his partners for fear of affecting their independence, Penney told Herbert he had decided to liquidate the wholesale business.

"I want an inventory taken," he told Herbert, "and I think I know where I can get a man to help you."

"Who is it?" inquired Herbert.

"A man named Bushnell, George H. Bushnell. I met him in Preston, a couple of years ago."

Bushnell, an accountant, was employed by a farm implement firm in Ogden, Utah. His business often took him to Preston, where Penney had located a store. Bushnell worked late at night and would frequently pass the store on his way to his hotel to find Penney still working.

One night—it was about one o'clock in the morning—Bushnell rapped on the store window. Thinking it was a customer, Penney unlocked the door to hear Bushnell introducing himself, and asking, "You're Mr. Penney, aren't you?"

"Yes."

Bushnell remarked on the similarity of their working hours. Penney invited him inside. It was the first of a number of similar visits, during which Penney explained his partnership idea and during which Penney and Bushnell came to know each other pretty well.

Then, there was another meeting, this one accidental. It was in a railroad station in Pocatello, Idaho. Penney was waiting for a train due to arrive at two o'clock in the morning. Unwilling to spend money for a hotel room for part of the night, he went to the station. It was winter; outside, the thermometer registered forty degrees below zero. Inside the station there was no fire in the round-bellied stove; and Penney was huddled on a bench, his overcoat collar around his ears, when Bushnell came in to wait for the same train.

In reply to Penney's query as to why he had not taken a room in the hotel where he would be warm, Bushnell answered he thought it a waste of money to rent a room for a night and surrender it without getting full value. The merchant was impressed because it indicated a desire to save an employer's money. It was this incident that Penney recalled when he decided Herbert needed help in making an inventory of the merchandise in the Salt Lake City warehouse.

He wrote Bushnell to offer him the job, told him it was an opportunity, said he would pay him $80 a month, and added it would be necessary for Bushnell "to find night work to make ends meet."

Bushnell replied, telling Penney he was getting $175 a month, plus expenses, and much as he appreciated the offer he did not wish to work for less than half as much money as he was getting. Just as promptly as Bushnell had replied, Penney wrote back again, this time offering $90 a month, and closed his letter by asking Bushnell when he would report for work.

Bushnell took that second letter home. He showed it to his wife, agreed with her that it "was ridiculous for Mr. Penney to expect any man to work for him for $85 a month less than he was getting," but told her, "Somehow, I am attracted." He recalled his conversations with Penney after hours in the Preston store, particularly Penney emphasizing, "If a man is not willing to come with me for less money than he is getting, this same man does not have the proper insight into the opportunities offered in our partnership plan."

Bushnell went to see a friend who was a state senator, showed him the two letters, and asked, "Do you know anything about this man Penney?"

The legislator told Bushnell he knew "Guy Johnson intimately, knew Callahan fairly well, and knew *about* Penney." He strongly advised Bushnell to take the job, saying, "If I were you, I would go at any price. Callahan and Johnson were Penney's first partners in the Golden Rule stores. They say he is a hustler."

In Bushnell's words, here is the rest of that story:

"I wrote Mr. Penney that I would try and sell my home, come down there, and take my chances on the future, whatever it might be. When I didn't hear from him as soon as I expected, I went down to Salt Lake City to see him. He was not there. So I went back to Ogden and resigned my position anyway, after having been there nearly eight years. I just pulled up stakes and reported to Salt Lake City.

"I went into the office, a little room, thirty by thirty-five feet or so, with a cement floor, one flat top desk that had been loaned to Mr. Penney by a friend, and one of those old-fashioned standing desks designed to keep bookkeepers awake. 'There is your desk,' Mr. Herbert said, 'just get busy and do whatever is necessary.' He was passing along the only instructions Mr. Penney had given him.

"There were no inkwells or pencils or things of that kind, to say nothing of such a thing as a typewriter. As we absolutely needed them, we would go out and buy penny pencils and a single bottle of ink, a penholder and a nickel's worth of pens.

"Well, as I began looking for a place to live, after I had worked one day, I decided to take off a day. I went out and found a two room apartment for $25 a month. It was handy to the office so I took it, sent word to my family, and had them come down. When I got my first pay check, I found that I had been docked for that day."

Once the inventory was taken, liquidation was simple. The Golden Rule stores never had "sales." When stock did not move, the manager marked down his price and took his loss. Penney did the same with the warehouse merchandise. He told his partners of his investment. Without hesitation they appointed a committee to appraise the dead stock, and on this marked-down basis each manager agreed to take his quota for his store. Penney got rid of the warehouse, the stock, and the buyer.

Although the idea of a central buyer had soured, the idea of a central auditor was established.

When Penney opened his warehouse, he had wanted not only centralized buying but centralized bookkeeping, accounting, and financing; not only for the stores in which he had a personal money interest but for all the stores in the chain. None of the partners knew much about accounting procedures. All knew how to strike a trial balance, to make a statement, and to keep track of their bank accounts; but bookkeeping knowledge was limited to single entry.

Like Penney, most of the managers knew where they stood in individual stores; but they had no system by which they could tell about transactions in all stores in which they were financially involved. For his part, Penney wanted a system of accounting that would give him a consolidated total picture of the business in addition to a current analysis that would show where each store was strong or weak.

With the warehouse out of the way and with two auditors on his pay roll, Penney decided to set up a bookkeeping system for all the stores. That is another story Bushnell told:

"Few people can realize the difficulties John Herbert and I had to meet. We would go to the men in the stores—*They* were *Partners!* We would ask for definite information. We would suggest various things that would help us to keep the records clearly. The managers were very trying. *They* were *Partners!* They were not bookkeepers or accountants. They did not care two raps about accounting. They were interested in selling merchandise and they didn't want any red tape to get between them and their customers.

"It was only by hammering away at them, working anywhere between eighteen and twenty hours a day, year in and year out without any break for a holiday, that we were finally able to get our system to where it was in working order.

"Mr. Penney would come to the office when he was in the city. He would come in at eight o'clock in the morning, go to work on his mail, and at twelve o'clock he would put on his hat. 'Let's go to lunch,' he would say. We would rush across the street to a lunch counter, have a ham and egg sandwich and a cup of coffee or a glass of milk—Mr. Penney never drank coffee. Then we would rush back to the office, being gone barely ten minutes; and then the same hammering away. Along about seven o'clock we would go home for supper, but at eight o'clock we were back on the job again and stayed there until midnight, or later.

"We had absolutely no equipment. Mr. Penney would go over his mail and as he opened his letters he was very careful of the envelopes. He would turn them upside down on his desk, slit them, stack them in a neat pile, and then use the unused parts of the envelopes for memorandums. John Herbert and I worked out a consolidated statement system for the payment of bills of all stores [by this time there were twenty-two stores]; and the record will show that every one of those payments was made out in long hand."

Bushnell opened the bookkeeping system by furnishing for each store a set of books through which daily transactions could be recorded in the central office. Later he added a set of control books for the operating accounts of the stores, thus giving a double check on each transaction. Daily reports were sent to the comptroller's department—later these reports were sent in every ten days.

In 1916, when there were 127 stores in the chain, the banks suggested the desirability of an outside audit by a firm of certified public accountants. Bushnell's records were checked against a complete inventory of all stores. The public accountants went over the records of every single transaction of the stores. They took separate inventories. When they finished, not a single figure of Bushnell's records had to be changed.

Bushnell afterward became the comptroller of the company and its first vice-president. Because of his duties, he had no opportunity to manage a store, train a manager, open another store, and thus become a partner. Mindful of his obligation to his associates, Penney sold Bushnell an interest in the Kemmerer store and gave him opportunities to buy interests in other stores.

But, years before Bushnell became comptroller, many other things happened.

SEVEN

Putting Men in Business for Themselves

AFTER BUYING out Callahan and Johnson in 1907 and finding Earl Corder Sams, Penney really began to think about expansion. In Sams, he recognized he had his counterpart as a worker. Sams was equally determined to succeed; Sams also understood the needs, the habits, and the desires of people.

After Sams had been in Cumberland a year, Penney inquired about his savings and, learning they totaled nearly a thousand dollars, proposed that they open a store in Eureka, Utah, about a hundred miles from Salt Lake City. "I'll put up two-thirds of the money, you put up one-third, and you operate the store," invited Penney.

Excited over the partnership opportunity, Sams listened while Penney talked at length about his ambition to have "twenty-five stores." Referring to the time when, at the end of his first year in Kemmerer, Callahan had offered him the management of "fifty contemplated stores," Penney told Sams he had not accepted because he did not think he was ready for the opportunity.

"Something inside me told me not to do it," Penney confided in Sams. "I have realized since then that the temptation to accept was really a temptation to fail. Had Callahan gone ahead with his projected plans, I would have failed. Despite my showing in Kemmerer, I still had a lot to learn. My first job, learning how to manage a store, was unfinished. I did not realize how unfinished it was until my second and third years in Kemmerer. I discovered then that I was learning more and more about how to operate a second store by operating my first one."

In a quiet voice Penney added, "I am ready now to do what Callahan wanted, had he and Johnson remained in partnership. I have started Mudd in Bingham and Neighbors in Preston. I want you to be the third of my partners."

Penney held nothing back. He was planning to invade Mormon country. He reviewed the warnings he had received that "the Mormons will not trade with Gentiles" and dismissed them with a curt "I know better. I had a good many Mormon customers when I worked for Guy Johnson in Evanston. I have Mormon customers in Kemmerer. They are a fine, industrious people. I know of no more honest and no more God-fearing people anywhere."

"I know better, too," agreed Sams. "I have Mormon customers here in Cumberland. Honest themselves, all they require of a merchant is that he be honest with them."

Penney nodded, and went on to explain the partnership idea he had already put into being with Mudd and Neighbors. The plan, in its barest outline, permitted a manager who had accumulated sufficient capital out of earnings to finance one-third ownership in a store, to get into business for himself, provided he had trained a new man capable of managing and developing a new link in the chain.

"As I see it, Mr. Sams," said Penney, "I cannot succeed in building a chain of stores unless I can find men to help me, and these men cannot succeed unless I reciprocate their help. What I have in mind is this: You and I will own the Eureka store. You train a man there. When he is ready to be sent out to manage another store, I will put up whatever money may be required to finance the starting of that new store."

"How does the man I train become a partner?"

"The same way that a man I train becomes one," answered Penney. "He should save enough money out of his earnings to finance a third of another store, and if not, I will lend him the money. But before he can become a partner he must have trained a man to send out. The important things are to have the man in business for himself and another man trained in management."

"You mean that the man himself must make an investment of one-third of the needed capital?"

"Eventually, yes."

"What happens afterwards?"

"Managers can become partners only by training men to become managers and, eventually, only by making enough money out of earnings to establish themselves."

"I understand that, Mr. Penney—but, suppose I have trained men who are partners in three stores, and the manager in the third store has trained a man and has saved enough to entitle him to become a partner by starting a fourth store—who finances that fourth store?"

"You, the man you have trained who has become a partner, and the man he has in turn trained to meet partnership requirements. Or, if one of you want to drop out of the financing, I will take up the needed one-third." (He made this sort of offer to many groups at the same time.)

Sams thought quite a while before asking, "You mean, Mr. Penney, that you are willing to surrender a financial interest in properties that may be valuable for the sake of developing partners?"

"I don't look at it quite that way, Mr. Sams," returned

Penney. "I think, if we pick the right kind of men and train them the right way, they will all catch the spirit of the partnership idea."

"Yes, but you are still surrendering valuable properties."

"Yes," agreed Penney, "but I will be getting something more valuable. I will be getting men."

"Do you plan to put such men under bond?"

"No. Not if you mean a surety bond. I don't want men who must have halters around their necks to make them do the right thing. You don't need a halter around your neck, Mr. Sams. If you and I are careful enough in picking partners, we will have nothing to worry about on that score."

Sams again was thoughtful. "What you are planning," he finally said, "is an organization that will always be renewing itself from within."

"Yes."

That day in Cumberland Penney and Sams talked a great deal about the plan. They talked while they went to the creek half a mile distant, filled up the barrel with water, and brought it back to the store. They talked, while Mrs. Sams remained on watch inside, sitting out in back where, by turning their heads, they could see the town of Cumberland squatting in the sun—with entrance to it denied them by the mining company. It seemed ludicrous that two men should have their dreams in such surroundings and under such circumstances.

They knew there was nothing comfortable about frontiers; for Utah, Wyoming, and the rest of the high country was still the frontier. Only a little more than half a century before, 143 men, 3 women, and 2 children under the leadership of Brigham Young had broken winter quarters on the Missouri; inching their way, sometimes a few miles a day, once as many as twenty-three and three-quarters miles, they had crossed the plains, the rivers, and the mountains until their covered wagons rolled out of Emigration Canyon into the Valley of the Great Salt Lake.

In the years since, the Valley had been made pleasant and hospitable by the Mormons; but there still were deserts to cross and mountains to climb. Air-conditioned, streamlined trains were not flashing across that route in 1907; no warning beacons gleamed from mountain tops, guiding airplanes to their destinations! no automobiles penetrated the roads to Kemmerer and Cumberland.

These Western frontiers were hard and they were resistant. There was still some *free* land—except that it was not free. Men always had to pay the highest price for land that is *free*. They had to break it and bend it to their wills, and only the hardiest of pioneers was able to succeed.

Having lived in the country, Penney and Sams knew that with all its beauty and grandeur it was harsh and steep. They knew that to succeed in what they were planning they would have to break the trail and survive the first hardships. They knew, without mentioning it to each other, that they would have to be the sort of merchants who put their goods up for sale, but never their principles.

They deliberately decided to avoid the larger communities, choosing instead country towns of a thousand, two thousand or three thousand population. "I'm not ready for the big towns," Penney told Sams. "I know how to run a store of our type—the sort of store that appeals to small-town people. I know how to select merchandise for them. I understand them, and they understand me. I intend to build on that understanding."

Sams opened the Eureka store in 1909. Within a year he recommended to Penney that L. W. Thompson, whom he had trained, be sent out as a tryout manager. He went to a new store in Price, Utah. Succeeding Thompson as head man in Eureka was G. G. Hoag, an experienced dry goods man. Sams trained

Hoag in Penney methods, recommended him; and Hoag was sent to a new store in Provo, Utah, as partner-manager. Penney and Sams were the other partners.

In a community that was 95 per cent Mormon, the Provo store was successful. When Hoag had earned enough money to invest in a store, he recommended a man he had trained. A new store was opened in American Forks, Utah. The partners in this store were Hoag, Sams, and Firmage, the man Hoag had trained. Penney was not a partner, excepting in the sense that the store was a member of the Golden Rule chain. The moral bond in which Penney had high confidence was having its first test.

To indicate how the chain stores were developing, there follows a list of owner-partners of Golden Rule stores in the order of their opening from 1902 to 1912:

Year of Opening	Town	Partners
1902	Kemmerer, Wyoming	J. C. Penney
1904	Cumberland, Wyoming	J. C. Penney
1908	Bingham, Utah	Mudd—Penney
1908	Preston, Idaho	Neighbors—Penney
1909	Eureka, Utah	Sams—Penney
1909	Malad, Idaho	Neighbors—Penney
1910	Midvale, Utah	Mudd—Penney
1910	Murray, Utah	J. C. Penney
1910	Price, Utah	Sams—Penney
1910	Provo, Utah	Hoag—Sams—Penney
1910	Rexburg, Idaho	Woidemann—Neighbors—Penney
1910	St. Anthony, Idaho	Truex—Penney
1910	Bountiful, Utah	Mudd—Penney
1910	Ely, Nevada	Collins—Penney
1911	Mt. Pleasant, Utah	Hicks—Sams—Penney
1911	Lewiston, Idaho	Brown—Neighbors—Penney
1911	Moscow, Idaho	Coffey—Neighbors—Penney
1911	Spanish Forks, Utah	Hoag—Sams—Penney
1911	Richfield, Utah	Malmsten—Mudd—Penney
1911	McGill, Nevada	Collins—Penney

1911	Pendleton, Oregon	Frost—Penney
1911	Walla Walla, Washington	Hyer—Penney
1912	American Forks, Utah	Firmage—Hoag—Sams
1912	Mackay, Idaho	Woidemann—Neighbors—Penney
1912	Trinidad, Colorado	Kendall—Sams—Penney
1912	Richmond, Utah	Neighbors—Penney
1912	Montrose, Colorado	Horn—Mudd—Penney
1912	Gunnison, Utah	Malmsten—Mudd—Penney
1912	Athena, Oregon	Frost—Penney
1912	Dayton, Washington	Hooper—Hyer—Penney
1912	Wenatchee, Washington	Dimmitt—Penney
1912	Aguilar, Colorado	Thompson—Sams—Penney
1912	Grand Junction, Colorado	Joclyn—Mudd—Penney
1912	Great Falls, Montana	J. C. Penney—H. R. Penney

When he insisted that, to become eligible for partnership, a manager had to finance his share from the earnings of his own operation, Penney was applying one of his own yardsticks of good management. He watched closely to see (1) that merchandise was never overpriced; (2) that the manager was buying close to the local demand, hence was not loaded up with inventory; and (3) that the store was taking advantage of all discounts for cash.

Through experience he knew, almost to the dollar, the volume a store should do each year and how much each manager's share of the profits should be. If at the end of the year, or the agreed-upon tryout period, the manager met the figure Penney had in mind and kept a tidy store, that manager was almost certain to be chosen for partnership; if the manager fell below what Penney estimated should be his share of the profits and kept an untidy store, that manager was almost certain to be marked as not being qualified for partnership.

Penney had also learned that good housekeeping was a fundamental of good storekeeping. He never approached a store without looking to see whether the front sidewalk was clean; inside, he looked at the floor, peeked into corners and under the counters to see whether there was any dust; ran his fingers along the under edge of the counters, examined the shelves and the merchandise; dived into the cellars to note the condition of reserve stock and packing cases and particularly to learn whether scraps of paper or string had been tossed behind boxes.

He permitted no waste. The heavier boxes were broken up and used for shelving; the paper and string were set aside for wrapping and tying parcels. He was especially watchful of the manner in which clerks wrapped packages. More than once he pointed out to his salespeople that "every merchant has two chances at a customer—one when the sale is made and the other when the customer opens the package at home."

"Always remember," he told his people, "if an item looks as well when the customer makes an independent inspection at home as it looked during the sale, she will be pleased and will return to buy from you. If it looks less attractive, she will feel cheated and will harbor antagonism not only toward this store but toward every store that bears our name."

Frequently using a shirt to illustrate his point, he would roll it into a tight bundle, wrap it in a piece of paper, tie it up with a piece of string, and instruct a clerk to open it. Then he would take another shirt, lay it flat, wrap it up without mussing the collar. When the clerk opened the second package, the demonstration was convincing. He seldom had to make it more than once.

Once they had attained partnership, Penney had no objections to his associates expanding their store interests through borrowing. He had borrowed money to acquire a partnership with Johnson and Callahan in Kemmerer; and in 1909 he prepared to borrow again to consolidate his holdings in Golden Rule stores and incorporate himself as the J. C. Penney Stores Company.

Having the largest investments and expecting to so continue for an indefinite period, Penney had two purposes in incorporating: One was to protect his associates, as well as himself. The other was to arrange his assets so he could use them as collateral for bank loans.

Penney had formerly borrowed on his personal credit if any of his stores needed money. With his interests widening rapidly, the Salt Lake City banks informed him that legal difficulties prevented them from granting loans against the collateral of store equities held as partnerships. To surmount this difficulty Penney incorporated himself. For the next few years, bank credits so established were used in the interest of all the partners and for all the stores no matter what Penney's personal interest.

By the end of 1910 the partnership idea had taken hold. There were fourteen stores and eight partners. The partners were all small-town and country boys, "some of whom," as Penney wrote, "had made fumbling starts, but who worked hard and caught the fire of an idea.

"The partnership idea was what supplied the spark. We were inspired by the consciousness that we were a fellowship every member of which was dependent upon the energy, integrity, and loyalty of every other member for security and success. We knew that in small towns gossip moved fast and that, unless we served in one town as in another, we all would suffer—unless our personal lives were as exemplary in one place as in another, all would be hurt.

"We realized that the partnership idea, to be effective, had to be carried over into our relations with our customers—that there could be no lasting prosperity for us unless the people of our communities were better off and happier for our being among them. For our part, we were among them to stay. To stay, we had to build upon satisfaction and goodwill."

Here were some Penney prices in 1910:

Children's underwear	7¢ up
Children's wool underwear	25¢
Double fold wool serge	14¢ yard
44" all-wool suitings	49¢ yard
Ladies' 50" brown fancy cloth coats	$2.98
All-wool broadcloth coats, full satin lining, velvet trimmed	$9.90
Cotton sheet blankets	39¢ pair
Wool blankets ... the $4 kind at $2.98, better ones from $3.98 to $7.90	
Men's blanket lined duck coats, corduroy collars	98¢
Men's ties	15¢ and 24¢
Men's heavy cassimere suits	$4.98 to $6.90

To those prices Penney added a postscript: ". . . Buy here and save 20 per cent on your purchases. Look around you! Money doesn't grow on trees."

Eight years after Penney located in Kemmerer, he suggested to his wife that they take a long-postponed wedding trip. "To Europe," he told her. "Let's pack up right after Christmas, and start out."

Like her husband, Berta Penney had gone west on doctor's orders. She had what her doctor called "an asthmatic condition," and the dry air of the mountainous country was recommended. Before she took the sea voyage with her husband and traveled in Europe, a Salt Lake City physician urged a tonsillectomy.

Wanting nothing to interfere with the vacation, Berta Penney had the operation performed while her husband was absent from Salt Lake City on last-minute business. On her way home from the hospital she was caught in a sudden heavy storm. She developed pneumonia, and Penney scarcely reached her side when she died.

After the funeral Penney plunged into work, opened stores in rapid succession, but found no escape from the tragedy. He went to New York on a buying trip, remained there a few weeks, decided against returning to Salt Lake City for a time, and, instead, went to Europe.

The system he had established went on working without him. Upon his return he learned that managers whom he and Sams and his other partners had sent out were ready to become partners on their own account. In 1911 and 1912 twenty additional stores were opened. In all, thirty-four Golden Rule stores now dotted eight Western states—two in Wyoming, thirteen in Utah, seven in Idaho, two in Nevada, two in Oregon, three in Washington, four in Colorado, and one in Montana.

Need for Specialists

RETURNING FROM Europe in 1912, Penney had made up his mind to change the name on the stores from "Golden Rule Store" to "J. C. Penney Store." He had decided to incorporate all the stores into one company and, through the issuance of classified stock, to define and secure the interests of each partner. He was convinced that, although the central buying idea had once turned out badly, it was still the proper thing to do.

He started to persuade his partners, first talking with Sams. He pointed out that being identified as a Golden Rule store was largely meaningless. The slogan was in popular use in all sorts of companies in the West, and Penney was sure no business would be lost through a change in name.

There was no hesitancy in Sams's agreement. From the day of his employment in Kemmerer, Sams had often expressed his disapproval of the name, commenting that to hide behind such an identification was good grounds for suspecting a company's merchandise and ethics, even though both ethics and merchandise might be of the highest grade. Certain partners had to be convinced, but finally the name was changed.

With the business expanding so rapidly that it needed immediate money, Penney went to the banks thinking in terms of incorporation. He was told he had reached the limit of his personal borrowings. "But I have to have the money," he said, "to take care of expansion."

The bankers shook their heads and told him if he wanted to borrow beyond his established credits he would have to adapt his business to the customary corporate form of organization, convert individual holdings into common and preferred stock, and consolidate all assets and all liabilities.

It was Penney's turn to shake his head. "No," he said, "what you are proposing will destroy our greatest asset, our partnership arrangement."

"Well, perhaps," agreed the bankers, "but you're in business to make money aren't you? Isn't that why you want to extend your borrowings, so you can make more money?"

Penney did not give an immediate answer, but when he did answer, it was in words something like this:

"I suppose if I had a financial mind I would think of money as something to be invested in a going concern. I haven't that kind of a mind. I do not criticize those who have. But, as I see business—and certainly as I see our business—money is a tool. It is true I started out with the single idea of making money. Now I see our business as an idea that only produces money as a by-product; the direct result produces men to be my partners. Even at the risk of having no bank credits, I will not change that relationship."

Calling his partners together, Penney told them what the bankers had proposed and what had been his answer. They agreed with him. During the course of the meeting Penney suggested that his partners seek legal counsel of their own to learn if there was any way around the difficulty.

In a few days Sams came to Penney and told him a way had been found. The partners had joined in what the lawyers called a "subrogation agreement." Under it the managers had signed over all their interests in the stores; for most of them it meant everything they owned.

Having explained the action of the partners Sams turned

the documents over to Penney, saying, "Take these, Mr. Penney. Please sign them or do whatever your lawyer thinks is necessary to make them legal."

The J. C. Penney Stores Company was incorporated under the laws of the State of Utah on January 17, 1913. To meet the requirements of Utah laws, 10,000 shares of common stock, face-valued at ten dollars a share, were issued. These shares were nonassessable and carried no dividends. In other words, they were courtesy shares with no particular value. They were all issued to Penney, as trustee.

The preferred stock, which the partners called "classified stock," was issued to the partners in proportion to their store interests, with each store being identified on each stock certificate. The company owned no stock. Dividends were paid against the earnings of each store and distributed according to individual holding in each store.

The directors were authorized to supervise the opening of all new stores or discontinue stores, with the owners of discontinued stores paying the costs of liquidation. The freedom of the partners to train men and to open new stores out of earnings and to participate in the earnings of these stores was not changed. In the main, the partnership idea was not impaired.

With the company incorporated, Penney called all the partners and managers together. Being "country and small-town boys," the partners had some trouble with the formality and routine of corporate matters; but with the help of counsel they maintained the legal procedures, elected officers,* and disposed of other corporate business.

After two days these legalisms were out of the way, and they spent the balance of the week holding the first convention of

---

* President: J. C. Penney; first vice-president: Earl C. Sams; second vice-president: Edward J. Neighbors; third vice-president: Dayton H. Mudd; Secretary and treasurer: John I. H. Herbert. These same officers served as the board of directors.

Penney managers. They discussed individual store problems, initiated managers who during the year had qualified for partnership, and listened while Penney attempted to persuade them into centralized buying, and the training of specialists.

He found it difficult. Sams and other senior partners, following Penney's lead, had moved their headquarters to Salt Lake City. Having spent several years in small towns, mostly mining camps, they were comfortable in Salt Lake City and did not want their comfort disturbed. The senior partners rose against the idea of moving again. The other partners followed suit.

Now thinking in terms of a hundred stores, Penney continued to argue:

"What we must do is train men not only as merchandise buyers, men who have instincts for wholesale buying, but we must train other men who will be expert in the use of credit and trade discounts. After being trained, these men will have to be conveniently located so as to be able to move quickly in taking advantage of manufacturers' overstocks.

"In addition to these two categories of trained men, we must have other men who will have a thorough knowledge of shipping routes, of rail and express tariffs, and the relation of various types of shipping containers to these same tariff and shipping routes. We should have such trained men now, even with our present stores; we must have them if we are to reach one hundred stores."

The whole broad idea was so revolutionary that his partners rejected it flatly. He went back at them, again and again. With figures he demonstrated waste of time and money in their existing operations.

One night shortly after the close of the convention, he asked one of his banker friends to listen to his arguments. The banker, like his partners, was not convinced but realizing

Penney's earnestness said, "You feel pretty strongly about this plan of yours, don't you, Mr. Penney?"

"Yes, I do."

"Then why don't you go ahead with it? You own most of the stock in the company. You can compel your partners to go along."

Penney was horrified. "I couldn't do that," he protested.

"Why?"

"Because they're my partners."

"Even though you are sure you are right and equally sure they are wrong?"

"Yes."

"I don't understand that," shrugged the banker.

Penney smiled. "By the time we finish our discussions—they are still going on, you know—they might prove me wrong. That is one point, but not the most important one. The vital point is that they are my partners. We work not as several, but as one. You should realize that by now."

With his partners almost persuaded to his point of view after weeks of discussion, Penney encountered another obstacle. They were in the midst of a conversation about centralized buying when one of the partners said, "I suppose, Mr. Penney, you would want to locate such a headquarters in Salt Lake City, the way you did before."

"No," replied Penney. "Our buyers would have to be in New York, close to our sources of supply."

Immediately there was a chorus of strenuous objections. The partners were Westerners, small-town Westerners. They knew the ways of the West. That was where ground was familiar, not half explored, where they belonged, where their future was. They wanted no part of New York.

Repeatedly Penney pointed out that New York produced nearly every item they sold and that, unless buyers were located there, they would neither be able to move quickly in making purchases, nor be intimately informed as to trends. The partners remained skeptical but finally agreed to Penney's suggestion that he take Sams to New York on his next buying trip "and let Mr. Sams, when we return, report to you."

Sams and Penney went to New York. In the evening, after calling on manufacturers and wholesalers, and on the way to and from the plants and offices, they talked about Penney's plan. Sams finally became convinced as to the need for specialists in different phases of chain store operations but remained unconvinced as to the wisdom of centralizing buying in New York.

Near the end of their trip Penney and Sams left their hotel one evening and walked down Madison Avenue. As usual, they were discussing the matter of immediate importance. After several blocks they reached Madison Square where they traced and retraced their steps as they walked around one of New York's best known landmarks. Finally Sams stopped, broke into Penney's arguments by putting his hand on his partner's shoulder, and asked, "Mr. Penney, are you sure of your judgment? Are you still convinced that we ought to move our headquarters to New York?"

"I am sure," answered Penney.

"Then I will come down here." Sams paused, and with his hand still on Penney's shoulder, added, "Now about the men you want to train as expert buyers. You said in Salt Lake City, and you repeated it tonight, that for the time being they would have to be developed from the ranks of the managers themselves."

"Yes. I made a mistake when I set up that warehouse in Salt Lake City. I brought in a man from the outside to be buyer, and to run it. I should have selected one of our own people. He and the managers would have understood each other better."

Walking back up Madison Avenue to their hotel and in their room afterward, Penney and Sams made their plans. Together they would select and train the men. Penney was convinced that, having selected the men, the training in buying would not take long.

When he was with Johnson and Callahan, those partners had taken him on buying trips; and it was on one of these trips to New York that Callahan had predicted, "Jim, you will never be a big merchant."

Johnson, Callahan, and Penney had been in a warehouse looking at piece goods, and Penney had asked for samples. That night he was vigorously scrubbing them in a lather of soapy water in a washbasin when Callahan came into his hotel room.

Stopping just inside the door, Callahan cried in an astonished voice, "Jim, what in the world are you doing there?"

"I'm washing these samples, Mr. Callahan, to see if the colors in them are fast."

With disappointment on his face, Callahan looked at the samples Penney had pinned against the curtains to dry, walked across the room, and stared into the washbasin. Then, shaking his head, he informed Penney of his future as a merchant. With the gloomy prediction off his tongue, he asked, "Why are you doing that?" and motioned to the still limp samples against the curtains.

"Just as I told you, Mr. Callahan—to see if the colors are fast. How can I tell my customers they are unless I know?"

"The wholesaler told us they were. I asked that very question. Didn't you hear me?"

"I did, but I wanted to know for myself. I want my customers to be able to trust what I say. I've got to know before I can tell them."

Carrying on in the Johnson and Callahan pattern, Penney continued taking managers with him to market. On buying trips they always worked together on the same lines, but each went to different suppliers. At night, after returning to their hotel, they compared notes. With this information before them, they placed their combined orders with the supplier who quoted the lowest price, all other requirements being equal.

In this way they were able to make noticeable savings, even in so small an item as pins. They began buying black pins from one wholesaler and white pins from another. "This may seem like a very small matter," said Penney long afterward, "but it is the small discriminations that distinguish the good buyer from the poor buyer. They not only have a bearing on the retail price but they indicate a merchant who is aware of the fact that his first duty is to act as a representative of his customer."

In the New York hotel room with Sams, Penney's imagination reached out that night beyond a hundred stores to double that number. Penney recalled that "in 1907 there were two, now in 1913 there are forty-eight" and predicted "it will take us less time to reach the two hundred mark, after we have one hundred, than it will to reach one hundred."

With their buying completed, they returned to Salt Lake City. As expected, the other partners accepted the decision.

However, it was agreed that Sams should remain in Salt Lake City for the time being while Penney was to return to New York. Mindful of his losses on his first experiment in central buying, where on his own account he had stocked a warehouse and footed the bills, Penney decided to start more slowly.

Choosing an assistant from the ranks, he took the trainee to New York at his own expense and paid him out of his own funds. The partners objected, but Penney insisted, maintaining it was pick-and-shovel work he was undertaking and, as such, should not be charged against the company. In New York he supplied desk room in his office for his assistant and, together, they began organizing Penney's knowledge of markets and buying.

In 1914 the company took over the operation. Sams and two more men came to help. Thus the foundation was set for what would be within a few years the buying headquarters for the J. C. Penney Company.

NINE

Original Body of Doctrine

IN BUSINESS for himself twelve years although he was not yet forty, Penney was beginning to think about his successor as president. The action of his partners in turning over their store interests to his keeping so that he might extend his bank borrowings had affected him deeply. He felt that his original aims had been accomplished and was satisfied that his company was a genuine association of friends. He said nothing to Sams but decided that when the New York central buying headquarters was operating satisfactorily, he would step aside.

In twelve years, he and his partners had broken the hold of company stores on a good many towns in the West. First in Kemmerer, then in Cumberland, and afterward in other towns, his stores had forced mining companies to furnish better merchandise for less money, or go out of the retail business. That job was not easy; but with his partners he had bested the powerful local competitors by again proving that the business mind is not solely concerned with money.

The business mind starts instead with an idea, a willingness to put an idea to work, and a desire to keep it working. Saving is part of the job of keeping it working. Penney had to save to stay in business. A sheet of wrapping paper and a piece of string were the things that wrapped a package. A package represented a sale.

Years afterward, when Penney and Sams were reminiscing with George Albert Smith, president of the Latter Day Saints, about earlier days in Wyoming and Utah, Penney recalled, a little apologetically, "saving every piece of paper and every piece of string that came into the stores."

"We still do," smiled the Mormon leader, and Penney felt better about his frugality.

By 1914, he had also elevated the rule-of-thumb practices he had adopted in Kemmerer into what his partners were calling "The Original Body of Doctrine." Wording unchanged, the doctrine is now called "Penney Principles." These principles are:

"1. To serve the public, as nearly as we can, to its complete satisfaction.

"2. To offer the best possible dollar's worth of quality and value.

"3. To strive constantly for a high level of intelligent and helpful service.

"4. To charge a fair profit for what we offer—and not all the traffic will bear.

"5. To apply this test to everything we do: "Does it square with what is right and just?"

Penney had long and frequent conversations with his partners about "what is right and just." They never lost sight of the elementary fact that without customers they could not remain in business. They looked upon their customers as their *real* board of directors. They realized that the success of their stores and the security of their own jobs were decisions completely within the keeping of the public.

"We must never forget," Penney always told a new partner, "that you, and I, as two partners among many, are on trial every day, the minute we open our doors. There will be occasions when you will be tempted, as we all are tempted, to deviate from the principles to which you, as a new partner, have subscribed. Any surrender by you, however slight, is a surrender of some part of yourself, just as any surrender, however slight, by anyone of the older partners is a surrender of some part of himself. It is a surrender that will hurt not just the one who weakens, but everyone."

There were many occasions when Penney (through his knowledge of markets and customers) had opportunities to buy items that were almost certain to be in extreme demand. Such occasions were opportunities for "making killings" by lifting prices just a little beyond what had been established as a fair profit. The partners refrained from such practices. They looked upon themselves as the personal representatives of their customers in whatever purchases they made.

Thinking as merchants, Penney and his partners saw a store as a place where a town and a countryside could buy needed items. As storekeepers, they interpreted the collective job as being one of continuing service. To sell at the lowest possible prices, they had to work; they had to save; they had to turn over stocks from four to eight times a year. They had to ask their customers to pay cash and to carry their purchases. In advertising this customer-cooperation, Penney said:

"Let us assure you in the frankest possible manner that you greatly assist us in giving you the service we seek to give.

"You are always willing to carry your purchases home with you. That may not always be a pleasant thing for you to do, but it helps to keep down the overhead expense that would be necessary if you obliged us to maintain a delivery system. The fact that we do not have to hire extra men and keep an automobile for that purpose permits us to keep the expense of doing business down to the minimum. We give you the benefit which rightly belongs to you because you carry your own purchases home with you.

"We have no business, nor has any other mortal man, to charge you for a service we do not give you. To keep down prices and to play the game squarely with all our customers is our policy.

"Then, too, another element that works in your favor is this: You pay cash for all you buy at our stores. We have no charge accounts. That fact enables us to save the expense of a bookkeeper in each store. Consequently, we have no loss on bad accounts; and most of all it enables us to pay CASH for our merchandise which means thousands of dollars saved in cash discounts. All this makes it possible for us to know every night just where we stand in the business world—we have the goods in our store or the cash in our bank. And you are the direct beneficiary along with us of all these money-saving factors which we employ in our business.

"When you fully consider the things we are telling you, you will readily understand how it is that we are able to do the great volume of business we do at the prices quoted. And in the final analysis, you actually receive the benefits of a partner in our business. Your profits may not—do not—come in the manner of annual dividends but they nonetheless come to you—handed to you in every purchase you make."

In 1918, Penney stores were advertising:

STAPLES

American print calicos	6¢ yard
Apron ginghams	9¢ yard
Dress ginghams	12½¢ yard
Cheviot shirtings	15¢ yard
English longcloth	10¢ and 12½¢ yard

MUSLIN UNDERWEAR

Combination suits	49¢ and 98¢
Princess slips	49¢ and 98¢
Extra quality gowns	79¢ and 98¢
Corset covers from	25¢ to 49¢
Brassieres, good ones	25¢
Brassieres, handsome ones	49¢
Women's better sateen petticoat	98¢

HOUSE LINENS

Turkish towels, per pair	19¢
Turkish towels, better ones, per pair .	25¢
Extra large Turkish towels, heavy ones	39¢ and 49¢
Dandy 45 x 36 pillow cases, each	12½¢
Better ones, each	15¢
Special sheets .... 72 x 90	49¢
A dandy sheet .....72 x 90	69¢
Victoria .... 81 x 90	89¢
Extra quality linen	79¢
Better quality hemmed bedspreads ..	$1.25

DRESS GOODS

Storm serges, all colors	59¢ to 89¢
French serges	79¢ to 98¢
Crepe de chine, 40 inch	$1.25

LADIES' SUITS

We carry nothing but the newest styles, and will have suits from $9.90 to $25.00

NEW SPRING COATS

We have the latest New York styles. $4.98 to $18.50

NEW DRESSES

In silk poplins, taffeta and serges $4.98 to $12.50

CHILDREN'S DRESSES

Fancy trimmed in dress gingham ...... 49¢, 69¢ and 98¢

LADIES' HAND BAGS

25¢, 49¢, 69¢, 89¢, 98¢, to $1.49

KIMONOS

Made from crepe .... 98¢ to $1.98

LADIES' WAISTS

Jap silk waists $1.98

MEN'S SUITS

We carry blue serges and fancy mix-
tures .... $9.90 **to** $18.50

SUIT CASES AND BAGS

Matting suitcase .... 98¢
Leather case, with straps $3.98
Cowhide case $6.90

MEN'S HEAVY DENIM BIB OVERALLS, GENUINE INDIGO BLUE
.... Pants, 98¢; jackets, 98¢

BOYS' OVERALLS .... 49¢ to 69¢

MEN'S WORK SHIRTS .... 45¢

Penney felt that merchandise should be sold at the lowest possible price, every day. He was opposed to "special sales," under whatever name; opposed to them because he believed they were "nothing but a storekeeper's remedy for curing his own mistakes, with the customer paying the bill." In training his people to be merchants he dwelt on this subject a great deal, telling them:

"There are two ways to buy for a store. One way is to guess what your needs will be, and buy accordingly. If you guess too low, you will run out of merchandise and you will lose customers. If you guess too high, you will have to put on sales to get rid of your overstocks.

"That means you will sell identical articles for different prices, on different days. I don't like that way of doing business. Guesswork in buying calls for early mark-ups to take care of later mark-downs. It penalizes one customer in favor of another and worse than that, makes him pay for mistakes not his own.

"The other way to buy for a store is to study your customers' needs, study your markets, pay attention to your shelves, and watch your inventory. If you will study and watch all those things, you will learn to be able to estimate pretty close to your customers' buying habits.

"In fact, you must learn to estimate closely if you expect to stay in business. At the prices we establish there are no allowances for mark-downs."

Being practical, Penney knew buying mistakes would be made, but he saw to it that they were never made in volume. In his first store in Kemmerer, if an article did not move off the shelves as quickly as he thought it should, he moved it to a different place. If after several moves it still did not sell, he cut prices on it until it did move.

By trial and error in his first years as a merchant he learned to estimate, closely, the needs of his customers. He took care of increasing volume by being in the buying market almost continuously and by watching to see that his shelves were always stocked and his cellar always lean.

"There are more merchants than merchandisers—and therein is your opportunity," Penney said on more than one occasion to prospective managers. He invariably added, "There are more sellers than salesman—and therein is another opportunity.

"What I am looking for—all the time, are people who will go about their business of becoming merchandisers as a farmer follows a plow. I want people who will put themselves between the handles of a plow, and stay there. Learning to be a storekeeper, or a merchandiser, calls for nothing more than persistence based on knowing what you are doing, and why you are doing it.

"Making a customer is more important than making a sale. As we try to buy intelligently for our stores, so do I expect you to teach your customers how to buy intelligently. When you do that, they will remember you; and when they need something, they will look you up.

"Now I am not going to guarantee to you, if you do these things, you will get ahead in this company; all I am going to say to you is that those who have done them have gone ahead."

Penney had learned a lot since starting in Kemmerer—a lot about merchandising, a lot about people, and a lot about himself—sufficient for him to write more than forty years later:

"In looking back on my career as founder, then president, then chairman, and then honorary chairman of the board of directors of the J. C. Penney Company, I am conscious of owing so much to my associates that it is not easy to estimate what, apart from them, I owe to myself."

In 1914 Penney was beginning to see the company in wider perspective, and beginning to admit, now that there were stores in seventy-one towns doing an annual business of $3,560,293.75, that his was a going concern. He was positive that "a national organization of hundreds of stores—beyond two hundred, perhaps as many as five hundred—was not an impossibility."

He was becoming concerned with the training of additional people; as soon as he was finished with setting up the central buying organization, he intended to devote the greater part of his time to that training. He had firm ideas as to the type of people he wanted. He felt strongly that he had "no more right to introduce damaged goods into the body of our organization than I have to place damaged goods on the shelves."

His own training methods, as well as his thinking, were grounded in self-help. He saw no way for an individual, or for a company, to progress without self-help, his reasoning being, "Unless I can train men to help themselves, how can I expect them to help others?"

What Penney was planning, of course, was a business organization composed of men who would think of the business as their whole lives. He wanted men—and he had them with him—who would sacrifice their stores before they would sacrifice their principles.

In many ways, Penney believed that the philosophy of a business was more important than any other consideration. There was nothing new in that approach. The unusual thing was that Penney began to see it in his early days in Kemmerer. Many men have failed to see it after spending lifetimes in business; few politicians ever see it; book-bred minds are seldom even aware of it.

In that first year in Kemmerer when he turned over his stock nearly five times, Penney began to understand money was a tool that had to be kept busy—that it was useful to him only when the dollar sign was taken off and it was converted into things he could sell. He also began to see that by working money harder he could turn over stocks not five times a year but six times, or seven times, perhaps eight times.

He realized, of course, that he would have to be sure his stocks would sell, that he could take no chances on over-buying, that he would have to sell on close margins if he was to attract sufficient trade. Thinking that way, he perceived the difference between a speculative dollar and a working dollar. In his mind he defined a speculative dollar as one a merchant used in order to buy more than he needed, planning to first mark up for quick profits and then to mark down for quick sales.

Years afterward, economists, measuring the stock market crash in 1929, discovered that some 60 per cent of the nation's money in 1929 was speculative money and that this squandering of dollars in speculation was responsible for the collapse of the nation's economy. Penney was not thinking in such broad terms; he was only concerned with his own business.

He saw that as the money came in, it went out again for yard goods; as it came back from yard goods, it went out for men's suits and women's dresses; as it came back from men's suits and women's dresses, it went out again for shoes, children's clothes, overalls, neckties, thread, pins, needles, all the hundreds of items that go to make up the stock of a department store; and that this chain of events was an established order. The instant a man became a seller, he became a buyer, then a seller, then a buyer—and money was the endless belt over which trade moved.

Observing this cycle, his greatest need was apparent. In Kemmerer he and Sams used to sit long hours after the store closed discussing ways to develop trained men—just as they talked about them on that day in Cumberland, before Sams began his first partnership in a store in Eureka.

Later Sams added up their talks in these words:

"Money is not, and never can be, the one principal object of our business. We place the greatest stress and give the foremost place to the training of men and the giving of service. *This is the business insurance of producing producers.* The essential duty of the manager is clear. He becomes a manager not alone because he gives evidence that we can trust him to conduct the affairs of a store but, beyond that, because he has proved to us that he can build another man to take his place.

"This is the true J. C. Penney Company endless chain; the training of men on down the line to make every man as capable as his teacher in the ability to handle every essential of this business and to make every man the teacher of the man beside him.

"Once a business is wise enough to do this, the financial income of that business is assured."

After three years, Penney had the central buying headquarters in New York organized. Men were trained and the work was divided among the hands of experts. Four older partners headed up the different groups, with Penney acting as general counsel. True to Penney's prediction, as special skills developed, they found they were buying to better advantage than when Penney and Sams spread themselves across the entire field.

However, the development of specialists did not remove from managers and partners the responsibility of decision as to the merchandise that went into their stores. Managers continued to visit New York twice yearly, but instead of going to the wholesalers and manufacturers they made their selections from samples on display in their hotels. They saved time because there was no shopping around and no evenings spent in comparing prices.

Under the plan Penney had worked out, buyers, being responsible only for prices and deliveries, were little more than leg men for the merchants. They had no authority to make commitments until managers and partners had made their selections and signed their orders. Penney had no intention of permitting encroachment upon the freedom of a manager, or a partner, in the operation of individual stores.

Inevitably, as the buyers became more experienced, managers and partners began depending upon their judgment. Closely watching this growing confidence, Penney suggested late in 1916 that the time was close by for a reversal of the process; instead of managers coming to New York, buyers should go to the stores taking their samples with them.

"By doing it that way," he said, "we will save a lot of time for the managers and partners. Instead of spending a couple of weeks twice yearly in New York, they will be able to be in their stores devoting their time to their customers and to the development of their assistants. Besides," he added, with an eye on expenses, "doing it this way will save money."

In 1917 they tried the experiment by sending out buyers to

a number of stores. The idea worked so well that it spread and was made permanent.

Near the close of 1916, with 127 stores doing an annual business of $8,428,144.34, Penney went to Salt Lake City to the annual convention of the partners and announced his wish to be relieved of his duties as president.

"This is not a sudden decision on my part," he explained. "For some time it has been clear to me, with the growth of our business, with the changing conditions brought on by our expansion and with the economic setup in the various towns where we are doing business and where we expect to do business, that mine is no longer a job one man can handle.

"We have established the partnership idea. The central buying headquarters has been set up and is functioning. I have done what I could along those lines. Now I want to devote my time to company policies, and particularly to the training, as well as the finding, of future executives for our organization. Something must be done to centralize and professionalize this problem in a way corresponding to what has been done in our buying activities. That is the problem toward which my mind is turning.

"Besides, I feel the day is now here when I should retire from the active leadership of this company and yield the presidency to one of my associates. It seems to me it will hurt the spirit of the partnership plan to let the idea grow up in the minds of my associates, or in my own mind, that I am indispensable. To let the idea of indispensability grow would spell failure of my own faith in the men I have selected and trained.

"I have never forgotten the effect upon me of the faith and freedom of initiative Mr. Johnson reposed in me when he sent me to Kemmerer. I want other men in this organization to have that same experience."

The partners objected, but Penney insisted. He placed in

nomination the name of Earl Corder Sams as president and one by one asked his partners to make his selection unanimous. They did.

On the same day, January 1, 1917, Penney was elevated to the chairmanship of the company.

Buying Out His First Employer

WHEN WORLD WAR I ended, Penney stores were in 197 communities, doing a business of $21,338,103.60 and had spread to 25 states. The average business per store had increased from $28,898.11 in Kemmerer in 1902 to $108,351.24 in 1918.

In the years since Kemmerer and Cumberland, Provo, Eureka, Spanish Forks, and Trinidad, the character of the stores had changed from the typical Penney store as described in "J. C. Penney, A Man With A Thousand Partners": *

"The stores were not palaces. The merchandise hung from the ceilings. The counters were usually homemade. The desks of the managers were usually boxes, covered with oilcloth and supplied with some improvised pigeon holes and drawers. Merchandise hung outside the stores, anything to make the stocks look as large as possible."

As president, Sams decided to get rid of the impression of "junkiness," as he called it. Better locations began to be chosen, better-looking stores began to be opened.

In earlier days Penney and Sams and the other partners had little money, let alone time, to share in community activities. Their first responsibility, as they saw it, was to their families and their partners to make their businesses secure. The limit of their community fraternization was on occasional Sundays and on occasional holidays when they hired, or borrowed, a

* An autobiography, published 1931.

horse and buggy from the livery stable, or a friend, and called on their customers, sometimes as many as fifteen or twenty in a long afternoon.

With the business on a sound basis, Penney and Sams began thinking in terms of debt to the communities as a regular part of company policy. Together, they now saw money and their partnership plan—both!—as by-products of rendering a service to the public. To each it seemed not enough to supply customers with merchandise for less money; just as it seemed not enough to furnish opportunities for men to get into business for themselves.

Having been farms boys and having spent practically all their lives in small towns, a sense of neighborliness was born in Penney and Sams. It was a natural thing for them to be interested in the community life of the towns in which they did business. They sat down to identify approximately two hundred towns in terms such as these:

How many people are there in the immediate trading area? (Much of this information they had.)

What do the people do—are they grain growers, stock raisers, fruit growers, miners or industrial workers? (Much of this information they had.)

How active is the interest of the people of the community in schools, churches, libraries, local newspapers? (This information they did not have.)

How much are the people of the community interested in local charities, such as hospitals? (This information they did not have.)

How strong are the banks in the town, the chamber of commerce, and other civic and fraternal organizations? (This information they had in part, particularly information regarding the strength of the banks.)

They notified their store managers to gather the necessary

information and to participate in every worth-while community activity.

As Penney afterwards wrote:

"We told our store managers that, unless they knew their communities and unless they were prepared to enter sympathetically into community life, they could not make a success of their stores. We pointed out to them that the men who represent our organization before the public are under much the same obligation to take the public into their confidence with respect to their public interests and the motivation and conduct of their enterprises as are men who enter public service in the more restricted political sense of that term.

"We reminded them that the privileges of private initiative are not without their public responsibilities and obligations; that, just as we must understand the attitudes, interests, and needs of the communities in which our stores are located if those stores are to prosper, so also must we know that we cannot conduct the kind of service in which we are interested unless the public understands our policies and methods.

"And, finally, we made it clear to them that our conception of partnership was not limited to the men within the organization; it was a partnership between every store and its community, with the essential condition of sound and serviceable merchandising being one of mutuality of interest between seller and consumer. Both must profit by every transaction across our counters if each is to be rewarded."

Penney and Sams also suggested closer cooperation between their managers and other merchants in each community along lines similar to those which Sams expressed before members of the National Retail Dry Goods Association in New York, in 1928:

"One merchant cannot stand as the only prosperous one very

long. . . . The business center of an American town is an association of general mercantile business to improve mercantile methods and prices so as to make available their services to an ever enlarging circle of customers in town and country. Merchants who associate with one another to improve merchandising methods are working directly for themselves by building their own communities. Any merchant who contributes good values to his customer and brings down the cost of merchandise is a benefit to the town and to the competing merchants as well."

All this would indicate that Penney and Sams were acutely conscious of public relations. They were, in the sense that in their business they had relations with the public. They were not public relations minded in the present-day professional use of that term. They had no outside advisers and no public opinion polls to influence their thinking. Together they kept watch over everything. Although one was chairman and one was president, no distinguishable lines of demarcation separated their work.

When Sams followed Penney to New York in 1914, the advisability of establishing credit in a New York bank became clear to them. They decided to divide the neighborhood banks into two groups, with Penney calling on one group and Sams calling on the other, and to make a choice on the basis of the bank which offered the best terms. This was how they bought merchandise, by calling separately on wholesalers and comparing prices, and they saw no reason why it should not work with banks.

One morning they set out and visited the banks separately. In one or two of the banks the answer came quickly. In others the bankers examined the incorporation papers with curiosity, saw that the common stock had no value, discerned that the preferred, or classified, stock was distributed according to store interests, with dividends being paid accordingly, and questioned, "What kind of a company is this?"

"A very good company," they were assured.

Politely the moneylenders gave their answers—and by noon Penney and Sams had visited all the neighborhood financial institutions, and at noon they compared notes. Everywhere the answer was the same. It was "no."

They widened their search for credit until one day Sams went into the Harriman National Bank on Fifth Avenue above Forty-second Street. A vice-president listened to his story, appeared interested, and, after asking what seemed to Sams to be innumerable questions, said, "How much money do you want, Mr. Sams?"

"Seventy-five thousand dollars."

"And you want to borrow this money so you can pay cash for merchandise?" inquired the banker, going over the ground again.

"Yes, sir."

"You think it will be more convenient than drawing on a Salt Lake City bank and giving those checks to your wholesalers and manufacturers?"

"Yes, sir. Besides, as I have told you, we need the money in our operations."

"You said seventy-five thousand dollars?"

"Yes, sir."

Once more the banker went into his round of questions, completed it, told Sams to come back the next day, and remarked, "This is a pretty wild and woolly proposition, Mr. Sams, but maybe we can help you."

Sams went in the following day, was introduced to the president of the bank, questioned at length, and got the money. Penney's signature, along with his own, went on the note.

This was their first line of credit in New York. It served for a time; but with the business expanding from 71 stores in 1914 to 177 stores in 1917, and with the Federal government imposing war taxes, the company needed other sources for borrowings. This time Penney and Sams went together to see the bankers. They were advised to have the incorporation papers changed to conform to common corporation practice, under which the company would own and control all the shares in its own name.

"If you do that," the bankers advised them, "a line of credit sufficient for your needs will be forthcoming."

Penney and Sams objected, pointing out that the strength of the company was in the partnership arrangement that distributed stock in ratio to store earnings. The bankers insisted, and recommended that Penney and Sams consult a particular legal firm in New York.

Penney flatly refused, telling the bankers that he would not trust such important business to strangers. Quite as bluntly the bankers informed Penney that a choice of lawyers was up to him but the company had no choice but to change its articles of incorporation if it expected to establish further credit.

Earlier in that same year Penney had met, through one of his western managers, a young New York lawyer named Ralph W. Gwinn. After the meeting with the bankers he sought out Gwinn, told him his troubles, and asked the lawyer to study the problem and make recommendations. Gwinn did, and accompanied his recommendations with a bill for $400.

Outraged over such a bill for just a few paragraphs of suggested changes in the articles of incorporation, Penney dismissed Gwinn and employed another firm of lawyers. When this firm charged him $2,500 for what looked to be a similar amount of work, Penney reemployed Gwinn.

Following Gwinn's advice, they changed the preferred, or classified, stock to common; and the board of directors was authorized to issue a limited amount of preferred stock for public sale, with the money so received being used for meeting tax burdens. The common stock was issued only to partners and was used for purposes of expansion. Actual earnings controlled the issuance of common stock; and the condition was imposed that, if a partner wished to dispose of any part, or all, of his holdings, he had first to offer them to the board of directors. Thereupon the book value of the stock was computed, after which the board of directors was empowered to offer such stock for sale to other common shareholders. If stock so offered was not disposed of within thirty days, its owner was permitted to sell wherever he chose.

The bankers were satisfied with the changes.

The company extended its buying activities to St. Louis and St. Paul; and, with style becoming an increasing factor, customers were assured: "We have our own buyers in the market every day and we have our own shipping department that does nothing but receive, examine, wrap, and start out to you the seasonable articles, via express, for sale in our stores. Thus you can have garments that are just as stylish as those of the well-dressed men and women who parade along Fifth Avenue or Broadway, for you are not more than six days removed, at the most, from New York style and fashion."

That was quite a change from the kimono and wrapper days of Kemmerer and Cumberland.

Included in the company's purchases in 1921 were: Handkerchiefs: 2,119,068 hosiery: 9,053,972 pairs; knitted undergarments: 3,133,300; corsets: 262,296 pairs; bathrobes: 13,546; blankets: 125,619 pairs; women's and children's ready-to-wear garments (suits, coats and dresses): 747,499; cotton thread:

4,000,000 spools; hair nets: 1,600,000; women's hand bags: 400,000; men's shoes: 2,731,738 pairs; hats and caps: 1,010,364; men's suits: 57,332; men's and boy's shirts: 1,945,986; men's and boy's overalls: 1,467,000 pairs; and 11,066 men's overcoats.

Included in the company's sales were: Muslins and sheetings: 4,183,300 yards; ginghams: 3,748,050 yards; percales: 2,554,360 yards.

As for prices, the customers paid: "Spring dresses (flat crepe de chine, canton moire silk): $9.90 to $49.75; women's spring coats: $9.90 to $49.75; popular Lady-Lyke corsets: 98¢ to $4.98; silk hosiery for women: 98¢ to $2.98; dainty white waists: 98¢ to $1.98; women's attractive kimonos (colorful crepes): $1.98 to $6.90; smart flapper dresses (silk crepe, printed silk crepe, taffeta, canton crepe): $14.75 to $22.50; girls' spring dresses: $5.90 to $14.75; stylish spring suits: $24.75, $34.75, $39.75."

Six years after Sams assumed the presidency, or at the end of 1923, when Penney stores were in 475 communities, word had come to Penney that the store of J. M. Hale & Brother, in Hamilton, Missouri, was for sale.

J. M. Hale, the man who had given Penney his first job, had decided to retire. Penney acted without delay. He went to Hamilton, saw Hale, and bought the store. After the purchase arrangements were completed, Hale chuckled, "Jim, I've been thinking ever since we signed the papers about what the boys around town are saying."

"What's that, Mr. Hale?"

"Well, when it got around you had bought me out, the boys started asking, 'How do you suppose that happened—Jim Penney buying out Hale's? Beats all!' and some of them are saying, 'That Jim Penney's might lucky, the way he has come ahead.' Hearing those things started me thinking that maybe you should have come in here several years ago. Maybe you could have forced me to sell out to you, instead of waiting for me to retire. Maybe you could have made a better deal, if you'd done that."

Penney shook his head. "Up to now, Mr. Hale, we weren't ready to come into Hamilton."

"But it's always seemed strange to me, Jim, that with you opening stores all over, you never opened one in Hamilton. Been expecting you to do it. Seems like you would have wanted to, this being where you were born, where your folks lived, and where you got your start."

"I know; but as I said, Mr. Hale, we weren't ready," repeated Penney, and shifted the conversation.

What Penney did not tell Hale was that years previously he had decided there would not be a Penney store in Hamilton until Hale was ready to retire and take down his name. The only location Penney wanted was the Hale location. Now with it in his possession, he enlarged the store and in recognition of his first employer and his birthplace reopened it as the five hundredth store in the Penney chain.

In that same year of 1924 there was a young manager, later to become president of the company, who was getting his first opportunity to operate a Penney store. Employed as a tutor for Penney's two sons, A. W. Hughes persuaded Penney to give him a job in the company. He put Hughes in a store—and started him where he started all inexperienced help, at the bottom.

His undergraduate work completed, Hughes, early in 1923, was sent to Eureka. After a year as assistant manager he became manager of his first store. Anxious to get ahead, Hughes made a fine showing—too fine a showing; for on February 22, 1924, Sams wrote him as follows:

Mr. A. W. Hughes
Eureka, Utah

Dear Mr. Hughes:

I have just returned from the South where, as you may know, I have been for a number of weeks. I have been going over the figures with Mr. Bushnell and I must say to you that I am extremely pleased with the splendid showing you made last year. You did fine.

You did the most business that has ever been done in Eureka, and made the most money that has ever been made. You made this profit because you kept your expenses down to a minimum. You couldn't have done this had you not been on the job, and everyone doing his part. Again I say you have done fine, and I congratulate each and every one of you.

I don't want you to get the idea, Mr. Hughes, that we want to make too much profit. There is danger in doing that very thing. There is a certain service that we owe to our community and it is one of the fundamental services that we want to give, which is merchandise at a fair profit.

I recall a little conversation that we had at our last convention, when you were being urged to sell a certain number of Ladies Silk Hose at 98¢ when, as you said, you could just as easily get $1.19.

When I look over your showing for 1923, I am reminded of this incident and I have wondered if you are doing that thing too generally.

Now don't misunderstand me, I am not censuring you, but somewhere in the operations of the Eureka business there is a profit that we owe to our public. The finding of just where this profit is, is a problem, and I should like to have you think this matter over and write me at your convenience.

I realize, Mr. Hughes, that in conducting a business of a volume of around $150,000 it is difficult to have the results tally exactly with the thing we are shooting at. In other words, we are liable to vary around 1 per cent, one way or the other, but when we vary more than that it shows that we are adding on just a little more than we ought to somewhere.

As I said above, think this over and write me your impressions.

With very best wishes to you and all your associates, I am

Sincerely,

E. C. SAMS,

President

Distinctly, that was not the sort of congratulatory letter Hughes had been expecting from the president of the company. Having established a new sales record that carried with it a new high in profits for the Eureka store, he had anticipated the warmest congratulations. He had particularly anticipated them because, in spite of "adding on" a little here and a little there, his prices remained below what other stores in Eureka were charging for similar merchandise. In selling for less, he had believed he was living up to the spirit of the Penney company; instead, here was criticism for having made "too much money."

At first, Hughes was disposed to write Sams in defense of his position, but he sat down, as Sams had suggested, to think over the matter. When he did write to the president of the company, Hughes frankly admitted having put too much zeal into his efforts and promised to pay close attention in seeing to it that "results tally exactly with the thing you and Mr. Penney are shooting at."

Hughes received a promotion in the form of a larger opportunity a few months later.

"A Project of Interest"

IN 1926, T. M. Callahan who, with Guy Johnson, had established Penney in business in Kemmerer, approached his former employee with a proposition.

"I'm tired," said Callahan, "and I want to sell out. I have twelve stores. Will you buy them?"

When they split their partnership in 1907, Callahan and Johnson had sold Penney three stores, one in Kemmerer, one in Rock Springs, and one in Cumberland, and they had taken Penney's personal note for $30,000. In this transaction Penney gave Callahan cash.

Two years later Guy Johnson came to Penney with a similar proposition. He had twenty stores which he wanted to sell. Penney bought them, also paying cash.

However, before Penney bought out Johnson, even while the Callahan stores were being absorbed, it was apparent the company would have to revise its table of organization. At the end of 1926, there were 747 stores, and for the first time in its history the company had annual sales in excess of $100,000,-000. The exact figures were $115,683,023.37, as against a sales total of $91,062,616.17 in 1925.

Since 1902, with the exceptions of the temporary credits that have been mentioned, the business had been built out of earnings; the organization, so far as stores were concerned, had grown with scarcely any central planning. Partners had developed managers and managers had become partners. There were hundreds of them. It was a jigsaw type of organization, with partners sometimes dropping the names of contemplated stores in a hat, pulling out slips on each of which a name had been written, and investing in whatever store happened to be drawn.

For several reasons it was desirable that the company cease selling partnerships in individual stores:

1. To permit men to retire and still receive rewards for what they had helped to build.

2. To provide more opportunities to share in company expansion.

3. To permit the company to enter into large operations.

4. To finance warehouses and other large expenditures.

5. To keep pace with the growth of what now was a nation-wide organization.

To accomplish these things a tighter corporate structure was necessary; but Penney and Sams saw that it was equally necessary to protect the partnership idea that had contributed so greatly to the success of the company.

They worked it out, as Penney stated, in this fashion:

"All classified stock was retired in favor of stock in the company as a whole. In return for his common stock the manager-partner received common stock at book value and preferred stock at par, together equalling the book value of the classified stock he turned in, and sufficient additional common stock so that his common stock had the same earnings power as the original classified stock.

"We removed from the partner-manager the burden of supervision of any store other than his own, relieved him of the responsibility for opening new stores, and freed his entire time and energy for concentration on his individual store problems. He continued to train men, but the final selection for the new locations, like the selection of the locations themselves, was transferred to a headquarters committee on store operation, whose members drew upon the managers for advice and information.

"The new partner-manager was no longer required to find new capital with which to acquire an interest in a new store. Location, rent, merchandise, and operating capital were all supplied by the company, and out of earnings. Thus the limitations of the previous plan were removed, and its strength retained.

"The new plan provided the managers with two ways for deriving personal income:

"1. A salary commensurate with the volume of business obtained and the net profits made.

"2. A compensation guaranteed by contract for a share in the net profits of the store he managed."

This new plan of organization, while tighter, removed from young executives the necessity for risking their own money in order to obtain partnerships. Training remained in the keeping of the store manager, but the decision as to when a trainee was ready for managership was no longer his; nor was the selection of a store. With a personnel department established and staffed by experienced people, the store manager was required to make periodic reports, every six months, on the progress of people under him.

All employees were graded according to:

1. Character.
2. General merchandising ability.
3. Sales ability.
4. Ability to train others.

These records were submitted to the personnel department where they were analyzed and kept up to date. Continually in the minds of the senior executives was the problem of finding a man suited to the job, and finding him, placing him

where he would be happiest. Promotions were always waiting
for the capable.

There was a young assistant manager in a store in Minnesota. His record proved he was ready to manage an average
store and indicated he was qualified to be an executive in a
large store or in headquarters. He preferred a store of his own.
He was sent to manage an average store in Iowa. In making up
his pay roll in his new store he put himself down at $150 a
month, believing this figure was warranted because, as an
assistant in the Minnesota store, he had been paid $135 a
month.

Before long he received a letter from headquarters informing him that his salary for managing the particular store in
Iowa was not $150 a month, but $135 a month—"and please
refund the difference."

That letter caused him a great deal of anguish. He had married while getting $135 a month in Minnesota, and an indul-
gent father-in-law had helped him with his household expenses. Now, in Iowa, he had no handy relative. He went to
the local bank, explained his dilemma, borrowed the amount
of his "over-drafts"—thirty dollars—and sent the money to
New York. That year, he and his wife lived on $135 a month.
After the year was over, he received another letter from the
company, this one from the treasurer. It contained his "compensation guaranteed by contract for a share in the net profits
of the store he managed." The check was for approximately
$11,000.

That man is now manager of one of Penney's largest stores.

In 1917, when Penney insisted that a successor be named as
president of the company so he might devote his time "to company policies, and particularly to the training, as well as the
finding, of future executives for the organization," he located
the personnel department in St. Louis. It was a more conven-

ient location for stores that still were principally in the West and Middle West.

He was convinced that the selection and training of men could be done on a basis that would make the job more secure for the applicant, as was the case in the story of the $135-a-month manager. Penney had learned early that rapid turnover in merchandise was one of the keys to successful storekeeping. Now he was beginning to understand that slow turnover in employees also was a part of successful storekeeping. Often his thoughts had gone back to his first year in Kemmerer when he turned over his stock nearly eight times and his clerks twice as often. Long since, he had decided the initial mistake was his own: that he had not selected carefully enough, nor explained well enough.

Setting himself up in St. Louis as an employment agent for the company, he began advertising in newspapers. Within four months he received approximately five thousand applications. Three hundred were selected for interviews. Sixty-three were employed. Very few of the sixty-three had experience. He selected them on what he saw—neatness in appearance, courtesy, a face of character; and on what he heard—they *wanted* to become merchants and were willing to start at the bottom for their learning.

Without exception, he tried to discourage them, warning them they were letting themselves in for hard work, and told them: "I believe work to be the solvent for all our troubles. Unless you are willing to spend long hours in the store studying what is there, I do not want you at any price."

Having selected sixty-three, he decided that something more than the personal attention of a store manager was needed. There should be as much coordination of training as there was coordination in buying. He initiated the writing of a manual; drew on the experiences of the company; and went into such subjects as the principles of the company, merchandise, sales, suggestion selling, stockkeeping, lost sales, service, the relationship of the store to the community, and other subjects he considered vital in the training and development of a merchant.

The practical Penney and the equally practical Sams agreed with George Washington who, from Valley Forge, wrote to John Banister:

". . . men may speculate as they will; they may talk of patriotism; they may draw a few examples from ancient store, of great achievement performed by its influence; but whoever builds on them as a sufficient basis for conducting a long and bloody war will find themselves deceived in the end. . . . I do not mean to exclude altogether the idea of patriotism. I know it exists, and I know it has done much in the present combat. But I venture to assert, that a great and lasting war can never be supported on this principle alone. It must be aided by a prospect of interest, or some reward. For a time it may, of itself, push men to action, to bear much, to encounter difficulties; but it will not endure unassisted by interest."

As Washington saw that patriotism needed to be reinforced by self-interest, even in so great an adventure as the War of Independence, so Penney and Sams saw that "a prospect of interest, or some reward" was necessary to sustain loyalty within an organization. In Kemmerer, Penney applied this principle to his partners; now he realized its proportionate application to all employees.

Beyond the management group, provision was made for paid vacations and, under a "sick benefit plan," for the continuance of salaries to all other employees during a reasonable period. An insurance policy for all employees with records of twelve months' continuous employment provided for "an amount equal to the salary drawn during the previous twelve months (not to exceed $1,800) in the event of death." Costs of these benefits were paid by the company.

In addition, a "Thrift and Profit-Sharing Retirement Fund Plan" has been set up (1939) providing for (1) regular savings; and (2) profit sharing. All full-time employees excepting store managers and central office executives are permitted to allocate a percentage of their salaries to this plan.

In 1917, when Penney was thinking about these plans and beginning to put them into form, he only considered that they would be good business. He recognized, as did Sams, that good will was their greatest asset; and they defined good will as "the earnest cooperation of a loyal staff of workers." They did not confine it within the narrow boundaries once marked out by a decision of the Supreme Court of the United States: "Good will is the desire of customers to return to a source that has served them well."

Penney, Sams, and the other directors recognized that a source that serves well is a source that is supplied by the efforts of many rather than by the efforts of a few.

They saw job security as an important part of employment and, with security, the promise of rewards and the opportunity to progress. In putting into the store manual experience gained in years of merchandising and in conducting training classes within the stores, the company was offering everyone on its pay roll the opportunity to learn and to get ahead.

Here, for illustration, is the outline of one of those store meetings:

Subject: How to Know the Needs of Your Community.

1. Rendering a superior merchandising service depends upon knowing, first of all, what kind of merchandise is needed in the community. A survey of the community, taken before merchandise is ordered, will include:

   a. A visit to the other leading stores in the town.

b. Observation of the quality and style of clothing worn by adults and school children.

c. Conference with the secretary of the chamber of commerce, the visiting nurses, and officials of similar organizations.

d. Study of map to determine the tributary trade territory.

e. Visits to the local industrial plants to determine the quality of clothing the community can buy.

f. Attendance at public meetings—church, social gatherings, athletic contests, or any other group gatherings.

g. Repeated walks through all sections of the city—to determine the standard of living in the community.

h. If in rural sections, observation of the standard of living and special clothing needs, because of climate or unusual occupations. Getting acquainted with the men who are working and finding out what they need and like in clothing, shoes, rubber footwear, and the like.

i. Study of newspaper files and the advertising of competitors. It is worth while to form the acquaintance and friendship of the local newspaper editors. If the right approach is made, these men will be glad to have you examine their newspaper files for this purpose.

To use Penney's words, the company was offering:

"A four-year business administration course, tuition free, reasonable living expenses paid while attending school, business taught by actual practice and practical application. The student must be willing to work hard to complete the course satisfactorily. The graduate will be set up in business. He will not be required to make any cash investment. He will receive a share of the net profits of the store. Once he attains managership he must be willing to continue to work hard to meet the demands of success."

It was as though a college or university advertised for students, offered to pay them while attending classes in business administration, and guaranteed, upon graduation, to set them up in business for themselves.

There never was any doubt in the minds of the partners that the idea would work. Farm boys, most of them, they saw business and the people in it much as they saw a wheat field. Every stalk of wheat had its individual roots in the soil, and every stalk was a separate growth; just as every associate had his individual roots in the company and found there sustenance for his separate growth. That was the reason for making each manager responsible for his store and each individual responsible for his own advancement.

Penney expressed it this way:

"No one is wise enough to solve another's problems, nor to relieve him of the responsibility for making his own decisions. However, misdirected work is waste work. Inexperience needs counsel. My father believed in work and taught me to believe in it, but it had to be work with an intelligent purpose. I remember that once, when I was talking with him about the meaning of work, he told me how one of his early teachers made him shift a heap of stones from one side of the road to the other and then had him lug them back again to teach him the importance of work as a discipline.

"That was senseless instruction. Memorizing lessons for no other purpose than mental discipline is equally senseless instruction. The fact that such discipline is practiced in our schools, colleges, and universities is not flattering to our educational system. Mental discipline should always be directed at useful results.

"We are continually discovering that the educational process in business can never be fixed. It is constantly changing, improving, adapting itself to circumstances as these same circumstances change with the evolution of the business.

"I am sincerely of the opinion that the finest education for the young man or woman is that education which springs from the demands of the job itself. When the job is analyzed into its components and these components are made the basis of constructive study, then, in my opinion, education has become an influence in business that is as constructive as any other department of its activity. But—this education must start with a job. That is what we set out to establish in the Penney company.

"A number of years ago William J. Cameron had as his subject 'The Power of the Job' on one of his Sunday evening broadcasts for the Ford Motor Company. Mr. Cameron expressed it well when he said:

" 'The job lays down its own terms; it inflexibly requires every element that contributes to it to be as nearly right in all its relations as it can be at the moment, and to continue becoming nearly right. No matter what the job—baking a pie, digging a well, building a skyscraper—this law must be obeyed. In industry you must deal with it ever more rightly with men, you must deal with it ever more rightly with materials, you must deal with it ever more rightly with money, or the job penalizes you.

" 'The job is the voice of natural law which we do not break, but it breaks us. All the contributing elements—the human physical, the human psychological, the human spiritual, if you will; the material, technical, and social elements—must sustain ever more refined and just and reciprocal relations with each other, or the job dismisses you.

" 'To say that progressive management heeds this law is not necessarily to credit it with conscious social idealism—let us say it merely indicates intelligence and plain common sense—but it does lift the social level and it does put solid, sustaining, material foundations under it.

" 'And this process continues.

" 'Following the requirements of first-class work, industry will build many another social improvement into its method —things that no demagogue has dreamed of—for the things that are good and remain are built. They cannot come by command or demand or compulsion; they grow by the inner necessity of the job.' "

While these policies were being worked out and put into effect, Sams received a letter from J. B. Byars, operator of 116 chain stores extending across the Western and Far Western states. Like Callahan and Johnson, Byars wanted to dispose of his stores because, he informed Sams, "I am concerned over my people. I have been watching the Penney company's operations for quite a number of years. I like the way you treat your people and I feel with you they would be in good hands. If you are interested in buying my stores I am interested in selling them to you."

Negotiations were under way for this absorption when Sams received another letter, this one from F. S. Jones, principal owner of the F. S. Jones Company, fifty-four stores located mostly in the Northwest. On May 5, 1927, Sams wrote Byars in Denver, Colorado, saying, "I just returned from St. Paul . . . where we put the final touches to the F. S. Jones Company deal. All their managers were on hand, fifty-four in all, and we inducted them into the J. C. Penney Company. . . . The new men seem highly pleased with the merger and took a quick hold of the situation attesting to their unqualified approval."

Approximately two years later Byars announced to all his managers:

"Here is some good news for you as manager of a Byars Company store. . . . After much time and due consideration, we have just succeeded in getting a better deal by far . . . from

our friends the J. C. Penney Company for a merger of the two
companies. You can rest assured that all good managers will be
retained as managers for their present stores under a mana-
gerial contract on the same basis as the J. C. Penney Company
managers. . . . Full details of the merger plan will be explained to you in person in the near future. Every stockholder
who was present in New York at the time the deal was outlined
has given his hearty approval to the plan."

Like the Penney company, the Byars and Jones organizations all grew from one store; and as Sams noted following the
Jones merger:

"There is no magic and there are no special secrets about
this phase of store distribution. There are only the open secrets
that lie at the heart of any healthy, growing business. The field
has always been wide open. Any merchant may take the profits
of his single store and, with the men he is able to train in that
store, open up a second store, then a third store, and so on until
he has a chain, if he chooses to develop his business in that
direction.

"His limitations are almost entirely concerned with the development and training of men. This is an educational problem, not a financial one. Since the independent store and the
chain store are essentially alike in the beginning and since
their differences develop only in the nature and extent of their
growth, it follows that the success of one depends on identically
the same fundamental business principles as the other. Both
profit continually by the interchange of ideas.

"Chain stores and single stores are affected equally by the
application of common sense principles, and benefit to the
same degree that they are applied. The same principles that
governed the success of our first store in Kemmerer now govern
all our stores. Success in operating a large number of stores
does not lie in the great number itself, but in the definite and

practical knowledge of how to operate a single store in a single community.

"As Mr. Jones and Mr. Byars knew, the application of common sense required that we pay men and women liberally for their work and do everything we could to promote their advancement. For this reason, from the very day a man or woman enters our employ, his or her educational, civic, and financial well-being are carefully considered. This means we must have superior type of people.

"As it is impossible to standardize a business without standardizing its working organization, so is it impossible to standardize the working organization (that includes everyone in our company) and assure its prosperity without providing for the education, training, and success of the individual. That was what was in Mr. Penney's mind when he decided to devote himself to policies and to the finding and training of future executives of the company.

"To establish and maintain a standard of operation, we begin with the person who, upon employment, gives promise of capability. His well-being we assume as our responsibility from the day he comes with us. There is thus established a bond of mutual interest that works for the good of the three parties concerned in what we call our partnership setup. That bond is: The Public, the Company and the Man."

Offers of Mergers

AT LUNCH in New York one day late in 1928, Marshall Field, Chicago merchant and banker, suggested to Penney the possibilities of a merger between the J. C. Penney Company and Montgomery Ward & Company, a Chicago mail-order concern which was expanding its operations into the retail field. At the time, there were 1,023 Penney stores, doing a gross business (1928) of $176,695,989.14. Montgomery Ward & Company had a total volume of approximately $500,000,000.

Penney was interested and gave Field permission to convey his personal interest to Montgomery Ward, but explained that nothing could be done "without the consent of my partners."

Field appeared puzzled. "Don't you control the company?" he asked. In reply Penney told Field that 'control' was not a one-man prerogative in the Penney company, that there had to be general approval, and said, "I am convinced that our plan of sharing responsibilities is the reason for whatever success the Penney company has had."

That afternoon Penney called his directors, told them of his conversation with Field, and expressed the opinion that the proposal was worth exploration. A few days later George B. Everitt, president of Montgomery Ward & Company, came to New York, met with Penney executives and discussed, at some length, the possibilities of the merger Field had suggested. Later Sams communicated with Everitt as follows:

New York City
January 25, 1929

Mr. George B. Everitt, President
Montgomery Ward & Company
Chicago, Illinois

Dear Mr. Everitt:

After our meeting here with you recently we discussed, at some length, among ourselves your outline of the advantages and savings to the public and to our companies that could be effected by some sort of combination.

You did not suggest any ways and means of bringing about such a combination, so we are uncertain whether your thought was that Montgomery Ward & Company should buy the J. C. Penney Company, or whether the J. C. Penney Company should buy Montgomery Ward & Company.

Regarding the first possibility. The J. C. Penney Company's principal assets, as you have stated, are trained store personnel and good will. In our judgment it would be impossible for us effectively to convey these values to you. We have hundreds of men who have worked with us from two to five years to whom we owe very definite obligations to provide them with the same opportunities that the older men now enjoy, to say nothing of our obligation to maintain the present plan of operation for all classes of our store personnel, new and old.

We could, of course, sell you our leaseholds, fixtures, stocks of merchandise, warehouses, and the services of certain general personnel whose positions would ordinarily not be affected by any such proposed sale or merger. But the board of directors of our company, all of whom are active in the business, feel themselves in a peculiar position of trust with regard to the preservation of the J. C. Penney Company plan of work and compensation. Knowing the situation as they do, they would be unwilling to take stock in a combination that might endanger the continuation of such a plan.

. While, of course, your organization would try to preserve what in your judgment seemed to be the value of the J. C. Penney Company, we think it would be well-nigh an impossible task, especially throughout the stores. To state the proposition in another way, we neither could sell you the value which we now enjoy nor could you fully realize upon such values in the event that you should purchase.

I trust that this statement of the case will not seem altogether too sentimental to you. Your own operation in the store field may not yet have brought you to a full realization of the truth of this statement.

Now with regard to the possibility of the J. C. Penney Company purchasing the Montgomery Ward & Company business. From our point of view you have the following assets that we might acquire:

First: The good will value of Montgomery Ward & Company. The extent of that value and the power of it we should, of course, want to examine carefully.

Second: Your organization and experience in buying and distributing lines of merchandise that we do not now handle. The value of this asset would depend upon our ability to enlarge our retail outlets so as to add these additional lines to those we now carry. The possibilities in this direction, from our point of view, would need considerable study. To add these lines may involve, possibly, the extension of the department store idea to the small as well as the large city. We are not prepared to forecast that this will be the logical course of merchandising for the next ten or twenty years.

Third. The mail-order business. Its future value must be appraised. If the department store type of merchandising is to persist indefinitely, such a combination involves the study of lines of merchandise that may be best handled in such stores. All of this, as you can well appreciate, covers somewhat new territory for us and would require a very careful and detailed survey of the facts which you alone have developed.

We want to assure you, Mr. Everitt, that we are not disposed to treat your suggestions casually. Neither do we want to assume that you would consider selling your business to us. If you would, and if your organization believes, as we understand it does, that the bringing together of our two enterprises is so much in line with the inevitable trend of the times, and you are willing to designate two or three members of your company to work with an equal number from ours to make a thorough-going study along the lines above indicated, we shall be glad to pursue such a study with you.

Very truly yours,
E. C. Sams

In reply (February 5, 1929) Everitt stated: "It has not been our thought that the J. C. Penney Company could be purchased, nor is Montgomery Ward & Company for sale. I judge in actual practice what we might do would be to form a new company, to which both of us would contribute all of our assets and experience. There could be no absorbing of one by the other. We would both throw our entire efforts into the new company and our stockholders would receive new stock in proportion to the values we brought to the new company.

"You speak of your board's obligation to preserve the Penney plan of reward and compensation. As I understand it, what you do is to reward people in relation to what they produce. Montgomery Ward & Company does that exact thing and the new company would have no difficulty continuing such a soundly economical basis of compensation."

There was considerable correspondence between Everitt

and Sams across the ensuing weeks. An investigating committee was appointed, which held a number of meetings. Penney, Sams, and the other directors in the Penney company finally decided against the proposition. Behind their decision (and they had no critical thoughts of Montgomery Ward in reaching it) was their feelings of obligation toward their personnel and desire to protect their job security.

Scarcely had negotiations between Montgomery Ward ended when Sams received a letter from R. E. Wood, president of Sears, Roebuck & Company, another Chicago mail-order concern which was also expanding into the retail field. Like Montgomery Ward, Sears saw advantages in a merger with Penney; and, as with Montgomery Ward, Penney executives gave serious consideration to the proposal.

After an exchange of correspondence between Sams and Wood, the latter wrote (October 29, 1929) telling Sams, "I had a talk with Mr. Julius Rosenwald . . . and I find him sympathetic to the idea, as he has a great admiration for your organization and its methods." In this letter Wood told Sams that the chairman of Sears was planning to be in New York, suggested a meeting, and advised that, "while Mr. Rosenwald would not undertake any of the actual negotiations himself, I think you would enjoy meeting him as he is a delightful gentleman of sterling character." Closing his letter, Wood stated, "Our position is that we are ready, if you are, on any fair basis."

In reply Sams expressed his pleasure over the opportunity to meet the chairman of Sears, Roebuck & Company. Referring to Wood's statement, "We are ready, if you are, on any fair basis," he said that his own company was "interested, and it would seem . . . that we ought to arrange to meet at an early date and discuss the problems in mind."

In preparation for this meeting Wood wrote Sams, outlining in much detail advantages Sears and Penney could bring to such a merger, and proposed, if the merger was effected, dividing the operating functions of the business into three divisions: "a mail-order division; an A store division, which would include stores in the large cities; and a B store division, which would include stores in the smaller cities and towns."

Because of Sears's experience, Wood proposed that the mail-order division should continue under the management of Sears's trained executives. The personnel in the A stores was to be absorbed, while all B stores were to be placed directly under Penney-trained merchants. Merchandising organizations were to be combined, with all heavy lines, or lines not carried by Penney, "under the jurisdiction of a merchandising manager, or vice-president, who would be a Sears's man, and the textile and shoe buying under a merchandise manager, or vice-president, who would be a Penney man."

Wood detailed other functions and, aware of the attitude of Penney and Sams toward their own organization, expressed the opinion "that so far as the Penney corps of managers is concerned, they have everything to gain and nothing to lose by such a combination." The President of Sears, Roebuck & Company closed his long letter by observing that he was "simply thinking on paper . . . my ideas are subject to modification, and I am quite willing to work toward a fair solution."

Sams and Wood met in Chicago, spent hours discussing the proposed merger; and at Sams's suggestion, Wood appointed a number of Sears's executives to work with an equal number of Penney executives as a committee to explore every possibility.

Sears committeemen went into and through the Penney organization, studying methods of operation, buying, management, merchandise, testing, personnel, training—every operation was thrown open for their scrutiny and inspection. Penney representatives went into and through the Sears organization the same way. Merchandise was taken from Penney stores by Sears committee members and tested in Sears laboratories. Merchandise was taken from Sears's stores by Penney representatives and tested in Penney laboratories. Nothing was withheld by either company.

After weeks of investigation, the reports of its own committee members were turned over to the top executives of the Penney company. In part, they said:

The proposed merger immediately raises the fears and complexities that mere size suggests. But our experience, in our own growth, shows that not only with the inevitable increase in size, are we permitted to effect economies and afford opportunities for managers and executives in an increasing ratio. Whether we merge or not, the problems of size will be about as great with us as with the merger. Some of the advantages and problems are:

1. Possibility of creating in each town the dominating store, with wider range of selection, the drawing magnet, so to speak, of the community. Because of outstanding plants and locations made possible again by the variety of lines carried from basement to catalogue, the mail-order houses are setting up big stores with resources of all kinds, the like of which we have never competed with on a nation-wide scale.

2. Size permits well organized districts such as A&P and Woolworth now provide, which we find rather difficult to do with our present volume. A business that is susceptible to districting and subdividing reduces the problem of size.

3. Size not only attracts the public, but possibly what is more important, it attracts outstanding personnel whether in buying, selling, advertising, style, finance, etc. A combination like the one proposed should attract the most capable managers, as well as candidates for first, second, and third positions.

If we do not merge and if it is desirable to add to our present lines in order to enjoy a reasonable degree of growth, then it is obvious that we must consider the cost: first, of developing these lines; secondly, of entering into direct competition with the mail-order houses.

Unless this merger is consummated, Ward or Sears would have no particular reason for avoiding towns where the Penney company is operating its present type of store with limited lines. In fact, these very towns offer Ward or Sears wonderful opportunities because, as a rule, the hard lines are being badly merchandised by local hardware or old-style general country stores.

Up to the present we have been more nearly the "family" store than have most of our competitors. In many towns we are, even with our limited lines, the "family" store. But it is perfectly obvious that we cannot maintain this position against the wider family appeal of the Sears and Ward stores.

We can get into no argument with the Sears company. They have been quite as free to point out their problems and difficulties as we have been eager to find them. They know the hardships of having to start from "scratch" with no personnel. In spite of that, they point to a volume of business at retail that is little short of amazing. Sears will do this year approximately $195,000,000 of retail business.

They claim that their success in this direction lies fundamentally in the same state of facts that Mr. Penney and the earlier founders of our company found. Namely, that retailing is so poorly done and merchandise is at such a high price, especially in hard lines, that with inadequate personnel and plant, the people come and take the merchandise out of the basement and from the counters.

Your committee recognizes that there are many difficulties to be met and many personal inconveniences in such a merger. These will come out of the discussions later. However, it is our conviction that when advantages and disadvantages to our organization over a period of years are carefully weighed, the tremendous economic advantages and possibilities which are apparent in this merger warrant favorable consideration for the proposed merger.

With their committee's report recommending the merger, Penney senior executives met again with senior executives of Sears, Roebuck & Company. Lawyers and public accountants were called in to render legal opinions and to make findings relative to the financial worth of each company. With every available fact before them, the representatives of the two companies went into discussions that lasted through several weeks. A great deal of searching was done to establish equality of position for each company in the event of merging.

Because Sears was much the larger, the problem of establishing the Penney company in an equal position was difficult. However, before that problem was fully answered, the Penney company, through Sams, expressed its conviction that it "could not deliver to a new company the values we now enjoy." Sams went on to identify these values, just as he had identified them to Montgomery Ward & Company.

There were no further negotiations.

In talking about the two proposals, Sams afterwards said: "On the surface it would appear that a great deal of time and

The first Penney store, called the "Golden Rule," brought hundreds of value-hungry families of Kemmerer, Wyoming, down this wooden sidewalk in 1902.

After Penney's fast-growing business had outgrown the first store, he moved to this larger and more modern store building.

Feminine fripperies in 1902 looked very much as they do today, with another cycle of fashion completed.

Over this small counter in Penney's first store, passed more than $28,000 in merchandise in its first year. At 1902's prices, that meant many, many sales.

Penney Engineers and Architects today design stores such as this.

...nney emphasis on big values for America's dollars brings crowds into over 1,600 stores.

Another example of the modern Penney store. Design takes into account locale, environment, climate, so each store fits into its surroundings.

One of the company's largest units, a west coast store on one of the country's busiest corner

One of the J. C. Penney Company's metropolitan stores does business in this building.

Not all new Penney stores are as modern as this, but each fits its neighborhood.

A men's clothing department in a Penney store of today.

Penney's is known coast-to-coast for the high quality and low price of its yard goods.

J.C. Penney Co.

THE GOLDEN RULE
175 BUSY STORES

KEMMERER, WYO.   KEMMERER, WYO.

......THE STORE OF.....

HIGH QUALITIES AND LOW PRICE

YOU ASK: "How can they sell at *low prices* when merchandise is continually *going up?*" Our answer is this---through the elimination of many costs that go into an article before it reaches you and being satisfied with a reasonable profit. **Now let us explain this to you!**

First—We operate 175 stores and we buy in large quantities direct from the manufacturer in many lines, and all buying together gives us the lower cost on the article.

Second—Selling for cash! Do you realize that the person who buys on credit and pays his bills must help pay the bills of the one who does not or will not pay them? That's another saving to you.

Third--By eliminating all unnecessary expense, made possible only by selling for cash. We do not deliver--eliminating the entire delivery system. Selling for cash, we do not have a book-keeper to see that _____ properly charged and all the bills paid that can be collected. This is another sa_____

Fourth---We b_____   _____ou ask; "How much more will my dollar buy at the J. C. Penn_____   _____y them and compare them with any catalogue o_____   _____ the values we give. To see is to be_____   customer, always a_____ or next week or th_____

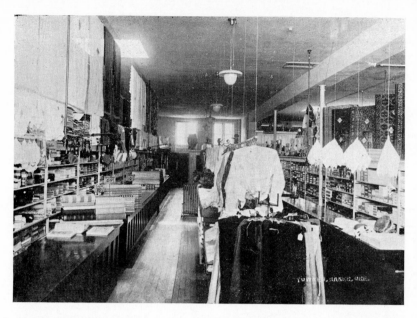

Interior of a typical Penney store of the early 1900's. In those days it was smart to hang merchandise from the ceiling.

The modern Penney store is spacious, orderly, beautifully lighted.

effort on the part of a lot of people were wasted in what appeared to have been a foregone conclusion. It was not a foregone conclusion.

"As Mr. Penney has said, so many times, the first duty of a merchant is to serve the public. Feeling that to be our duty, it was incumbent upon us to explore, fully, any proposal that indicated savings to the public. We did so. With all the facts before us we were satisfied that savings to the public would be negligible.

"Having learned that, we then investigated the possibilities of greater opportunities for our people. That investigation was just as searching as our investigation into savings to the public. In spite of the report of our own people, we felt that our younger executives would have lessened rather than greater opportunities. There would have been great expansion in operations but that very expansion would have handicapped our people.

"For one thing, we would have had to provide, at once, nearly 250 managers had we merged with Sears. We could not have done that. Such men were not available within our organization. We would have done a partly trained man a great disservice had we asked him to accept such a responsibility, to say nothing of the greater disservice to the public and to the new company. Nor could we have asked trained Penney managers to assume a load that, probably, would have been too great to handle.

"I would like to add that the termination of negotiations did not result in loss to Montgomery Ward & Company, to Sears, Roebuck & Company, nor to us.

"Montgomery Ward & Company and Sears, Roebuck & Company are merchants. Good merchants. They are interested in the same thing that interests us—bringing good merchandise for less money to more customers. In the negotiations representatives of those two companies were given full opportunity to study our methods, and the things we sell. If they learned some things from us that helped them to be better merchants, that was gain for them and gain for their customers. If we learned some things from them—and we did!—we were helped. That was gain for us, and gain for our customers."

Sams could have mentioned two other factors that were present in the negotiations, one of which Penney executives had discussed.

With Ward and Sears going into the small-town retail field, Penney, being much smaller in volume than its competitors, appeared to be caught between them. Sams and the Penney directors were aware of this. During the negotiations there was a memorandum before them which said:

"At the end of this year, the J. C. Penney Company will have approximately 1,300 stores, mostly in small towns. Montgomery Ward & Company will have 500 so-called chain stores in small towns and 23 department stores in the large cities. Sears, Roebuck & Company will have 70 large department stores in the large cities and 21 C stores, which are tire and accessory stores, also in the large cities, and 225 so-called B stores, which are located in the small towns.

"Montgomery Ward & Company are going ahead on their idea of building their chain to 1,500 stores. To maintain their position, Sears will be forced not only to increase the number of its stores to over 500 but also to add textiles, shoes, and other style lines which it has not done up to the present time or, at least, only to a very small extent.

"With these three chains in towns of from 5,000 to 25,000, the sales of all three companies will suffer.

"If Montgomery Ward continues, as they give every evidence of doing, and if Sears is forced into the position not only of increasing the number of its stores in the small towns but also of carrying complete lines in these stores, it looks as if Penney would eventually be in the weaker position because Ward and Sears, with complete lines, would have an edge with the buying public."

Had Penney, Sams and the other directors of the Penney company not been conditioned to fighting against odds, they might have given this memorandum more consideration. Had they had less vision of the possibilities of their own lines; or, had they considered that the purpose of competition was to kill off competitors, they might have gone into one of the mergers. They had not been brought up on such a strategy of politics and high finance. They did not believe that competition meant killing off rivals—or, as the saying goes, "If you can't beat them, join them." Competition, as they understood it, meant seeking with other merchants what was better for all consumers and all stores.

The other factor never mentioned was that Penney, Sams, and the other senior executives of the Penney company had the opportunity to sell out, in each and every case—for a large sum of money. This was in 1929, when they realized that difficult times were ahead for both the company and the nation. Instead of retiring in ease, they chose to be loyal to what they had helped to build and to their obligation to their organization—and did not quit.

Challenge to Depression

On October 23, 1929, the J. C. Penney Company ceased to be a closed corporation. On that day, common stock in the company was listed on the New York Stock Exchange. With the exception of a small amount of preferred stock issued for payment of tax levies following World War I (preferred stock that was afterward retired) this was the first public participation in the corporate affairs of the company. Although there was no connection of course between the two events, a few days after the listing of the common stock for public hearing the market collapsed. The depression of the thirties was under way.

The following year, the company for the first time in its history failed to show a gain in sales. In 1930 its total sales dropped to $192,943,765.42 from $209,690,413.77 in 1929. In 1931 sales again dropped, to a total of $173,705,094.52. In 1932 they fell off again, this time to $155,271,981.19—a difference of $54,418,432.58 from 1929.

Instead of going into a cellar, the company marked down its merchandise, sold it, wrote off the losses, and restocked at lower prices in 1930. Having completed these preparations, it moved against the depression and expanded its operations, increasing the number of its stores from 1,392 in 1929 to 1,473 in 1932. It was Sams's and Penney's conviction that the depression gave the company three major opportunities:

  1. Because each manager was responsible for his own store,

depression forced both him and his personnel to become more resourceful if they were to survive, thereby helping to solidify them as a team.

2. It enabled the company to introduce itself into new communities at costs that would represent savings later on.

3. By offering merchandise at prices that represented savings (in times when savings were increasingly important) new stores were able to establish themselves sooner than in ordinary times.

With ten million jobless, political minds (unaware that the program they were ballyhooing would reduce production and drive the depression deeper) were urging employers into a "share-the-work" program. By opening new stores in 78 cities in the first three years of the depression, the Penney company frankly admitted that, if "the way to help the country was to curtail production," it did not know how to do it.

In 1932 the voters, tired of the hard times that followed the stock-market collapse, chose a new Congress and a new President. With the new administration in power, it soon was apparent that politics was in control of the nation's economy; apparent that the future—the immediate future, at least—was dependent upon expediency rather than upon "the disposition," as Edmund Burke, the English statesman, phrased it, "to preserve and the capacity to improve."

Having obtained political responsibility for ten million jobless, the political minds reached for weapons to defend their newly won position. One weapon was propaganda; the other weapon was money. Propaganda was used successfully to discredit private ownership of business; money was used unsuccessfully to buy back prosperity.

Propaganda was used successfully to discredit private ownership of business largely because the popular mind had been conditioned to thinking critically—by the depression, by the mistakes of bad management, and by the publication in the twenties and early thirties of such books as *Sixty Families,* whose themes were taken from Karl Marx's *Das Kapital,* which claimed that in a capitalist society all wealth concentrates in fewer and fewer hands.

Despite a family heritage of generations of rabbis who were true spiritual leaders of their people, Marx, while still a youth in Germany in the early nineteenth century, dedicated his mind to materialism * and outlined the pattern of communism.

Seeping out of intellectual sewers for seventy-five years and flooding out of Moscow after the communist revolution in 1919, the Marxian philosophy had its followers in Washington. The winds of communism were blowing around the world (they are still blowing). In Washington there were those who maintained that permanent unemployment was, as Marx said, "a condition of existence of the capitalist mode of production." These men subscribed to the same ignorance out of which Marx wrote when he disclosed his discovery that "all profits are based on work hours maintained by human labor," that the use of machinery destroys profits, and that, since capitalism cannot exist without profits, it was destroying itself by the use of machinery which eliminates human labor.

As in Moscow where the communists broke with the past

---

* "Representation, thought, the intellectual behavior of human beings, arise as the direct outcome of their material behavior. The same thing is true of mental production, as displayed in the language, the politics, law, morality, religion, metaphysics of a people. Even the phantasmagorias in the human brain and enforced supplements of man's material vital process. Morality, religion, metaphysics, and ideology in general, with their appropriate forms of consciousness, thus forfeit the semblance of independence. They have no history, no evolution of their own. Human beings, developing material production and material intercourse, and thus altering the real world that environs them, alter therewith their thoughts and the product of their thoughts. Consciousness does not determine life, but life determines consciousness." Karl Marx, *German Ideology.*

and with God and celebrated their independence by butchering priests and desecrating altars, so in Washington there were
those who sought to break with the American past of free competition and substitute for it a government-planned economy.
Educated in sophistry, they had no "disposition to preserve
and [no] capacity to improve."

Because the nation's economy had been built by free competition, businessmen were publicly branded as enemies of social
progress. Political investigations into business were constantly
in the headlines. Accompanied by press releases, laws were
written to restrict and punish. When the National Industrial
Recovery Act gave the President control over industry it
promptly froze competition and just as promptly froze recovery.* There was legislation against chain stores; there were
discriminatory tax laws; there were all sorts of laws, all written,
according to the publicity, in the name of "social progress."

Although the American people were a solvent people, even
in the depression, the planners argued: "Granting our standard of living is much higher, there are still too few of our
people who have enough of the good things of life. We must
have more electric lights, more automobiles, more food, more
clothing, more homes, more everything for everybody."

But, instead of merely talking about "social progress," private business had been steadily producing more of those "good
things of life" until, in this country, there were more electric
lights, more telephones, more bathtubs, more radios, more
automobiles, and more of almost everything else, distributed
among more people, than in all the rest of the world. Without
being told by the politicians, businessmen realized, however,
that they had still not produced enough. They also knew that

* When the National Industrial Recovery Act was declared unconstitutional by
the Supreme Court of the United States on May 27, 1935, indices recorded that
business as a whole had only recovered to the extent of one per cent in the
twenty-three months of the law's existence.

"production and distribution" was the solution, not "social progress." Such a term was too high-toned for their vocabularies. The political solution to "we must have more [of] everything for everybody" was legislation designed to hamstring production lines and distribution methods.

There will be those who will not agree; but private business has been responsible, within itself, for more and greater social gains than all the politics that have been indulged in, and all the politicians who have lived in this nation since its beginnings. The greatest social advance ever made in this country occurred when industry moved out of the home and into the factory, thereby making the home a home. That was a contribution of business, one of the many advances—advances that are always made by people in their private capacities as citizens.

The only way social advances ever find their way into law is through their introduction and practice in business; practice that leads to acceptance by enough people so that the seeker after public office, depending upon votes to be elected, can safely embrace them.

Largely because of restrictive legislation, the years of the thirties were all depression years, with as many jobless when the decade ended as there were in 1932. Prosperity was not bought back by political spending. No government has yet brought prosperity by grinding its people between the wheels of taxing and spending. Prosperity, like a home or a business, has to be built by the people themselves.

No one has yet built a home on money. A home must have within it the love of a man and his wife and his children. No one has yet built a business on money. A business must render a service and, if a business is to prosper, it must have principles to govern it. Love in a home and principles in a business are separate and apart from the kitchen and the ledger, but they rule both.

This is not to be interpreted to mean that all businessmen believe these things, and live them. There are sharps and there are crooks in business, as in everything else; but, all enlightened business minds believe in the ruling principles, and try to live them.

Having a completely materialistic approach to life, the communistic mind contemptuously dismisses law, morality, and religion as "having no history, and no evolution of their own." The book-bred mind, whatever its approach to life, contemptuously dismisses business as being beneath serious study and fit only for sociological experiment. As with the communistic mind in its denial of the spiritual, so with the book-bred mind in its attitude toward business—neither "can learn," as Emerson said, "what he has not preparation for learning, however near to his eyes is the object."

But despite propaganda against the private ownership of business, despite sociological experiments with business, despite the sheltering of communists within government in Washington, and despite the enactment of restrictive and punishing laws against the private ownership of business including specifically the Penney company—the Penney company went ahead in the depression years of the thirties.

It went ahead by the mere act of going to work.

The widening opportunities of their contracts encouraged the store managers to work harder in order to meet the challenge. The underlying purpose was to put more money in their pockets by making the following changes in their contracts:

1. In the years between 1927 (when the company ceased to sell partnerships in individual stores) and 1937, expansion stock was sold six times, each time at a figure below the market price, so as to give the managers more opportunities to invest in the company's future.

2. Since 1933 managers have shared in all profits but have not paid for store losses.

3. Tryout managers have also been given a share in store profits.

4. Since 1944 managers moving to other stores have received credit in their contracts for previous management.

5. Profit sharing is no longer limited to managers but is distributed among assistant managers and others.

6. Since 1939 the profit-sharing retirement plan has added much to management's future security and its share in the company's earnings.

The company in turn benefits because:

1. It assures the continuous influx of new blood and new merchandising ideas—both so essential to any continuing and developing business.

2. It assures the stockholders "of the same, or even greater, degree of loyalty," as Sams pointed out in a message to the owners "on the part of those who are handling the business."

In 1937 there were 1,523 Penney stores and a sales volume of $275,375,137.32; in 1940 there were 1,586 stores and a sales volume of $304,539,325.64; and in 1941 there were 1,605 stores with total sales of $377,571,710.99. In only one year of the nine years immediately prior to 1941, did sales fall below the previous year. That was in 1938 when they dropped to $257,963,-945.53. In the nine years, the average sales per store increased from approximately $105,000 in 1932 to approximately $235,000 in 1941.

As Sams and Penney had expected, depression taught their people to be better merchants.

Since it was not classified as an "essential industry" during the war years, the company lost many of its key personnel to the Armed Services. It replaced them with women; to whom Sams, in the third year of the war, paid this tribute:

"Hundreds of our stores do not have a single trained Penney man besides the manager. Women are writing orders, trimming windows, making show cards, keeping the stores clean, selling most of the merchandise, doing every job in the stores. In one city the Penney women went back to a store at night in a flood, moved the merchandise out of reach of the water, and kept the store in business. That was a dramatic performance, but day in and day out Penney women have kept the company in business."

With all the perplexities of government wartime controls being superimposed on the political restrictions of the years preceding the war, with acute shortages in personnel and in merchandise, the company kept moving ahead to a sales volume of $549,149,147.67 in 1945, although it had dropped back to 1,602 stores.

The $500 cash investment Penney had made in one store in Kemmerer had grown in forty-three years to a surplus of $68,409,390.53. With the difficult years of depression and war behind them, Penney and Sams, following the annual stockholders' meeting in April, 1946, were promoted again. After twenty-nine years as chairman, Penney became honorary chairman of the J. C. Penney Company, and Sams became chairman. A. W. Hughes, the young merchant in Eureka, Utah, who in 1923 had been criticized by Sams for "making too much money," was elected to the presidency.

Characteristically, Sams wrote to all managers and all associates in the company:

April 23, 1946.

To the Managers and Associates:

You men are, undoubtedly, aware that our company's annual stockholders' meeting was held on April 20. At that meeting the present members of the board of directors were re-elected. At the same time, the stockholders, by an overwhelming vote, approved our company's "General Office Compensation Plan." This plan had been approved by the stockholders originally in 1927. However, it was felt desirable to submit the plan in detail and in its present form to all stockholders for formal ratification. Needless to say, we were pleased by the confidence expressed in the stockholders' action, because it reflects the jobs that you folks in the stores, as well as the associates in the central office group, have done. Furthermore, it provides stockholder endorsement of the fundamental principle which has built this company—the principle of men sharing in the results they produce.

A meeting of the directors was held immediately following the stockholders' meeting. At this meeting a number of changes were made in the officers of this company.

These officers were elected:

Honorary Chairman of the Board of Directors, J. C. Penney; Chairman of the Board: E. C. Sams; President: A. W. Hughes; Executive Vice-President: W. A. Reynolds; Second Vice-President: F. W. Binzen; Treasurer and Third Vice-President: G. E. Mack; Secretary: A. J. Raskopf; Comptroller: R. C. Weiderman; Assistant Comptroller: G. M. Campbell.

I am happy to write you men regarding this change in our official setup. It seems particularly fitting that in designating Mr. Penney as Honorary Chairman of our Board, we shall pay deserved tribute to the man who has made "honor" so real in his own life and in the life of this company. For thirty-nine years I have found inspiration and strength in working side by side with our Founder and I look forward to the same fine fellowship in the years ahead.

With respect to the other changes, I think that my feelings can best be expressed to you men in a letter I addressed to the other members of the board, since I was unable to attend this meeting:

"First, let me say that I desire to be relieved of the responsibilities incumbent upon the president of the J. C. Penney Company. For nearly thirty years I have served the company as its president. I have slipped by the 'milepost' that provides for retirement from such intensive activity and it is high time for another to take over. I hope and expect to remain a part of management—exercising that great privilege of a continuing association with a body of folks that, to me, are tops from all points of view.

"The company is particularly fortunate that it is filled with men who are entitled to increasing recognition. The men who compose our executive group are indeed a 'pillar of strength.'

"Mr. Hughes has served the J. C. Penney Company for twenty-six years—as store manager, personnel director, assistant to the president, and as executive vice-president. His abilities are well known and he has demonstrated a great quality of leadership. He is worthy and entitled to be designated president.

"Messrs. Reynolds and Binzen have contributed so much to our progress and success that words of approval from me would be only repetition. They have served for some years as second and third vice-presidents and, of course, they should be advanced to first and second vice-president respectively.

"There are a number of men from whom we could choose a third vice-president. Any of these men would serve with ability and distinction. It seems to me that the man who handles our finances could well be designated as third vice-president. Mr. Mack has a fine record of accomplishment over a long period of years with the company and his responsibilities seem to suggest this designation.

"I will be back to my office a few days following the above-mentioned meeting and I shall be happy to get back. In the meantime, I trust the board will give due consideration to the suggestions contained herein. These recommendations are made with only one thought in mind—viz., that which is best for the greatest organization in the world. Great opportunities lie ahead. This company has just begun to scratch the surface of its possibilities. There is no such thing as reaching or even approaching the 'top of the ladder' of accomplishment and achievement—greater—greater things lie ahead always. The best way to do anything has never been found.

"With such a group as we have to carry on, no goal can be set; new blood mixing with the old, bringing new ideas to dovetail with tried and tested methods—all this makes for progress. What has been, will seem of small consequence as we move forward into the realm of possibilities that I am confident lie ahead.

"This is a great world and it's a great time to be alive. As we move forward I hope to continue to serve with value—thinking always in terms that whatever it is our company undertakes it must tie in with our motto—Honor, Confidence, Service and Cooperation."

Cordially yours,

E. C. SAMS

In the tradition of Penney and Sams, the new president, A. W. Hughes, informed Penney managers:

"Many shares of Penney stock are held in the portfolios of estates, institutions, and individuals. These folks are not speculators; they are investors. The investment advisers, who make their living by guiding people in safeguarding their funds, check and follow closely the companies in which they put their money. They make periodic visits to our offices and ask a great many questions about sales, conditions, profits, prospects, and a hundred detailed matters. They are, as a group, keen, intelligent men.

"When they have finished their questions I always try to send them away with one final thought. I say to them something like this:

" 'You've asked about a lot of things, but you have missed the most important factor in our business. Our biggest asset is not shown in the company's balance sheet or in the figures. The Penney company's greatest asset is the Penney manager.'

"I make that statement to these men because I believe it. Furthermore, whenever a Penney manager has happened to be visiting the building while one of these analysts was in the office, I have called the manager in and told my investment friend, 'This is Jim Jones, the Penney manager from Blankville. I want you to meet him so you will realize what I have been telling you about Penney managers. Maybe you'd like to ask him some questions.'

"Each time this has happened, the investment man has said to me after the manager left the room, 'Thanks so much for the chance to meet Jim Jones. Now I understand what you mean. If all Penney managers are like him, I can easily understand why Penney's is recognized as it is in the merchandising field.'

"Maybe they say that to please me, but they back their statements by investing in our company."

FOURTEEN

Cutting Across Buying Patterns

THERE IS nothing new about the chain store method of distribution.

In China, more than twenty-one hundred years ago, a merchant named Los Kass established a distribution system involv-
ing a large number of stores. Centuries later, in Japan, the
Mitsui group put together a chain of apothecary shops which
remained powerful in the drug business from the time of organization in 1643 until the end of World War II.

The Fugger family in Augsburg, Germany, in the eighteenth
century, were chain store merchants; and, in 1670, the "Company of Gentlemen Adventurers of England Trading in Hud-
son's Bay" were given a King's charter to set up the first chain
store organization in America. John Jacob Astor, with his fur
trading posts in the West, was a chain store operator. One of
our presidents, Andrew Jackson was a partner in Jackson and
Hutchings, operators of a small number of retail stores in Ten-
nessee more than a hundred years ago.

In the United States the oldest national chain organization
still in operation is the Great Atlantic & Pacific Tea Company,
which grew out of a little store on Vesey street, in New York
City, owned by George F. Gilman. A hide and leather merchant, Gilman abandoned that business in 1859 to open a tea
store "to do away with," as he announced, "various profits and
brokerages, cartages, storages, cooperages and waste, with the
exception of a small commission paid for purchasing to our

correspondents in Japan and China, one cartage, and a small profit to ourselves which, on our large sales, will amply repay us."

In partnership with Gilman was George Huntington Hartford, who had been his representative in hides and leather in St. Louis. The profits Gilman was determined to eliminate had been going to factors in Chinese and Japanese ports, to importers in New York, to bankers in foreign exchange, to speculators, to wholesalers, to carters, to coopers and to merchants, all of whom cut in on every pound of tea until tea was retailing at $1, and more, a pound. By reducing the number of middlemen, Gilman cut the retail price to 30¢ a pound.

It was the beginning of a business that soon extended its buying methods into coffee and spices, and from coffee and spices and tea into all lines of groceries.

Following A&P came Woolworth, McCrory, Kresge, Kress, Kroger, W. T. Grant, Sears, Montgomery Ward, and scores of others along with Penney, all working to the same end of bringing necessities to the consumer at lower prices.

In the West when Penney started there were a number of small chain store groups, but for the most part the retail trade in the small towns were controlled by mining companies or by general store merchants who went to market once a year and never more than twice a year, buying on these visits requirements for six months or a year hence. Drummers were few; peddlers and their team-driven wagons were familiar and welcome sights in the remote settlements.

Crude as they were, the general store and the peddlers were the beginnings of retail merchandising in this country. The general store, more often than not, was in "dingy, wooden structures, either with rough counters or no counters at all, which offered consumers every conceivable kind of merchandise from dry goods, hardware, chemical fireboxes, and notions to such patent medicines as Steer's Maccaboy and Caphalic snuff. The peddler ranged the countryside with a pack on his back or penetrated deep on horseback, or in his painted wagon, to dispose of ginghams and cottons, needles, thread and pins, boots and shoes, and patent medicines.

Peddlers, like the general merchants, charged as much as they could get. Up to the time of Gilman, there was no such thing as a common price to all customers in retail establishments; and when Gilman with his partner, Hartford, expanded into general groceries, that common price affected only the grocery business. It was not until John Wanamaker opened his "Grand Depot"—which was the first real department store in this country—in Philadelphia in 1876 that "one price for all" came into general merchandising. Wanamaker also took another idea from Gilman and Hartford. He eliminated a number of middlemen in his purchases, and passed along savings to his customers.

For doing these things—opening a department store, selling for less and at a common price—the merchant was given rough treatment by a Philadelphia newspaper editor. He was excoriated as being "grasping and greedy" and accused of having "squelched hundreds of small dealers without compunction."

Disliking the idea of reducing prices, although not admitting it, other merchants appealed to their legislative listeners to pass laws outlawing department stores. A bill was introduced into the Pennsylvania Legislature calling for the licensing of department stores and the collection of $100,000 in yearly fees. Although it did not pass, a law was created in Missouri, levying a tax of $500 a year on each and every classification of merchandise sold in a department store.

The agitation died down when the department store proved its place, to be aroused again against mail-order houses. This clamor reached its zenith or its nadir, as you choose, in a small town in Montana. Here a motion picture theater exchanged admission tickets for mail-order catalogues and turned over the catalogues to town authorities for burning in the public square, thus insuring a continuance of "freedom of opportunity in America."

It could not have occurred to Gilman and to Hartford in their little store on Vesey street in New York, nor to John Wanamaker in his "Grand Depot" in Philadelphia, that the day would come when government would penalize merchants for selling for less. It could not have occurred to Penney in Kemmerer in 1902 when, to be in business for himself, he furnished his home with an empty dry goods box and two empty shoe boxes; nor to Sams in Cumberland in 1908 when, to qualify for a store of his own, he and his wife lived in a lean-to and went to a creek half a mile distant for water.

These men did such things because they realized the job of getting ahead was one they had to work out for themselves. In those days, there was no one around to tell Penney that to be thrifty was to be evil, nor to warn Sams against working overtime. In those days, people simply would not have been persuaded that they could rid themselves of all economic problems by dropping them into a ballot box where they would disappear in the radiance of a political sunrise.

Did government by decree single out Galileo and order him to invent the pendulum? Did government say to Elias Howe, "Produce a sewing machine"; to Cyrus McCormick, a reaper; to Edison, an incandescent lamp; or were these, and thousands of other inventions, the products of patient investigation by patient men?

It is very easy, once a thing has been accomplished, to say that it was waiting to be done, all the time. Of course it was— but it needed some specific person to do it. Usually it was one man: such as Henry Ford who worked out, in 1893, a simpler way to make gasoline, doing what he had watched at the Columbian Exposition in Chicago. In the kitchen of his home in Detroit, while he turned a flywheel, of a little engine made from a piece of gas pipe, as his wife stood by dropping gasoline in an intake valve, Ford proved an idea that led to the building of the automobile industry.

Pioneers in the chain store field were not inventors in the mechanical sense. They did not bring low-cost transportation to the family garage, but, being merchants, they did bring merchandise at low cost to the family itself.

They did it by cutting across a long-established buying pattern (into which was woven half a dozen, or more, middlemen) and by going directly to the manufacturer and passing along most of the savings to the customer.

To do these things they had to know markets; they had to know merchandise; they had to know their customers. This was what Penney was talking about when he established centralized buying in New York. He was confident that, by having trained men on the spot, they could take advantage of many buying opportunities that otherwise would be lost. The company's experiences proved that he was correct:

There was a doll manufacturer who had to shut down his factory because he was unable to obtain firm orders from wholesalers. He went to the Penney company and received orders for his entire output. The plant was reopened. People went back to work. The dolls were delivered on a weekly basis and were in the Penney stores in time for the Christmas trade.

There was a blanket company on the edge of bankruptcy. It was an old established firm which had refrained from manufacturing for chain stores. A representative of the company approached the J. C. Penney Company, received an order sufficient to keep his working organization together, received a larger order when the first one was filled, and so on down through the intervening years.

A hosiery manufacturer had a great many idle machines. Knowing that idle machines were costing the manufacturer a great deal of money (which idle machines always do) the Penney company approached him with a proposition to make full-fashioned silk hose to retail for 95¢ a pair.

The manufacturer was amused. "You mean, you seriously mean you want me to make you full-fashioned silk stockings at a price that will permit you to sell them at 95¢ a pair?" he repeated, laughing.

"Yes."

"It can't be done. I can't do it, nor can anyone else. What you are asking is ridiculous. Who ever heard of full-fashioned silk stockings selling for 95¢ a pair, even at wholesale prices?"

"We think it can be done, and we think you can do it," the manufacturer was told, and before him were placed specification sheets showing the construction desired by the Penney company.

The manufacturer studied them and agreed to take a small contract of several thousand dozen pairs as an experiment. For its part, the Penney company agreed to work with him. Together they found a way to manufacture a full-fashioned silk stocking that could be sold at retail for 95¢ a pair.

Before long the manufacturer's plant was working three daily shifts. All his machines were busy. His overhead went down and, while his profit per dozen pairs of stockings was not large, his over-all profit was substantially increased.

Wanting a better quality in a man's union suit to sell at retail at a particular price, the Penney company sought out a particular manufacturer. As in the case of the hosiery manufacturer, the Penney company was told that its requirements could not be met for the price it was willing to pay. Again specifications were given to the manufacturer. Like the hosiery manufacturer, he studied them and agreed to experiment.

The experiments proved the requirements that had been submitted to him, and he accepted an order, "to keep," as he said, "my plant from shutting down during the dull season."

He made some money on the contract; not much, but some. "Of more importance," he said when he had completed the contract, "was the fact that I learned the advantages of continuous operation."

As the manufacturer's technique improved, the Penney company kept improving the garment to obtain greater and greater value. With manufacturing costs still going down, Penney reduced the retail price correspondingly.

"These illustrations—dolls, blankets, silk hosiery, underwear—indicate what we mean when we say that the first business of a merchant is to act as the representative of his customer," said Penney. "To represent the customer properly, a merchant must be intelligent about the goods he sells. He must have a professional concern about the intrinsic values in the goods he offers. He must be able to understand manufacturing to the point where he can show a producer how to produce for less and, at the same time, turn out a good article.

"In the case of silk stockings we simply did not agree they were a luxury item, as manufacturers and merchants thought them to be. We believed a person of moderate means had the same right to have her desires satisfied as did the person of substantial means. We set about to prove that belief, and the mere fact that silk hose had never been sold for as little as 95¢ was of no importance.

"There were obstacles in the way of making them so they could be sold at that price, but removing those obstacles was not the customer's job. It was our job and the job of a manufacturer with idle machines and an active mind.

"So it was with men's underwear. So has it been with a lot of things we have on our shelves and on our counters. It is upon such values that our business has been built. It is the steady striving to raise standards that brings to the merchant the keen satisfaction of the professional spirit."

Before going to a manufacturer, the Penney company estimates the retail price for the item it wants made. This requires study of every phase of manufacturing from the cost of raw materials to the cost of finished goods, as well as additional studies into warehousing, distribution, and turnover. All these and other factors enter into price eventually fixed, which must contain a saving for the customer, a profit for the company, and a profit for the manufacturer.

We still hear it said, although not so frequently, by those who oppose chain stores, that they first get the manufacturers dependent upon them, then chisel down prices year after year until they force the supplier into bankruptcy. How could Penney, or any other chain store merchant, stay in business if suppliers were constantly being forced out of business? The fact is, the chain store is one of the supplier's best customers, if not his best.

By placing large orders in seasonally slack periods, the Penney company helps to reduce manufacturers' overhead by eliminating these slack periods—and, in many instances, pays for finished merchandise well in advance of the delivery periods contracted for.

As for driving suppliers into bankruptcy, here are two typical stories among hundreds. The first concerns a manufacturer who supplies overalls to the Penney company. From the day he started in business in 1918 until 1925 he made overalls for independent merchants. His average yearly net profit was less than 1 per cent; to be exact, his average yearly net profit from 1918 through 1922 was .66 per cent.

In 1922 he contracted with the Penney company to supply a certain number of overalls and he has been a supplier for Penney ever since. His average yearly net profit on these contracts since 1922 has been several times as much as he was formerly making. His business has expanded; he employs more people; the work is steady, twelve months each year. His wage scale since 1925 has been substantially above accepted standards. He now makes a better overall. The Penney company sells this better overall for less money.

A sidelight of a Penney buying operation is found in an experience of a blanket mill. In 1938 The Penney company was approached by a representative of the mill. He had a problem, and a plan.

The problem:

The mill was losing money, and had been for some time. Its product was good, but, because blankets are seasonal goods, merchants were reluctant to place orders for their manufacture during the months of December to May. As a result, during those months the mill was closed, or partially closed. In addition, despite the profitable working months from May to December, the mill was operating at an annual loss. Credit was extremely limited. The common stock had not paid dividends in years. Dividends on the preferred stock were badly in arrears. The company was threatened with bankruptcy.

The plan:

If the mill could secure an order sufficiently large to be kept running full time during the otherwise quiet months, it could afford to take that order at a smaller profit than it would normally expect. By so operating, the organization could be kept together and be maintained on an annual profitable basis from the results of the later months when there was a heavy demand for its product.

Penney asked for samples and prices. The representative gave both. The Penney company agreed upon the quantities necessary to keep the mill working when production was needed. The Penney company also agreed to the prices that were submitted. Penney's relationship with this mill has continued. Today, the mill is one of Penney's most valuable sources of supply.

As a result of this relationship the mill has been able to dispose of all of its old machinery and now has a production line that is entirely modern. Within a few years all the back preferred dividends were paid, and the common stock went on a regular dividend basis. Several hundred people now have steady jobs at greatly increased wages and salaries; and, on top of the increases in wages and salaries, an annual bonus plan in which all employees participate has been inaugurated.

Some will say that in the whole scheme of a nation's economy the restoration of one small blanket company was not important; that if it was forced out of business only a comparatively few people would have been affected—the stockholders and the employees, altogether only a few hundred persons.

The Penney company was not then—and is not now—sympathetic with that point of view.

It saw the people in the blanket company—stockholders and employees—as individuals, as members of individual families who, in turn, were members of the larger family known as the community. As such they were people whose economic well-being was not only highly important to them as individuals but, in a larger sense, was important to everyone else in the community.

By enabling the blanket company to once more become a going business, the Penney company did more than merely preserve a business.

It enabled the employees to be self-supporting, protected the stockholders against loss of their savings, and through the distribution of pay checks, bonus checks, and dividend checks enabled the company to become an asset rather than a liability to the community—through the payment of local taxes for the support of local government and the maintenance of property values upon which the cost of all government, in large part, depends.

Here again, as in all dealings with suppliers, the Penney company was in its proper role of helping the supplier to solve his immediate problem for the ultimate benefit of the consumer.

FIFTEEN

Serving 35,000,000 Customers

Before the final shaping of Federal legislation to impose punishing taxes on chain stores, one of the men involved in the political transaction dropped in to see J. C. Penney. He was concerned, he said, over "the plight of the little fellow" and began a long dissertation on that subject.

He repeated all the familiar arguments: Chain stores had an unfair advantage over the small retailer and the small manufacturer. Buying as they did in large quantities, they were able to buy for less and sell for less, thus forcing the small merchant into bankruptcy. As for the small manufacturer, he was compelled to sell for a lower profit; and, since he could not survive long in a price war with the chain stores, he was eventually forced to sell out his factory.

As his visitor concluded, Penney observed, "Of course, what you say is only half true." After agreeing that buying in large quantities enabled the company to buy for less, he went on to say, "That is not what *really* permits us to sell for less. We are able to sell for less because, as a group, our managers are better store operators than are the average storekeepers, and, beyond that, our managers are backed by better buyers.

"The advantage we have in quantity buying is a sword with two sharp edges. One edge cuts through costs, and the savings are passed along to the customer. But what happens to us if our buyers buy merchandise the public doesn't want—and we have on hand a million dress shirts, a million pairs of shoes, or a hundred thousand dozen pairs of stockings? You might consider that, and after you get through thinking about how these large quantities apply to all the items in our stores, take some time and conduct your own survey of all our suppliers—most of whom are small businessmen—and see what they have to say about doing business with the Penney company.

"My own opinion of the legislation that is being proposed is this:

"You can write laws that will tax the experienced out of business but you cannot write laws that will keep the inexperienced in business. It is inexperience, not the 'little fellow,' you are trying to protect with this legislation. The 'little fellow,' if he is a businessman, doesn't need protection. The law you are proposing will have one result, and only one result. Everyone will be paying for the losses of bad management and, worse still, the public will be forced to pay higher and higher prices for eveything it buys.

"The fact is, by the passage of such a law government will make it harder for the little fellow to succeed. What you are proposing in this measure is really a law to keep the owner of one store from using his savings to open a second store—and, by decree, punish him for trying to get ahead."

As said in another chapter, thousands of suppliers—most of them small, although some have become large—supply merchandise to Penney stores. Here are some typical stories to explain how some of them became affiliated with the J. C. Penney Company:

A few weeks after the stock-market collapse in 1929 a small shoe manufacturer was forced to liquidate his business. Going to his creditors he promised, if not pressed into bankruptcy, to pay all he owed. The creditors agreed. Hearing of his promise and of their confidence, the Penney company was attracted by the man's integrity and invited him to call.

As a result of that conference, the man set up a factory in a loft building and began making slippers and play shoes. He paid off his debts, and today he has a modern plant, has tripled his production, greatly increased the number of employees, and has repeatedly refused higher prices for his product than those paid by the Penney company.

In 1903, a year after Penney started in business, two men formed a partnership to deal in scarfs and handkerchiefs and to be converters of piece goods. Their capital was $6,000. To-day, they are among the largest suppliers in their line; they still are suppliers to the Penney company.

In 1910 a glove manufacturer, since grown into one of the country's largest, began selling to Penney stores. At that time the company had one small factory and Penney was its principal customer. As the years passed it grew larger, but in 1921 it was in financial trouble. The owner saw Penney, told him, "I haven't enough money left to keep open thirty days," and wondered if the Penney company could help him out temporarily.

He was asked whether it would help if his bills were paid "every ten days, instead of every thirty days as your invoices provide."

"It will keep me in business," answered the manufacturer.

That owner tells this story: "Many a time when we had the pay roll come due, the Penney check would come in just in time. I had a couple of tough years, and the Penney company sent in a lot of orders and kept the check coming every ten days. I have never forgotten it, and never will. We have 3,100 accounts today and we have two new factories; thirteen in all."

There is a trunk company in a mid-western city that has among its possessions a canceled check for $86.98. It is a check drawn on the First National Bank of Kemmerer, Wyoming, under date of March 29, 1904, and signed by Johnson, Callahan and Penney. It was the first check a small trunk-maker received from a Penney store. The Penney company's dealings are now with the second and third generations of a family-owned business, with the account growing, in 1947, to $258,612.

Fifteen or twenty years ago, a suspender manufacturer was working at a machine in a company of which he is now president. In that first year the company was very small and Penney placed a $2,000 order with it. In 1947, the company was large in its field, with approximately one million dollars of its yearly volume coming from the Penney company.

More than forty years ago, Penney placed an order for work clothing with a Western company having one small plant in Denver. As Penney's business expanded, so did the manufacturer's. The company now has three large plants and does a business each year of many millions of dollars, much of which is with the Penney company.

A quarter of a century ago, a hat manufacturer in New England sent a representative to the Penney company in search of business. He received an order, in 1922, for 36,000 hats. At present, Penney is selling 1,000,000 hats a year from the same manufacturer. One of the new plants built by the company operates almost exclusively filling Penney orders.

In 1928, the Penney company wanted to sell rayon underwear at a certain price. Having established the specifications, the company followed its practice of studying costs and approached a manufacturer. The manufacturer agreed to experiment and was given approximately $50,000 worth of business that year. Today, twenty years afterward, he has a large new plant, and his volume of business with the Penney company exceeds $3,000,000 a year.

A sweater manufacturer received his first Penney order in 1941. In that year his volume with the Penney company approximated $52,000. Seven years later, his volume was over $600,000. . . . In 1938 a merchandising man who was familiar with the needle industry presented a proposition to the Penney company. He wanted to establish a new dress house and was encouraged to go ahead. Having that encouragement, he interested a partner with substantial capital and a company was formed. In 1947, this company sold Penney more than $1,000,000 worth of dresses. . . . In 1920, a woman's coat business was organized. One of its first customers was the Penney company, with which it now does a volume business of close to $3,000,000 annually.

In 1937, a young man decided to leave an advertising agency and go into business with his father, who made foot appliances. In business a short time, the son saw the limitations of his father's company and began designing a soft-sole shoe for babies and infants. Completing a model, he took it to the Penney company for criticisms and suggestions. The company supplied worked-out improvements in the model, then gave the young man his first order for babies' and infants' kid leather shoes.

The shoes turned out so well from the standpoint of construction that the company gave him a babies' and infants' hard-sole shoe to make. The results again were good. More and more business in shoes of different types and patterns was turned over to the former advertising man until he had exhausted expansion possibilities in the neighborhood of his father's plant and was forced into meeting the problem of building a new factory.

Going to the Penney company, he expressed a desire to locate in some small Midwest community. The company made several suggestions, and he chose a small town in Missouri where, as he said, "the people who work in the factory can have homes and gardens and their kids can have room to play." The real-estate department of the Penney company helped him in his choice of a site, and in the design of his new plant.

Within two or three years he needed another shoe factory in which to make Goodyear welt shoes in misses' and children's sizes so that he would have a complete line of misses' and children's shoes. Again the company consulted with him in the selection of lasts and patterns and types of shoes to be manufactured. Now he is planning a third factory, this one to manufacture additional children's shoes. Once more, with the company, he is going through the same careful preliminaries.

Starting in 1937, this former advertising man has become one of the largest producers of babies' and infants' shoes. The Penney company remains his principal customer, and the shoes it helped design are sold in department and shoe stores all over the country.

In 1932, an account was opened with a comparatively small manufacturer of women's hats. As a condition of placing the order, Penney buyers went into the factory to work with the foremen on some of the finer details of this high-style merchandise. The hat company now has three factories producing nearly 10,000 hats daily. Penney buys about 25 per cent of this output. . . . A supplier of women's coats and suits started as an errand boy with another supplier in 1923. He now has his own company. His volume of business with Penney in 1947 was a little more than $750,000. . . . Twenty-five years ago, a boy got a job with a dress company as a follow-up clerk on the delivery of reorders. His efficiency and courtesy attracted the attention of Penney buyers. A few years later when he decided to go into the dress manufacturing business for himself, Penney was his first account. . . . In 1918 another boy was in the delivery department of a shirtwaist and dress manufacturer. He came up through that firm to reach a partnership, to leave and start his own business in 1944. Both his old firm and his new firm are Penney suppliers.

These are but a few of the many, many stories of small companies—some now large in their field—employing mostly 75 or 100 or 150 people that have been started by men who wanted to be in business for themselves and who were able to get their start because a Penney company was waiting to buy from them.

Altogether there are more than 7,000 merchandise suppliers to the Penney company. Among them, each year, are distributed checks totaling millions of dollars; in 1946, checks for more than $400,000,000, and, in 1947, checks for more than $500,000,000. This is money and employment that finds its way into every nook and cranny of the United States.

In many cases, Penney merchandise accounts for 50 per cent of a manufacturer's output. Sometimes it runs to more than that; often it runs to less. Penney has two reasons for operating this way. As a buyer, the company does not consider it sound business to be too dependent upon one source for what it buys; and, in reverse, it does not consider it sound business for a seller to be too dependent upon one outlet for what he sells.

Buying as it does large amounts of merchandise each year, ordinary business prudence requires Penney to buy intelligently. Business is as exacting a profession as is pursuit of the arts, or law, or education, or government—and, in our present-day civilization, is the supporting structure under all. In one way or another, business is what furnishes the pay rolls, endows the universities, subsidizes the arts, and provides the taxes that permit government to function. The same law which rules business rules every other human activity—the law of mathematics.

In its dealings with its suppliers, the Penney company is also aware that the laws of mathematics govern them. It knows it must watch their profits as well as its own profits, and regulate both so that the customer shares with both.

This does not merely mean savings for a customer and profits for a manufacturer and a merchant, but it starts a whole chain of events. By saving on what he buys, a part of the customer's dollar remains in his pocket, which he can use to spend or to save for other things.

A few years ago a customer came into the Penney store in Wenatchee, Washington, went to the manager, and said, "Come outside and see the automobile the Penney company bought."

Somewhat mystified, the manager followed the customer outside where a new car was standing by the curb.

"You bought that car for us," explained the customer. "When Penney's opened a store here, my husband and I started to trade with you. We decided to keep track of how much we saved. Last week we bought and paid cash for this car out of those savings. It was fun to watch the savings, but Penney's paid for the car."

Although most customers of Penney's do not keep such close track and do not know exactly how much they have saved, the savings are always there, and are used. They contribute to a higher standard of living for the 35,000,000 customers of Penney stores.

As for the Penney company, profits enable it to remain in business, thus furnishing regular employment to 50,000 people and part-time employment to more than 75,000 people. The wages of these people, in addition to providing homes and education, food, clothing, and recreation, help to support every other business, every profession, and every home in every community where a Penney store is located.

In addition to approximately 7,000 merchandise suppliers, another 4,000 firms supply fixtures, counters, and other necessary articles. In turn these 11,000 suppliers are able to remain in business and furnish employment to more than 1,000,000 people. The wages paid these employees flow through the same channels as do the wages paid Penney employees.

Beyond these channels are other channels; one called "taxes." In 1947, the Penney company paid $28,212,465.69 in direct taxes to Federal, state and municipal governments. It is impossible to estimate how much it paid in indirect taxes (those taxes that are hidden in the cost of everything the company buys) but, certainly, a very large sum. The suppliers paid further millions directly and indirectly; and, on top of these, were all the direct and indirect taxes paid by Penney employees and all the employees of 11,000 suppliers.

To state it in one sentence: A company cannot continue in business, hence continue to employ people, unless it makes a profit.

A tree doesn't mind if the fruit is taken from it. It doesn't live on its fruit. But take the soil from its roots, and there will be no fruit on its branches.

SIXTEEN

Protecting Moths with Hospital Care

A WASHBASIN, a cake of soap, and a pitcher of water were the tools; and a room in a small hotel in New York was J. C. Penney's first testing laboratory. You remember the story: Penney, sleeves rolled up, busy scrubbing samples, and his employer, T. M. Callahan, standing inside the doorway, inquiring, "Jim, what in the world are you doing there?"

Today, test tubes, chemicals, microscopes, launderometers, fadeometers, machines for testing tensile and bursting strengths, steel balls, indelible inks, washing machines, abrasives, and a room filled with other equipment have taken the place of a room in a small hotel. Today on the eighth floor of the J. C. Penney Building on Thirty-fourth Street in New York City is located the research laboratory of the J. C. Penney Company.

The research laboratory has three assignments: (1) the maintenance of merchandise standards through control testing; (2) the development of new and desirable products; (3) the adoption of new materials and processes to company merchandise.

The purposes are two: (1) to aid buyers in selecting quality merchandise; (2) to make sure that deliveries from manufacturers meet the standards upon which the merchandise was purchased.

Whereas more than forty-five years ago, Penney used soap, water, and a washbasin for one test—to see if colors were fast in the samples he had—merchandise is now tested in a multitude of ways, among them being tests to determine not only fastness in the colors but the weight of materials, wearing qualities, composition, resistance to fire, susceptibility to water, warmth, and, as in the case of woolens, tests of methods for rendering materials moth resistant.

Many tests determine the quality of a piece of merchandise, and it is emphasized by the researchers that no material can be judged properly "from one or two isolated facts. All facts developed by a whole series of tests must be known before conclusions can be reached."

Here are some of the many tests to which material is put, and here are what the tests tell:

One of the first questions a merchant asks about material is its weight. This applies to materials whatever their width, with weight being expressed in yards per pound. This, of course, means the actual number of yards required to weigh one pound.

Thread Counts: A microscope is used to determine the number of warp yarns and the number of filling yarns per inch in a woven fabric. The thread count tells the researchers the construction balance. This balance has a bearing on the serviceability of the fabric.

Fiber Identification: Fibers are important in the wearing qualities of materials. They are identified under microscopes and by chemical analysis.

Per Cent Sizing: The fabric is weighed and then put in a chemical bath. The chemicals remove starch and other sizings. After having its bath the material is weighed again. The weight difference tells how much sizing was in the material.

Shrinkage: A ten-inch square is drawn in indelible ink on a piece of material. One side of the square is drawn parallel to the warp; another side is drawn parallel to the filling. The sample is washed and ironed and the marked square remeasured. Loss or gain in the dimensions of the square is calculated against the quantity of material needed in a garment. Thus the company is able to determine the fit of a garment after it has been washed.

Tensile Strength: A machine determines the breaking point of material. For the average garment, a tensile strength (warpwise and fillingwise) of twenty-five pounds is sufficient. For work clothes, the required tensile strength is much higher. To be noted is the laboratory caution that tensile strength does not determine durability.

Bursting Strength: On the machine used for determining the tensile strength of knitted goods a special attachment is placed containing a one-inch steel ball. This ball is pushed through the material. The machine records the amount of stretch and resistance there is before the material is ruptured.

Wear Tests: Two types of machines are used. On one machine the fabric is stretched across a spool which is covered with an abrasive. As the spool moves back and forth, the oscillations are recorded until the fabric is worn into two pieces. On the other machine the fabric revolves under two off-center wheels. These wheels give a sidewise rubbing action, and the machine records the number of revolutions required for the wheels to wear a hole in the material. The second machine is also used for testing shoes. The durability of the shoe is determined by the amount of leather rubbed off in a given period.

Launderometer: This is the machine that has replaced the soap, water, and washbasin of Penney's early tests to determine the fastness of colors. In loading launderometer jars for a test, a two-inch by four-inch piece of white test cloth is inserted with the material under scrutiny. This white test cloth contains all the common textile fibers so that stains are quickly detected. In the jar with the test cloth and the fabric is a measured quantity of soap solution and ten one-inch steel balls which pound the sample under test.

Fabrics are submitted to four types of washes:

1. Solution, neutral soap; temperature, 100°F.; time in solution, thirty minutes. Merchandise failing to pass this test is considered unsatisfactory for any type of washing.

2. Solution, neutral soap; temperature, 120°F.; time in solution, thirty minutes. Merchandise which passes "wash one" but which fails to pass this test (that is, merchandise which does not stain any of the fibers in the test cloth and which shows no appreciable change in color) is labeled with washing instructions as follows:

a. Make rich warm suds (wrist temperature) with mild soap. Do not use strong soaps or bleaching agents.

b. Wash by hand, squeezing the suds through garment. Do not rub, twist or wring.

c. Rinse in clear water of the same temperature until all soap is removed. Gently squeeze out excess water.

d. Dry in shade.

e. Under this heading are given any special instructions that are needed. As, for illustration, acetate rayons: "Iron when almost dry, using warm, never hot, iron." In case of sweaters: "Do not hang, but dry flat. Shape to size when almost dry."

3. Solution, soap and washing soda; temperature, 160°F.; time in solution, forty-five minutes. Merchandise which passes "wash two" but which does not pass "wash three" is labeled: "This article can be washed at home or in a commercial laundry under careful methods. The temperature should not exceed 120°F. (slightly warmer than lukewarm). Strong soaps or bleaching compounds should not be used. Do not dry in direct sunlight."

4. Solution, soap, washing soda, and chlorine bleach; tem-

perature 185°F.; time in solution, forty-five minutes. Merchandise which passes "wash three" but which does not pass this test is labeled: "This article can be washed under normal commercial or home laundering conditions. It should not be boiled or washed with bleaching compounds. Do not dry in direct sunlight."

Materials which meet the requirements of "wash four" will stand up under almost any kind of washing. No washing instructions are attached to such materials.

Fadeometer: Samples of materials are put in this machine and subjected to exposure stronger than June sunlight. If the materials withstand forty hours of continuous exposure without showing appreciable color changes, they are considered satisfactory for outer garments. Materials used for draperies must withstand eighty hours of continuous exposure without color changes to be acceptable. (The same machine is used for testing plastics. Such materials are acceptable if they do not become brittle, or change color, after eighty hours of continuous exposure.)

Treatment of Woolens to Resist Moth Damage: According to estimates most frequently quoted by reliable authorities, moth damage to apparel and housefurnishings amounts to $200,000,000 a year. The principal species are the webbing and case-making moths, and the equally common (and harder to get rid of) carpet beetle, also known as the Buffalo moth. Yearly, in dollars, the estimated damage of the different species is: Webbing and case-making moths, $80,000,000; carpet beetles, $120,000,000.

The webbing and case-making moths differ little in appearance and concentrate on breeding and laying eggs in their two to four weeks of adulthood. The four species of carpet beetles commonly found in homes are the furniture carpet beetle, the common carpet beetle, the varied carpet beetle, and the black carpet beetle, the last-named being the most destructive of the lot. The period of adulthood of each species varies from three days to five weeks and, like the webbing and case-making moths, is a period spent in breeding and laying eggs.

Popular belief to the contrary, adult clothes moths and carpet beetles do not feed on fabrics or fibers. But they do deposit their eggs in fabrics, yarn, fur, feathers, or anything containing keratin, a protein which exists in all such materials. Ordinarily, they do not molest cotton, linen, rayon, or vegetable fibers.

When hatched, all the larvae go to work; and the softer the material the quicker the destruction. The larvae of the webbing moth spins threads which often form webs on infested material; the case-making moth indicates its presence by constructing small, tightly woven cylindrical cases. The carpet beetle larvae live longer and leave no betraying webs but do cast their shells of horizontal stripings into the material, while they themselves often crawl and squeeze into wall spaces to lie dormant and out of reach of any cleaning which is less than thorough.

However much you dislike and kill these destructive insects in your home, they are protected with hospital care in the research laboratory of the Penney company. From the moment the eggs are laid until the larvae appear, they are watched over and kept under scrupulously ideal conditions. They are fed the choicest dog food (dog food of a particular make, although they will eat any kind) and allowed to gorge themselves until they are about five months old, and about a half inch long.

Reaching this stage, which is the peak of their virility, they are deposited, ten to a group, on a piece of wool cloth about two inches square and invited to make themselves at home. A glass sealer is clamped over them to confine them while their habits and the rate of their destructive progress are closely watched. It has been learned they can cut through soft fabrics in a couple of days while hard-twisted fabrics sometimes keep them chewing for twenty-eight days or longer.

Other moths are not so lucky. After gorging themselves on dog food for the allotted five months, they are segregated into other groups of ten and deposited on woolens that have been chemically treated. By repeated experiments with successive families of moth larvae, Penney researchers have learned how to treat wools so they will be completely unattractive to moths for five years and more—that is, providing the wool is kept clean. Grease stains or dirt are more attractive to moths than the wool fibers themselves.

There is no known way, say Penney researchers, to impregnate wool fabrics to keep moths permanently discouraged, that is, if the clothes or fabrics are hanging loose. By sealing up freshly dry-cleaned or washed fabrics or clothes in airtight bags and putting a few moth balls in each bag before sealing, moth damage can be prevented so long as the articles are so protected. Sprays and other so-called moth-destroying agents may destroy eggs and larvae already deposited and hatched, but the clothes or fabrics will remain uninfested only so long as an adult moth does not visit the place where the clothes or fabrics are.

But, even without the visit of the moth there can be damage (in the sense that "moth-proofing" is interpreted to mean complete protection). This is better understood when it is realized that larvae can, and do, often clip their way through cotton fibers, through glass fibers, and through fine steel wire.

The researches into moths and moth damage have progressed to the stage where the Penney Company now gives five-year guarantees against moth damage on all-wool blankets and on some part-wool blankets. The number of returned blankets has been negligible; and in the blankets returned it was discovered that moths had first attacked not the blankets, but grease spots on them.

Fabrics are now being treated while in the manufacturing process. The fight against the moth continues.

Insulation Tests: The purpose of these tests is to determine whether the material in a garment, or a blanket, or any other item, will be warm enough when in use. In conducting this test a cylinder suspended in a machine is kept at body temperature while the interior of the machine itself is kept at 25°F. The amount of electricity necessary to keep the cylinder at body heat for one hour is known. The cylinder is wrapped with the material to be tested and the amount of electricity required to keep the cylinder at body heat for one hour is recorded. The reduced amount of electricity needed to maintain body heat when the cylinder is wrapped enables the researchers to calculate, percentagewise, the protection offered by the material.

Test for Rain Wear: One test subjects the fabric to hydrostatic pressure. This determines whether the material is waterproof, water repellent, or unsatisfactory. The other test is a spray test. This tells the researcher whether the surface of the material will still wet out when subjected to spraying water such as is encountered in a rain storm.

Sanitized: Suspecting, years before, that absorbed perspiration in shoes did much to destroy their wearing qualities, one of Penney's first suggestions when the research laboratory was established was, "When I was a boy I was always needing shoes. See if you can't do something to make shoes last longer."

The researchers went to work. It wasn't long before they learned a great many things about the effect of absorbed perspiration not only on shoes but pillow tickings and materials that were not subject to washings. They set about to control the bacteriological growth that fed on absorbed perspiration and

worked out with outside researchers a sanitizing process that
does these things:

1. Keeps bacterial growth at a minimum in shoes, pillow
tickings, and materials not subject to washings.

2. Prolongs life of shoes by preventing disintegration of
textiles and leather and tends to prevent insoles from becoming hard and brittle and from shrinking.

3. Delays bacteriological action in absorbed perspiration in
linings of shoes, in pillow tickings, and materials not subject
to washings, thus reducing odors.

Flammability of Materials: All textiles will burn, but some
fibers are more combustible than others; and with the introduction a number of years ago of buttons and ornaments made
from cellulose nitrate, accidents from fire became increasingly
numerous. They were accidents that were highlighted by
death, or injury, to small boys playing in cowboy suits that
were highly flammable.

Greatly concerned, the National Retail Dry Goods Association began a series of investigations. One result of the investigations was the appointment of a committee of the American
Association of Textile Chemists and Colorists to use the
Penney laboratory in the development of what is called a
"flammability tester."

By use of the "tester" most hazardous and relatively non-
hazardous materials have been identified, although no standard testing method has been established. In one series of tests,
seven laboratories analyzed like portions of thirty-three different fabrics, getting like results in some and unlike results
in others. More and extensive work will be required before
conclusions can be reached.

Hosiery Tests: To meet required specifications, the gauge
of the hose is determined, also type of yarn, yarn size, twists per
inch, the number of needles used in knitting, the number of

courses, length of the hose, and many other factors. Inasmuch as stockings are made in a number of mills, control testing is important to insure a uniform product.

Penney researchers are less concerned with original research into new materials than they are with original investigations into ways to make existing materials wear better and last longer. Researches into moth prevention illustrate that point, as do researches into ways to make shoes last longer or materials less flammable.

Items that go into family washing machines, or that are sent to public laundries, are now getting a lot of attention. In collaboration with other testing laboratories, the company has conducted an extensive survey in an effort to learn why, generally speaking, washable articles do not stand up as well after public laundering or private washing as they do after the washings to which they are submitted in the laboratory.

The early suspicion was that harsh washing compounds were mainly responsible for the quicker breakdown in materials. That suspicion was verified in some cases; but, for the most part, it was learned the principal cause was the failure to use sufficient soap and water. Articles were packed too closely into the machines. Lack of liquid permitted them to rub together, or against the sides of the machines, thus fraying materials or fading them.

With costs of living having greatly increased as the result of two world wars, heavy taxation, and lack of production per man-hour of work, the company is deeply concerned over the value of the customer's dollar, as well as its own. The program of the research laboratory is tied into the buying and merchandising programs, with the buying and merchandising efforts being keyed to savings and the laboratory efforts being keyed to lengthening wear.

SEVENTEEN

Promotions Are Not on an Escalator

TWENTY-EIGHT years ago in a Penney store in Moberly, Missouri, a salesman was fitting a pair of shoes when the customer suddenly inquired, "Young man, isn't that a Phi Beta Kappa key hanging on your watch fob?"

"Yes, madam."

"Is it yours?" There was suspicion in the customer's voice.

"Yes, madam."

"You don't mean to tell me!" Still incredulous, the woman asked, "If you are a Phi Beta Kappa why are you working in a small store?"

After the customer had gone—with a package under her arm—the clerk looked down at the key that had attracted her attention, stared at it for a moment, then slowly detached the watch fob, and put both the key and the fob in his pocket, thinking as he did so, "She bought a pair of shoes . . . but that key didn't make the selling job any easier . . . made it tougher . . . and this job is tough enough without parading any college decorations."

When A. W. Hughes, who succeeded Sams as president, recalled that incident, he said: "As I grew older I realized something that was not in my mind at the time. I realized I had earned the key in a classroom because I had teachers who were there to teach me what they thought I needed to know. When I got away from school and into a store, I was measured differently. In the classroom I was measured by what I didn't know; in the store I was measured by what I knew.

"The customers measured me by what they assumed I knew. The manager and the other employees measured me by what they thought I should know. In the store I had to learn with my hands as well as my head. I had to have a lot of help. I got it from everybody.

"Naturally, I am not subtracting from the advantages of an education. An education is a short cut into a job, whether the job is farming, manufacturing or store-keeping. But it is well to realize that, once he is out of school, the world accepts the individual as being ready to go to work. That is what I meant when I said in a classroom teachers are there to teach what they *think* the individual needs to know. In Penney stores we continue to teach, but the teachers teach what they *know* the trainee has to know.

"In selecting men for training, we are more interested in desire to become a merchant than we are in college degrees. By experience, we know the man who has done well in college is a more desirable applicant—providing he displays an equal urge to succeed—than is the applicant with less formal education. However, if he evidences less desire to succeed, he will not be selected. We are always mindful that the two greatest merchants in our entire organization are two men who did not go to college: Mr. Penney and Mr. Sams.

"Mr. Penney and Mr. Sams were natural learners. They were determined to become merchants, and they never let up. When the store was closed at night they remained behind, often until one and two o'clock in the morning, fixing what had to be fixed, shifting displays, figuring out ways to do things better. Such men are exceptional. Most of us are not exceptional. Most of us are not natural learners and need all the teaching we can get.

"But an education, no matter how extensive in school or in business, is of little value unless it teaches an individual to think—and, in thinking, develops within him an ability to stand up against discouragement.

"Some time ago at a dinner I sat next to a young man who had been with the company a few years. He was looking forward with great anticipation to the day when he would have a store of his own. We were talking about our training program when he said:

" 'The company is doing so many things and furnishing so much help that I know, when I get a store of my own, I will only have to follow directions and I will be a successful Penney manager.'

"At first I thought he was engaged in a little apple polishing. Then I realized he was serious. Somehow he had picked up the idea that management was an escalator and all he had to do was to keep his feet on a step in order to be carried upward. I spent an hour trying to get that idea out of his mind. I pointed out to him that was not the way this company was built.

"Mr. Penney found no ready-made escalator in Kemmerer. If he had, the Penney company probably would have stopped right there. He did not seek men who simply followed instructions; he did not put Mr. Sams on an escalator in Cumberland, nor did he put such a lifting apparatus under anyone else. What he did was to give men a place to start. The rest they had to think out and do for themselves. That is still the challenge within this company.

"A year or two ago Mr. Penney returned from one of his trips and told me of a young man in one of our stores who was much discouraged over his 'inability to progress in the Penney organization.' Mr. Penney asked the young man how long he had been with the company and was told 'four years.' Questioning developed that in the four years the employee had earned three promotions with corresponding increases in salary.

" 'Why are you discouraged?' asked Mr. Penney.

" 'But that isn't all the story, Mr. Penney,' explained the young man. 'I want to get into the advertising end of this business. That is what really interests me. I have studied our advertising, studied other advertising, and have submitted a number of ideas that the manager thought good enough to send on to New York. I have been doing that for some time and now I am plain discouraged.'

" 'Over what?'

" 'Because I can't seem to break through and get a job in the New York office.'

" 'What does your store manager think about it?'

" 'He tells me to "keep right on pitching." '

" 'And, of course, that is what you are doing.'

" 'No, sir, I'm not. I decided about three months ago I was wasting my time.'

" 'I think you are making a mistake. If I were you, I would keep right on, as your manager says, "pitching." '

" 'I can't, Mr. Penney. I'm so discouraged that I have lost all my steam. I was talking with the manager last night about it; and, when he told me you would be in the store today, I asked if he had any objection if I talked to you about this personal problem. He told me "none whatever." I didn't want to bother you, Mr. Penney, but in a big organization like this it's awfully hard for a fellow like me who is out here in the sticks to break through and into the big league.'

" 'I talked to that young man,' Mr. Penney told me, 'and tried to persuade him to keep on trying, and assured him that if he did he would wake up some morning and find himself getting off a train in New York. I tried to impress on him some of the things that were involved in the promotion he was seeking—that, although he might think he was ready for such a promotion, someone else had to concur in that decision; and that, in addition, there had to be an opening in the desired department. I doubt if I was successful, but I wish you would check and see if our advertising director knows about him.'

"I checked and learned that the advertising director did know about the young man, had been watching him for some time, and had complimented him on some of his ideas. About five months after Mr. Penney returned to New York, there was an opening in the advertising department; and the advertising director, in spite of the fact that he had received no further communications, got in touch with the store manager, requesting the release of the young man at a starting salary that was double, and more, than the salary, the store was paying him. The candidate was no longer available. A month before the request was made he had quit—discouraged, as he told the store manager, 'because of his inability to get ahead.'

"Hearing about his lost opportunity, the young man persuaded himself that he was the 'victim of a tough break.' I can sympathize with that point of view without agreeing with it. As I see it, he quit too soon."

Twenty-eight years ago when Hughes started in Moberly, the Penney company had approximately three hundred stores. There were four trainees in the store. They all were troubled because they were afraid that most good Penney locations had been covered and that the real opportunities within the company were in the hands of men who would hold them permanently. They kept plugging, and all moved ahead.

As Hughes indicated in his warning to the Penney trainee, promotions within the company are not on an escalator. The training programs and the literature sent out from headquarters are designed only to help. "Doing" is up to the individual. Beyond a certain step, the step that is at the bottom of the escalator, it is not the policy of the company to spoon-feed its people.

Once they are given responsibility, they are expected to carry it. They are expected to make decisions, and to rise or fall on those decisions. A highly decentralized organization, the directors and senior executives intend keeping it that way; but, as in all good organizations, executives consult with each other. However, if, without consultation, an executive decides on a certain course of action in his department or store his decision sticks so long as it does not violate company policy. Within the limits of sound business practices, the company insists on its executives and store managers having the highest possible individual freedom in the operation for which each is responsible.

At the head of every store and at the head of every department is an executive who has earned his job by coming up through the ranks and, along the way, doing every job he now has others do. These men, the company feels, have the experience to make their own decisions.

Here are the stories of some men who have been successful:

It was summer; the day was hot. A boy came into the Penney store in a midwestern town, a new cap on his head. Introducing himself to the manager, he said, "Mister, I've come in for that bookkeeping job you advertised."

Suppressing a smile, the manager inquired, "How old are you?"

"Sixteen."

"What makes you think you're a bookkeeper?"

"I took a bookkeeping course in high school."

"Oh, you did."

"Yes, sir. I graduated last week, and if you haven't filled that job I'd like to have it."

"Well, I haven't filled it, son, but I'm afraid it's a little too much for you to handle, in spite of your high school training."

"I can do it," insisted the boy. Finally, becoming convinced he had no chance to get it, he shifted his sights: "If I can't have that job, what job have you got you think I can do?"

"That's the only opening we have."

"Mister, I've got to have a job," persisted the boy. "I live in [he mentioned a community forty miles distant] and I came down here expecting to get that bookkeeping job. I spent $2.50 buying this cap and I haven't got enough money left to get home. I've got to have a job."

"Are you any good at washing windows?"

"Sure."

"All right. Come with me. I'll get you some water and window-washing tools, and you can get to work. Do that job, and I'll pay you enough money to get home on."

When the boy finished, the manager went outside, inspected the windows, shook his head, and said, "They aren't clean. See those streaks. Wash them again."

The boy had to wash the windows four times, on a hot day, before they were clean enough to satisfy the manager. Returning the tools and water pails to the storeroom, the sixteen-year-old reported to the manager's office for his money.

Handing him his pay the manager asked, "Think you learned anything about washing windows?"

"Yes, sir."

"Like to wash them again?"

"Now!"

"No. I told you when you came in here I had no openings. I haven't. But, I'll make one. If you want to stick around as a chore boy, I'll give you a job. Do you want it?"

"Yes, sir."

The chore boy has become manager of one of the company's largest stores.

A senior executive was once a clerk in a competing store, a store owned by his father-in-law. With his wife he went to a church dinner one evening to find himself seated next to the local Penney manager and his wife. The two men talked shop, and before the dinner was over the clerk was offered a job in the Penney store.

"How much will you pay me?" he asked.

When the manager named a salary, the clerk laughed. "I'm getting more than that where I am."

"So I suspected. What's your future—heir apparent?"

"That's the one thing I don't like about my job."

A month later, the clerk went to the Penney manager and told him he was ready to go to work.

A stranded musician took a temporary job; he is now a senior executive. . . . A director began as a clerk in Wenatchee, Washington, in 1911. One night a year later, while he was sweeping out the store and wondering if he should look for another job, he turned to Penney who was visiting the store and asked, "Mr. Penney, do you think this thing will hold together long enough for me to get a store?"

Instead of answering directly, Penney replied, "If we watch expenses, some day we might have seventy-five stores." At the time there were thirty-four stores.

A college graduate was working in a Pacific Coast store and wondering what he would do with a store of his own. While he was wondering, a district manager asked him if he would like to tackle a tough job. When he said he would, the district manager warned him it was a real tough job. He still wanted it. In his first year, he showed a large increase in sales in the store he was sent to manage. He has continued to move up into bigger managing jobs.

Failing in the automobile business, a man needed a job, any job. He got one in the Penney store in his town. Soon he was in charge of men's work clothes, then men's lines, then the piece goods department. He became first man, then manager, then district manager, and when one of the largest stores was opened he was made manager. He is now director, treasurer, and second vice-president of the company.

An Idaho schoolteacher wanted to make a change. Weighing about a hundred pounds and standing an inch or two above five feet in height, he had reached the conclusion he would have difficulty in handling some of his pupils in an argument. Going into a Penney store he applied for a job. Soon he became outstanding for his judgment in buying merchandise. After five years he became manager of a store that had slipped badly. In his first year, he almost doubled the volume of the previous year. He has moved ahead, steadily.

A number of years ago young managers about whom partners were still doubtful were sent to a particular town on the theory "they would make it, or quit." One such young manager was sent there and worked there late hours seven days a week for seven months. He was driving the last nail in a home-made glove rack one night when the station agent walked in with a telegram, shook hands with him and said "goodbye." The telegram was a call to another town. He now manages a large store.

There are hundreds and hundreds of such stories within the company. They are all in the same pattern, yet all different—as different as this one:

The president of the company was making a trip with a district manager, and the two men were discussing the capabilities of the various store managers. Finally one manager's name was mentioned. Without hesitation, the district manager declared, "He is the best manager in my territory."

"Why do you say that?" questioned Hughes. "His sales record doesn't show it."

"I know it doesn't, but he has developed more good Penney men than any manager in my territory. His personnel record shows that."

Hughes smiled. "That is my principal reason for making this trip. I want to see him and once more tell him how much the company appreciates the job he is doing."

As you might expect, there is a common spirit in this organization that is hard to duplicate. It is a spirit that has come as the direct result of giving responsibility—a type of decentralization Hughes defines when he says, "We men in New York realize continually, as Mr. Penney realized in the beginning, that the final answer to any company problem is the answer found by men in individual stores, or in individual plants. The key man in the Penney company is the store manager. All the rest of us do is help."

Or, as Sams puts it:

"There is fun in doing a job. Part of the fun of store management—fun that endures through the years—comes from knowing Farmer Brown and his family, from seeing their youngsters grow from childhood to youth to manhood as friends of you and your store. Just knowing your customers and making friends of them is fun.

"But the richest job is the finer form of fun that comes from the development of one's associates. To me, store management is never monotonous so long as the manager is thinking of his day's work, not as work but as an opportunity to meet new situations and new combinations, to find a better answer today than he found yesterday, and to build human relationships that endure.

"In a conversation with an executive of another company I was asked in all seriousness, 'How do you keep your managers from going stale and becoming indifferent without shifting them around frequently?' He went on to explain how his company checked its stocks, informing me that every three weeks a man from the district office checked every item in a store and told the manager what he had to order.

"What's the fun for a manager who has no responsibility? The Penney company never wants to take from a manager the thrill that comes from running the show in his own store. In Penney management, the manager is the coach, the captain and the man with the ball. The company provides a book of rules. The company provides the equipment. It may even lend coaching assistance through the district managers, but only the manager and his store group can put over the winning score."

Sams recalled talking with a Penney manager with a fine record as a trainer of merchants. "What's your secret?" Sams asked; and the manager answered:

"It's very simple. Before a man starts to work in my store I caution him that no man has yet started out with the intention of making a big mark—and made it! That sort of a man, I tell him, usually watches the mark so closely that he doesn't have time to do his job.

"I tell him that no business ever got to be a big business by starting out that way—that they all started in a small way and grew big because they had what the public wanted.

"I tell him that getting ahead means hard work, that by hard work and by close attention to small things, he will get started in the direction he wants to go. I tell him to do his job today, and do it again tomorrow, because there isn't any other way you can get to where you want to go.

"I tell him that I honestly believe personal growth and business profits are not accidents. They don't just happen—and when I get through telling him those things I remind him that personal growth and business profits are the direct result of well planned, hard work; and that they are only the reflection of good management and development of the individual in that business.

"When he understands those things, and does them, he is ready for promotion."

EIGHTEEN

The Job

BASIC IN the Penney company is the insistence that everyone understand the importance and the relationship of his particular job to the success of the entire operation. This insistence applies in equal measure to the store manager, to a clerk, to a stock room boy, and to the president of the company.

Whether it is the president of the company, the chairman, or a chore boy, every job is bigger than the person who fills it. Starting their thinking with that acknowledgment, the executives of the company are able to place the emphasis where it belongs.

"To my mind," says Sams, "one of the most destructive ideas that has been promoted in the recent years is that some jobs are menial. That type of drivel can come only from inferior minds. No work that is honest is menial; no job that is honest can be menial. The only thing about a job that is menial is the attitude toward it.

"A garbage collector or a street cleaner may be told he has a menial job. The health of the community depends, in considerable measure, upon the collection of garbage and the cleaning of streets. Is work upon which the health of a community depends menial work?

"To some, sweeping out a store or sweeping the sidewalk in front of a store may be menial work, but keeping a store and sidewalk clean is part of the job of good storekeeping. Many times Mr. Penney, upon visiting a store, has gone to the storeroom, picked up a broom, and walked back outside to sweep the sidewalk. I am sure it never occurred to him he was doing a menial job.

"I am equally sure that usually, in addition to wanting a clean sidewalk, he did the job himself in order to impress upon the manager his own laxity in good storekeeping. I said 'usually' because there was an occasion a number of years ago when Mr. Penney landed in a western town early one morning and arrived at the store before it was open. A stiff wind was blowing and a junior clerk was trying, with little success, to sweep sand from the sidewalk into the gutter.

"Watching the clerk's efforts for a moment, Mr. Penney inquired if there was a shovel in the store. When the youth nodded, Mr. Penney suggested he get it. Taking the shovel with which the clerk soon returned, the chairman of the company scraped up the sand in little piles, disposed of them, and then used the broom to sweep off the remainder.

"That done, he went inside and helped the clerk sweep up the sand that had sifted in on the floor. When the job was finished, the clerk, a grin on his face, inquired, 'You're Mr. Penney, aren't you?'

" 'Yes.'

" 'I realized you were when you followed me into the store. All the while you were cleaning the sidewalk, I kept wondering who you were. Then I knew. Your picture is upstairs in the front office. Now I know what to do the next time we have one of these windstorms. Thanks, Mr. Penney.'

"But, to get back to that destructive idea about menial jobs. I have expressed my disagreement; I have given brief illustrations to show why I believe as I do. I have said no work that is honest is menial. It is my opinion that, when a person protests that a job is beneath him, he really reveals that he is beneath the job. We believe in this company that every job is bigger

than the person who fills it. When we all look back at a job—
any job we have ever been in—don't we realize there were
things we could have done better?

"For a person to do his best in every job, three things are required: (1) understanding of the relationship of that job to
the next one; (2) opportunity for promotion into the next job;
and (3) proper reward for doing the job now occupied.

"Running my eye down financial statements, our own included, I find listed such things as cash in banks and on hand,
United States government securities, accounts receivable, merchandise, land, buildings, furniture and fixtures, and a lot of
other things that are always listed as 'assets.' What are called
'assets' are nothing more than accessories. The only real asset
that any business has is its personnel.

"Not long ago I was reading a story of a proposition that was
made to William S. Knudsen when he was president of the
Chevrolet Motor Company. A representative of the Russian
government came to him with an offer to buy tools to make
automobiles, a set of drawings for a factory, and a stipulation
that some people be sent to Russia to supervise the construction of the building, the setting of the tools, and the early
manufacturing processes.

"Mr. Knudsen protested, saying automobiles could not be
built that way, that to make automobiles people had to be
trained in the work.

The Russian disagreed, informing Mr. Knudsen that 'when
we have the tools over there, we have the people already there;
and once we get them together, we can make motor cars.' To
that he added, 'My government wants it done, and that is the
way it will be done.'

Whereupon Mr. Knudsen said, 'I will sell you the whole
Chevrolet factory, tools, machinery, and buildings on the
hoof if you will let me keep the people I have. Then I will

start all over and I will have new buildings, new machines, and new tools, and I will make more motor cars and better motor cars than you will make; and I will make them before you get started.'

"Mr. Knudsen declined to be a party to the proposition the Russian government outlined. So is it with the Penney company. If we kept our people, we could sell every piece of merchandise, every stick of furniture, and every fixture in any store, or all our stores; set up shop in a new location, or locations; and, excepting for the temporary inconvenience of stocking anew, go on as though nothing had happened.

"When one considers the importance of the people in the organization, it becomes clear that in order to do his best work a person must understand the relationship of his job to the next one. Take, for example, the job of a clerk who makes the sale and his relationship to the store and to the company.

"Every good merchant knows there are two points to a sale. One point is when the sale is made in the store; the other point is when the package is opened at home. If, when the package is opened, the customer finds the merchandise as attractive and as fresh looking as when she purchased it, she has an entirely different feeling toward both the merchandise and the store than if the package came to her with the contents in a mussy condition. Almost always, if the merchandise is attractive and fresh looking, she remains happy with her purchase; if it is in a mussy condition, she feels she has been imposed upon; and she has been.

"Those things are explained to a clerk when he, or she, starts to work in a Penney store. He begins to see the relationship of his job to the next job and the relationship of the next job to the sale. Thus he begins to realize his own importance to the success of the store. He is given no opportunity to think of himself as just one of many people who are employed. He has an identity. We do our best to see that he keeps that identity.

It is a mistaken belief that assumes only those who are in the arts have the desire for self-expression. All persons, whatever their occupations, have the natural desire to express themselves and to improve themselves. We try to encourage that desire and, at the same time, try to instill in the person that he, or she, is a member of a team.

"I am thinking of something that happened a year or two ago. One of our district managers called on a Penney store in a Western town. The store was closed at two o'clock in the afternoon when the local manager, unlocking the front door, admitted a sputtering visitor.

"Listening for a moment, the manager interrupted, saying, 'Did you see any other stores open in town?'

" 'Yes. A dry goods store, a drugstore and a grocery store, all down the street in the next block.'

" 'Many people on the street?'

" 'No. What's going on in this town today?'

" 'This is the opening day of the deer season,' answered the manager. 'Practically the whole town knocked off.'

" 'So you thought you'd knock off, too?'

" 'Well—yes. But not in the way you may be thinking. A month ago several of my department heads and their assistants came to me. They asked for this day off so they could go hunting. Finally I called them together, told them I couldn't let them all go, and suggested they call "heads or tails" among themselves to decide the winners. They made a counter proposal to the effect that I let anyone go who could increase his monthly sales quota by five per cent. That was agreeable to me and it is still agreeable, although I figured some would miss. None did. The department heads and their assistants have all gone hunting. Seeing as how the department heads and their assistants could not have exceeded their quotas without the help of everyone else, I told the rest of the force to take the day off.'

"In its way, that illustrates something of what I mean about working as a team.

"Now to the second point—the opportunity for promotion.

"I believe that, as a general rule, more people are interested in opportunities to get ahead than they are in wage increases. This must not be taken to mean that wages are not important. But I am confident that given a choice between a job at one wage, with little opportunity for advancement, and another job at a lesser wage, but with a real opportunity to get ahead, a majority of people would choose the latter.

"When a man is tied to a job with no future, it is very easy for him to begin thinking of himself as a machine very much like the machine he operates. Occasionally, too, some of our 'higher intellects' get together for the self-stated purpose of 'rescuing man from his bondage to a machine-made civilization.' These are fancy words having no meaning. There is no bondage in a machine; on the contrary, bondage would exist without it.

"The machine has reduced the workday from twelve and fifteen hours to seven and eight. The machine has moved industry out of the home and into the factory. By one man flipping a switch, a truck picks up loads that once had to be carried on the backs of men. The machine takes a man to his work and carries his family on vacation. The machine does the family wash, toasts our bread, cooks our coffee, and brings music into our homes.

"These higher intellects are confused. What they call bondage is really monotony—the monotony of doing the same thing over and over again, or in watching the same thing being done over and over again. I find it difficult to believe that monotony would ever be a serious factor in employment if there was certainty that good work would be recognized and promotion would follow.

"It is not the policy of the Penney company to hold out promotion as an inducement to coming with us. We do not believe in making such promises. If a person wants to come with us, he must make that decision for himself. When he is satisfied that we are the sort of people he wants to work with, then we must satisfy ourselves that he is the sort of person with whom we want to work. When these two decisions have been made and this person is placed in a job, his future, with us, is up to him.

"We believe promotions should be earned. We believe that to give a man a promotion before he is ready injures him just as it injures us, but that to withhold a promotion after a man has earned it does a disservice both to him and ourselves.

"When an applicant is accepted and goes to work, we believe it our obligation to supply him with the tools of merchandising and to teach him their use. As for the rest—well, he knows the opportunities for promotion exist because, whatever his job and wherever he is in our organization, he is surrounded by people who have earned promotions. In my correspondence with Mr. Penney before I went to Kemmerer, I was told, 'You can have all the rope you want, if you are competent.' That promise, if it is a promise, remains a policy of the Penney company.

"The third point—proper reward for doing the job.

"We do not believe 'proper reward' begins and ends with wages. The top salary paid in the Penney company has been $10,000 a year. And, while this is personal, neither Mr. Penney, nor I, have received any salary or any other compensation in many years. Anything beyond $10,000, paid to any executive, has been dependent upon a share of the company profits as earned each year.

"There is a little story behind that top salary bracket. When we first organized as a company, Mr. Penney, because of his financial interest in many stores, decided he should draw no salary. But we did have executives who received no interest from any stores. When the board of directors decided these men should be given top salaries, the question arose, 'What is a top salary?'

"In those years a top salary was $10,000 a year. Mr. Penney said, 'I think we can afford that much money, but not any more. If the salary is too high, we may run into lean times; and I do not want the company burdened with a top-heavy pay roll.'

"But, as I was saying, we do not believe 'proper reward' begins and ends with wages. We believe in sharing our profits with everyone in the Penney organization. Being selective in our personnel, we do not want people whose only interest is being on a pay roll. We want people who are enough interested in opportunities to take advantage of them, who are enough interested in bonuses to want to earn them. But we recognize that a feeling of financial security is necessary if an employee is to do his best. Consequently, the wages we pay are as high, or higher, than is the custom. The wages are constant, fifty-two weeks in the year.

"This same general plan is in effect throughout the organization. While we do not claim it is the best plan ever conceived, we do insist it is the best we have been able to work out. We are trying constantly to improve it."

When the company was incorporated in 1927 under the laws of the state of Delaware, some executives argued that money-making opportunities would be lessened because individuals would not be permitted to open stores of their own. Penney and Sams agreed and, to compensate partially for loss of individual ownership, they worked out the profit-sharing plan. Under this plan a manager shares in the net profits of his store. In practically all cases the manager's share of the profits exceeds his salary.

Individual opportunities have increased; company records show promotions have more than doubled since 1929. The reason is found only partially in the increased number of stores; in 1929 there were 1,395 stores; in 1948 there were 1,601 stores. The real reason for the greatly increased number of promotions is found in the increased volume of business done by each store.

In 1929, the average Penney store showed a sales volume of approximately $150,000. In 1947, the average Penney store showed a sales volume of approximately $500,000. The company's training program which develops more men to be better merchants is primarily responsible for gains in sales.

The company uses a fine net to screen applicants for jobs and a wider net to screen promotions, but there have been times when good executive material has escaped. One such case happened a few years ago. There was a clerk employed in a Western store, whose efficiency reports disclosed little or no possibility for promotion. In fact, the report indicated he was not even a promising clerk. The store manager advised other employment.

Discouraged, the clerk sought advice as to what kind of work to pursue. "I don't know," responded the manager. "I thought when you started here you had a great chance to get ahead. You get along well with people. Everyone seems to like you. When you started, I figured you were a cinch for promotion, once you got your feet on the ground and learned something about storekeeping. You've been here nearly three years now, and I'll bet you don't know much more about merchandise than you did the day you started to work. Do you?"

"No, I guess not," admitted the employee. "Somehow, I just can't seem to get the hang of it."

"Well, there you are. It isn't fair to you when you have practically no chance for promotion to keep you here. Nor, is it fair to the other people in your department because they have to depend on you to pull your weight. You've never done it."

"I know I haven't, but neither you nor they could feel worse about that than I do."

"What do you think you'd like to do?" asked the manager.

"I still think I'd like to be in a store."

The manager shook his head. "You're not cut out for a store. Why don't you try advertising work, or newspaper work—something like that? You have a good education; you've been through college. You like people and people like you. I think if you'd try advertising, or newspaper work, you'd do well. You've got something, even though I haven't been able to put my finger on it."

Although it was not necessary, the manager informed the district manager that he had discharged the clerk and, still distressed, wrote headquarters, berating himself for his failure to develop what he had earlier considered "a top notch prospect." He closed his letter by saying, "While I am sure he will never make a go of it in a store, I am equally sure he will be a top-notcher some place."

Correspondence followed between headquarters executives and the store manager. The company reviewed the discharged clerk's efficiency reports (rating reports, they are called in the Penney company) and suggested to the manager that he quit worrying about his decision. "It was the right decision," the manager was told.

Meanwhile, the former clerk, instead of going into advertising or newspaper work, left the Western city, located in a city in the Middle West, and joined another retail organization. He was placed in the personnel department. He moved up rapidly into the job of personnel director.

However, before he became personnel director, the Penney company, watching his progress, turned to its own rating reports, examined them and added five qualifications to its requirements in "standards of management."

Instead of restricting itself to qualifications such as (1) ability as a merchant; (2) sales-mindedness; (3) ability to organize; (4) ability as a trainer; and (5) ability as a money-maker; it added these: (1) leadership ability; (2) considerateness of others; (3) judgment (4) imagination; and (5) flexibility.

By adding these five categories, it opened opportunities for itself and for its people in fields other than storekeeping—fields such as advertising, personnel, finance, research, and all the other departments in a large organization where special training and knowledge are needed.

Business Is a Public Service

BUSINESS NEVER was and never is anything but a public service. For years, every enlightened businessman has been conducting his affairs with that knowledge.

Men with business minds—as distinct from the financier, politician, and mental shut-in—realized a long time ago that the cost of living was a business responsibility. Henry Ford began doing something about it in 1907 when he manufactured his Model T to provide people with low-cost transportation. But, even before then, in order to be in business at all, Ford had to challenge the men who had forced the automobile industry into a stalemate by a legal document known as the Selden patent. These financial minds sued Ford; and Ford won, although he had to carry his case to the Supreme Court, meanwhile filing bonds to the extent of his last dollar to protect his customers against other suits threatened by those who desired to monopolize the industry.

Penney also did something about the cost of living in 1902 when he risked his savings of $500 and borrowed $1,500 to provide people with inexpensive clothes; and before either Ford and Penney were born, George F. Gilman and George Huntington Hartford began the trend by reducing prices of the things people eat. How to lower costs and improve products—those are two problems the enlightened business mind never ceases studying.

Before proceeding to discuss the functions of business in terms of public service, however, it may be well to clarify what is meant by the *financial* mind, the *political* mind and the *mental shut-in.*

The financial means that type of mind which believes that "a business corporation is organized and carried on primarily for the benefit of the stockholder." *

The political means that type of mind which in its quest for votes promises one thing and delivers another—and ends up by lowering its own principles to the level of expediency and then by attempting by decree to extinguish the principles which guide everyone else.

The mental shut-in is that type which, after having read books, decides that modern business is too complex and yearns for days of simplicity when men were their own manufacturers and their own merchants. It is the type of mind which, when sitting under a lamp and reading a book, fails to understand that it is the very processes of business which have brought both book and lamp to him.

Possibly that mind prefers the simplicity of going into the woods and gathering a fagot of twigs and branches to make a fire to the complexity of pushing a switch and lighting a lamp; —or the simplicity of finding a cave in the side of a hill and squatting to study the chiselings on the walls to the complexity of sitting down in an easy chair and reading a book; the ease of raising, catching, and shearing a sheep, spinning the wool, weaving the cloth, cutting, measuring, and hand-stitching it into a coat and pantaloons to the hardship of going into

* Quotation is taken from a court decision rendered against Henry Ford in 1919, when a few financially-minded stockholders restrained him from plowing back company earnings into greater employment and new equipment. Ford solved that dilemma by buying out the remaining stockholders.

a store and choosing from a rack a suit of clothes. Perhaps, even, the joy of swinging a scythe and flaying the windrows to get grain, hand-grinding the grain to get flour, mixing the flour into dough to bake bread to the labor of picking up a loaf from a grocer's counter.

Dreaming of Elysian fields that never existed, these cloistered minds do not comprehend that, if each individual were his own manufacturer and his own merchant, he would have much less—and it would cost much more.

If he attempted to make all the things he needed, he would have that much less time in his fields to grow food for himself and his family. If he left his work to go to where the things he needed were made, he would have to walk or ride horseback because there would be no automobiles or trains. His trips would be few and far between. His purchases would be confined to those things he could carry on his own back or on the back of his horse.

"But," say these critical minds, "it costs money to manufacture and to merchandise, and the manufacturer and merchant charge too much of those who buy, and pay too little to those who make."

Without going into detail, let us examine these three criticisms:

1. It costs money to manufacture and to merchandise.

Of course manufacturing and merchandising involve certain expenses. The manufacturer searches the markets for raw materials, transports them to his factory, and converts them into useful things; and these operations cost money. But we buy the useful things that are manufactured at a fraction of what the cost would be if we had to make them—conceding that as individuals we could make them at all.

The merchant does much the same thing; he searches the

market places of the world and brings back to his store the various products for our selection. If these operations cost money, we are saved much time and effort and we can buy what we want by merely going to the corner store.

When we look at those manufacturing and merchandising processes clearly, we see that what the professorial and political minds label complex is actually simple and what they identify as cost is not cost but savings.

2. The manufacturer and the merchant charge too much for the things they sell.

No enlightened business mind will deny it. Nothing satisfies the financially-minded as much as the elimination of all competitors and subsequent mark-ups in profits. Nothing disturbs the financially-minded more than the very acceptance by enlightened business minds of the fact that goods cost too much, that the level of prosperity in this country can never be high enough until all the elements of business—management, labor and finance—join at the risk of personal prerogatives and work together, as associates, in preference to working apart, as groups.

"Working together" is one part of the solution to lower and still lower prices; "production" is the other. Political and professorial minds to the contrary, there never has been and there never will be overproduction. There can be no such thing as overproduction as long as need exists anywhere. What secluded minds call overproduction is nothing more than over-pricing.

The real trouble is within ourselves. We have never really put our minds to work but, of late years, preferred to hand the problem over to political minds. Their solution was destruction—the destruction of crops and the despoiling of foods—to the accompaniment of nationwide tax levies to pay the producer to raise weeds in his fields, keep his pig pens empty, and keep prices going up and up.

3. Wages are too low.

Again, no enlightened business mind disputes it. In manufacturing, wages have their base in production; in merchandising, their base in sales. Responsibility for both production and sales is not with labor, not with finance, not with government, but *is* with management.

In fact, the enlightened business mind was first to see that mass production and mass sales both raised wages and lowered prices. No political mind ever even thought of a minimum wage until years after Henry Ford had established his $5-a-day minimum wage plan and Penney began his profit sharing with his people.

High wages and low prices are products of natural law. Enlightened management, which trains men into their jobs so they can be worth more and which puts better tools into their hands so they can produce more and thus earn more, simply acts in obedience to this natural law. The drafting of artificial laws to meet election emergencies raises wages only temporarily; such emergencies create other emergencies which must in turn be met by writing artificial laws to raise prices.

Bad management in business is seldom able to raise wages and lower prices, even temporarily. Of what value is a law dictating wage scales if bad management forces a company into bankruptcy? Some persons may say government could take over the plant, operate it, keep people at work, and pay the prescribed wages. There is an example of such government control today in Russia. Under date of November 2, 1947, Leopold Schwarzschild, German economist and editor who was forced into exile by Hitler, wrote in the *New York Times:*

". . . Like all governments everywhere, the Soviet government is less efficient, flexible, rational and economical in investment and production than private enterprise must be under penalty of bankruptcy.

"The inevitable consequences followed automatically. For thirty years more 'surplus value' had to be withheld from the workers, and their so-called exploitation has been more ruthless than anywhere under the conditions of free enterprise. Hence the fact, confirmed by every honest statistical analysis, that the Russian masses not only live incomparably worse than those in the capitalist countries, but also that their 'real wages' are lower than even those of the Russian industrial workers in 1913."

Lately we have heard much about bigness in manufacturing, in finance, in merchandising, in labor unions, and in all the other efforts of people in their private capacities as citizens; the inference being that bigness itelf is evil and the only way to counteract this evil is through the establishment of a government bigger than everything else. Unhappily, that sort of reasoning has to assume that government, little and big, is without evil.

But, to get back to this question of bigness. The Penney company operates approximately 1,600 stores. These stores are in every state in the Union. All 1,600 stores in 48 states came from one store. All this was once a few hundred dollars worth of merchandise in a 40- by 20-foot room in a one and one-half story frame building on a side street in a Wyoming mining town of about 1,000 inhabitants. The present 50,000 full-time Penney people and more than 75,000 part-time Penney people owe their jobs to two far-seeing people—a man and his wife.

Nevertheless, the one store and the more than 1,600 stores *
were actually there in 1902 in Kemmerer at the same time. At
night in his room when everything was shut up downstairs,
Penney saw first ten, then twenty, then thirty, and dimly as
many as fifty stores all growing out of his one store if the conduct of that store was anchored in the right principle.

The principle was expressed a long time ago in the Golden
Rule. Applying it to himself as a merchant, Penney interpreted
it to mean sharing profits and training men to be merchants.
As long as he acted on that principle, there was nothing strange
in the development of more than thirty times the fifty stores
that Penney so dimly saw. As long as they stood close to that
principle, Penney and his partners knew their stores would
never be at the mercy of anyone but themselves. In sharing
profits by selling at lower prices, they have kept old customers
coming back and new customers coming in until individual
Penney stores now average approximately $500,000 a year in
sales as against an approximate volume of $29,000 in 1902.

* Here are the stores that Penney envisioned in 1902:

STORES BY STATES, Dec. 31, 1947

State		State		State	
Alabama	12	Maryland	5	Oregon	42
Arizona	18	Massachusetts	10	Pennsylvania	58
Arkansas	18	Michigan	52	Rhode Island	1
California	141	Minnesota	63	South Carolina	13
Colorado	48	Mississippi	19	South Dakota	27
Connecticut	6	Missouri	49	Tennessee	21
Delaware	2	Montana	36	Texas	119
Florida	19	Nebraska	51	Utah	30
Georgia	17	Nevada	7	Vermont	5
Idaho	35	New Hampshire	3	Virginia	13
Illinois	49	New Jersey	4	Washington	61
Indiana	52	New Mexico	17	West Virginia	12
Iowa	68	New York	32	Wisconsin	54
Kansas	77	North Carolina	31	Wyoming	22
Kentucky	21	North Dakota	33		
Louisiana	11	Ohio	61		
Maine	9	Oklahoma	49	Total Stores	1603

No one has tried to figure, and no one could figure, the dollar savings to customers of Penney stores since 1902. Unquestionably, since 1902, the direct savings have totaled well into the hundreds of millions of dollars; and the sum of the indirect savings is just as great. Through working on Penney orders, manufacturers have found better ways to make their products, and other merchants have become better businessmen because of a Penney store in their midst.

These savings may not be immediately spectacular but they are real and they go on day after day. That is the real meaning of the statement that every enlightened business mind accepts cost of living as a business responsibility. In Penney advertising to the public and in Penney promotional material to its own people, that responsibility is emphasized continually in such messages as these:

"Penney's is an old hand at saving you money." "Your cost of living is a Penney problem." "A Penney bargain is always price and quality."

It is true that when Penney started out in business his thoughts about sharing profits were confined to his customers and to himself. He quickly enlarged his scheme, bringing in by turn Sams and other partners, then executives who were not merchants, and finally, through a bonus and savings plan, including everyone in the organization.

His plan, of course, had to develop slowly. When he started out in Kemmerer, he had first of all to be a merchant. He had to assign himself humbly and prayerfully to the job; he had to study and he had to discipline himself. The more he studied and the more he disciplined himself, the more the job taught him. Finally he had no need to ask questions; if he listened, the job gave him the answers. Every advance in every field has come in the same way. The violin taught Stradivarius, and the power loom taught Cartwright; just as the file on a bench says to a mechanic when he picks it up, "No, use something else!" and forces him to take another tool.

As for profit sharing, there will be persons who will point to the surplus in the company's financial statement and to the dividends paid to stockholders and say, "those are profits. If Penney and his partners really believed in profit sharing, they would have divided those profits among their workers from the beginning."

The establishment of a surplus and the paying of dividends violated no principle. Violation would have been in *not* setting aside a surplus and in *not* paying dividends.

Assume that what the critics claim is true. Originally, the only persons employed in the Kemmerer store were Penney and his wife. Had they assumed the profits belonged to them and divided them, there would have been no money left for the hiring of a single clerk. Or, if the profits had been divided up every night or every pay day, after there was already one additional clerk, the personnel would never have been increased again because nothing would have been left over to hire a second clerk.

Had Penney operated on that theory, he would still be in Kemmerer, managing his little store and employing one clerk. Instead, Penney knew that profits—in addition to being used for wages and all other immediate operating expenses such as rent, light, heat, insurance, taxes—are necessary for growth.

The truth is the profits made during those first days or weeks, when Penney and his wife did all the work, did not belong to them exclusively. In part they belonged to the business. To grow and to gain strength, the business had to have its share of the profits; just as to grow and to gain strength, an infant has to have milk and an adult, meat and vegetables. And this is only another way of saying a business goes ahead on its earnings—earnings that become identified in a financial statement as "surplus." Wipe out the surplus of any company and it has the same experience as a family when its savings are destroyed.

Because it built a surplus—and Penney and Sams had their troubles, in the early days, persuading a few of their partners to build surpluses—the J. C. Penney Company, instead of hiring one person, furnishes full-time or part-time employment for more than 125,000 persons. All are employed at wages and with profit-participation plans that are better—much better! —than those paid to one clerk, in 1902. Beyond these wages are a multitude of other social benefits.

As for dividends that have been paid to stockholders, they are nothing more than interest payments to more than 20,000 persons who have invested their savings in the Penney company. These dividends, in whatever year, may be too high; they may be too low. That is a point of view, and on a few occasions there have been complaints, both ways.

But, whatever the dividends to the stockholders, and whatever the wages and bonuses to the employees, no one would argue that one particular group should receive all the profits. Any preachment which says one group—whether stockholders, management, labor, or government—should get everything, while other groups get nothing, ends up in no group getting anything.

Neighbors with Customers

WITH 1,603 STORES in the United States, the J. C. Penney Company is the largest retail department store chain in the world. By population groups, these stores are located as follows:

In communities under 1,000: 11; 1,000 to 2,500: 207; 2,500 to 5,000: 316; 5,000 to 7,500: 259; 7,500 to 10,000: 153; 10,000 to 15,000: 206; 15,000 to 25,000: 179; 25,000 to 50,000: 129; 50,000 to 100,000: 61; over 100,000: 78.

With such a large organization, it is natural for company executives to have some positive thoughts regarding what goes into the making of a store. Their first requirement is that the one chosen to be a store manager must be a merchant: not only a merchant in the sense of knowing merchandise, knowing his community, and being able to strike a balance between inventory and cash but, *importantly,* a merchant in the sense that he feels himself born to fill that job.

From his boyhood, Penney never thought of himself in any capacity and, with the exception of a brief excursion into owning a meat market, never was anything but a department store merchant. Since he thought of himself in such a way, he was sure there were others who felt as he did. From the time he opened his first store he set out to find such persons. The company still searches for them.

"Whatever his other qualifications, a man is not cut out to be a merchant unless he feels deep inside him no other job will fit him." That is Penney's conviction. To it he adds: "Wherever I am, I like to go into stores. I can detect a poorly managed store the minute I set foot inside the door. I can sense that it is being run by someone who thinks of his store solely in terms of making a living, or making money, instead of thinking of it in terms of 'I wasn't born to do any other thing. This is my job, my life's work. I can't give it as much as it can give me, but I can give it the best I have—and all I have.'

"I recall when I was working for Callahan and Johnson in Evanston, Wyoming, going to lunch one day with the chief clerk. After eating, I started back across the street to the store. The chief clerk stopped me. 'What are you trying to do?' he snapped. 'Impress the boss?'

"Impressing the boss had not occurred to me. I wanted to get back because nothing interested me as much as that store. I will grant that cutting short my lunch hour helped the boss, but I made more out of it than he did. In what was supposed to be my 'spare time' I learned a good many things about merchandising. Learning those things accelerated my own progress to the day when I would have a store of my own. And, in connection with that business of 'helping the boss,' I know no way by which a person can help himself without helping someone else.

"Often, I am asked about the Penney company. Some people seem to feel there is something mysterious, or lucky, about our growth. There isn't. The Penney company has grown because it has emphasized the selection and training of men who wanted to be merchants.

"The explanation is quite as simple as that; although, upon hearing it, some questioners seem surprised and say, 'Is that all?'

"That *is* all, but included in it is a lot of hard work. In becoming a merchant, a man has to see the Golden Rule beyond the catechism; he has to see it in the people he meets, and in his dealings with them. The intelligence he displays in being a merchant finds its expression in his store. That is what makes a store."

As Penney recognized more than forty years ago when he had only two or three stores, he was serving his own best interest by delegating responsibility to individual partners; so today: the company recognizes that, in continuing the policy of individual responsibility and delegating it to managers in more than 1,600 stores, it is serving its own best interest.

Being a merchant in his own right, a Penney manager hires and trains his people. He selects his merchandise, places his own advertising, and makes his own promotions within his own store. It is just as important for managers to do these things today as it was for Penney's partners to do them thirty and forty years ago.

In the beginning, Penney instinctively preferred the idea of individual independence for his partners. Today, with stores in every one of the forty-eight states, the company knows that independence of the individual is inherent in the better way of doing business and is typical of the American way of life. The company knows, too, that no single man, no group of men, and no central office is wise enough to do more than guide such an operation.

When he was talking with a group of managers one day, Hughes described being on a train between New York and Washington. "In the car," he recalled, "there was a group of men and in the center of the group was a man I recognized as head of a large corporation. I wasn't eavesdropping, but no one in the car could help but hear this man's oration.

"For an hour, he told his listeners of how he had reorganized his company . . . how 'I visited this plant, and jacked up the superintendent—visited that divisional office and fired a vice-president—visited another plant—another office—jacking up this one and firing that one, and so on and on and on.'

To me, it was the Hitler or Stalin technique applied to American business.

"In our traditional commitment of independence for the individual, I believe we, in the Penney company, are moving toward what American business will be. We now have it in substantial outline. We intend to protect it and to improve it. This is the true individualism that holds the company together—and, I might add, this same true individualism is what holds our country together. In a nation, or in a business, this is the individualism that is self-supporting, an individualism that knows it is only able to stand where it does because others have built the steps, and knows it has to build steps of its own.

"Many times I have heard Penney managers personally thank Mr. Penney for going broke in the meat business, explaining to him, 'It was the greatest break I ever had. As a butcher I would have been a wash-out.' Now, what has all this got to do with what makes a store? It has a great deal to do with it.

"1. A Penney manager joins in movements that build his town.

"2. A Penney manager contributes from the store's funds to those agencies that help his town.

"3. A Penney manager registers and votes in his town.

"4. A Penney manager guards the reputation and good name of his company and store as zealously as he guards the capital investment entrusted to him.

"These things cannot help but be reflected in the attitude of the community toward the store, and the attitude of the store personnel toward the customers. The Penney store reflects a manager on the premises and not a stranger in a distant office, pushing buzzers. Remote control is never subtle enough to escape customer notice. Usually it shows up first in the attitude of the clerks toward their jobs."

Having spent so much of its effort in selecting and training managers, the Penney company expects the managers to exercise care in the selection and training of store personnel.

One of the first things a manager evaluates in an applicant is that applicant's liking for people. In establishing that evaluation, the manager seeks answers to several questions. "Does the applicant like to work with people?" "Do people like him, or her?" "Do people like to work for him, or her?" Such things as neatness in personal appearance, courtesy, willingness to learn are secondary because managers have learned these things can be taught. The first thing—liking people—cannot be taught. Unless an applicant possesses it, his chances for employment are slight.

Having built a good organization, the responsibility of the manager is to lead it; to show consideration, to recognize without delay and to correct little annoyances which cause friction, to compliment good work, and to remember that his own friendliness with his own people is passed along by them in their dealings with their customers.

So, friendliness is another thing that goes into the making of a store.

Knowing merchandise and imparting that knowledge to subordinates is also extremely important. However, there have been Penney managers who were not experts in all lines of merchandise but who were successful merchants. They were successful because they knew people and furnished leadership. Such merchants met the formula once put into these words by John D. Rockefeller, Sr.: "The ability to deal with people is as purchasable a commodity as coffee or sugar, and I will pay more for that ability than any other under the sun."

But, as a rule, Penney managers know merchandise, much as Penney himself knows it.

A few years ago Penney was visiting a store and was standing near the main entrance when he saw two women hesitating after coming in through the front door. Approaching them he inquired, "Is there anything I can do for you ladies?"

Shaking their heads the women went toward the rear of the store. Feeling certain they were strangers, Penney watched. As the women paused, talked briefly with each other, and turned as though to leave, Penney circled around through another aisle. Stepping up to them again, he smiled. "I don't want to seem to be bothering you, but I do want to help, if I can. If there is anything you would like to see, or if there is anything I can get for you, I will be glad to do it."

One of the women disclosed they were strangers and explained, "We dropped in the store because we had a little time to spare. I thought I might like to look at some blankets, but I guess not. I can get them when I get home and we won't have to lug them back in the car."

"If you have a few minutes, I will be glad to show you some blankets," said Penney, turning and starting toward the blanket counters. The women followed. Reaching the counters, Penney displayed several different patterns and textures, all the while telling how the blankets were woven, identifying the materials, where they were made. He answered a lot of questions, including questions of prices. His knowledge was such that one of the women observed, "You seem to know a lot about blankets."

"Yes, I think I do," returned Penney.

"But how do we know you're telling us the truth?" interjected the other woman.

A bit nonplussed, Penney answered, "You don't, madam," and added, "but I know I am telling you the truth, and if you buy these blankets you will know it after they have given you years of wear."

The women were undecided. Suspecting what was in their minds, Penney asked, "May I inquire where you ladies live?"

They told him.

"And, you are wondering about the prices on these blankets?"

"Yes, we are," said one. "Before I left home I looked at blankets. These look much the same as the ones I saw, but they can't be the same because—well, because they're so much cheaper," and she identified the store of which she was a customer.

"That is a very good store," declared Penney. "The blankets they showed you are made by the same firm that makes these blankets. They are the same grade. We are able to sell them for less money because we have no charge accounts and no delivery services. Also, we save in other ways. I am sure, if you buy them here, you will find you have made real savings."

The women examined the blankets again, discussed them with each other, and each bought four pairs. While paying for them, one woman said, "When we get back home we are both going to write to the manager of this store and tell him how helpful you have been. What is your name, please?"

Not wishing to identify himself, Penney chuckled and passed by the question, "I appreciate your thoughtfulness but that is not necessary, really it isn't. As a Penney man, I am expected to know about these things."

The questioning and the evading continued while the blankets were being wrapped, with the woman who had requested his identity finally saying, "Even though you don't seem to want to give us your name, and I don't know why, I am going to write the manager and compliment him on one of his salespeople. I am going to describe you to him, too." The woman studied Penney for a moment, memorizing, "Medium-sized man, white moustache, blue eyes, a bright tie—if I tell him that much, he ought to be able to know which clerk I mean."

Still chuckling, Penney gave the women their receipts and helped them with their packages to the door.

After the personnel, the most important thing in the making of a store is the merchandise itself.

Sams often talks about that. "The future of any store," he says, "depends upon its increasing ability to serve the customer. The emphasis is on the word *increasing*. The job of a retailer is to get the merchandise people want; and, when a store has the things people want, the desirability of this merchandise must be enhanced by the surroundings and the manner in which it is sold. That would seem to be obvious—and, it is obvious!—but it is surprising how often storekeepers neglect it.

"A number of years ago one of New York's fine old stores was picked up by an investment trust and turned over to a woman to manage. The store had a fine reputation but was floundering in red ink and heading for the scrap heap. The woman took over her new job with keen awareness of its difficulties. Looking at the store through unprejudiced eyes, she began an investigation and quickly learned that, while the store had plenty of merchandise on its shelves, there was little the public wanted.

"In a few months she made that store one of the finest and most talked-of retail establishments in the country. She succeeded because she measured accurately the job that was being done and then proceeded to the limit of her ability to change it into the job that could be done.

"By changing the job that was being done into the job that could be done, this woman went to some of the fundamentals that make a store:

"1. Personnel.
"2. Well-selected merchandise stocks.
"3. A store not just well kept, but kept the best in town.
"4. A constructive part in the community life.

"We all recognize that the law of life is growth. After being in business a few years, too many men seem to believe their stores have franchises on immortality. They forget that a store justifies its existence only by increasing its ability to serve its customers satisfactorily.

"Among my acquaintances there is a man whose grandfather had a considerable fortune. It was invested in a company that operated ferryboats between Brooklyn and Manhattan Island. The grandfather put all his savings into this particular investment because, as he said, "There will always be ferryboats running across the East River. The population is constantly growing and this transportation company is bound to grow just as fast as the population."

"One day the grandfather read in the newspapers stories of plans for building a bridge across the river. He scoffed at them, but the Brooklyn Bridge was built. The bonds and stocks of the ferry company became worthless because someone had found a better way to do the job of transporting people from one island to another.

"As it was with the ferry company, so is it with a store. No store ever reaches its ideal in performance; but unless it constantly improves, it soon loses its usefulness. There isn't any such thing as a finished performance in storekeeping. Every day brings its new demands.

"Eighty per cent of all customers of all department stores are women. Housekeepers themselves, women are much sharper-eyed than men in detecting good and bad store housekeeping. They react to both. If bad housekeeping, they cease patronizing the store; if good housekeeping, they favor it with their trade. Good housekeeping includes cleanliness, courteousness, and friendliness. There must be items customers want, and customers must be able to locate them easily.

"We have learned, and so have other department store merchants, that most women turn left when they enter a store and most men turn right. For this reason merchandise of interest to women is found on the left side of a store while items of interest to men are found on the right side. These and other buying habits must be remembered if a customer is to feel comfortable while shopping."

The distinguishing characteristic of the pioneers of the Penney company was their lack of knowledge of the "niceties and theories of store operation." They left that knowledge to their competitors, most of whom have gone broke. Penney, Sams, and their early partners lived with their merchandise and their customers. They knew what wasn't selling and, of more importance, they knew what was selling. They concentrated on the things that sold.*

* Penney, Sams, and their early partners concentrated on the things that sold:

YEAR-BY-YEAR SALES FIGURES, 1902–1947

Year	No. of Stores	Gross Business	Year	No. of Stores	Gross Business
1902	1	$ 28,898.11	1925	674	$ 91,062,616.17
1903	1	63,522.95	1926	747	115,683,023.37
1904	2	94,165.49	1927	892	151,957,865.20
1905	2	97,653.54	1928	1,023	176,698,989.14
1906	2	127,128.36	1929	1,395	209,690,417.77
1907	2	166,313.82	1930	1,452	192,943,765.42
1908	4	218,432.35	1931	1,459	173,705,094.52
1909	6	310,062.16	1932	1,473	155,271,981.19
1910	14	662,331.16	1933	1,466	178,773,965.06
1911	22	1,183,279.96	1934	1,474	212,053,361.46
1912	34	2,050,641.99	1935	1,481	225,936,100.88
1913	48	2,637,293.72	1936	1,496	258,322,479.00
1914	71	3,560,293.75	1937	1,523	275,375,137.32
1915	86	4,825,072.19	1938	1,539	257,963,945.53
1916	127	8,428,144.34	1939	1,554	282,133,933.64
1917	177	14,881,203.14	1940	1,586	304,539,325.64
1918	197	21,338,103.60	1941	1,605	377,571,710.99
1919	197	28,783,965.42	1942	1,611	490,295,173.10
1920	312	42,846,008.53	1943	1,610	489,888,090.69
1921	313	46,641,928.20	1944	1,608	535,362,894.30
1922	371	49,035,729.06	1945	1,602	549,149,147.67
1923	475	62,188,978.73	1946	1,601	676,570,117.03
1924	569	74,261,343.00	1947	1,603	775,889,615.00

The best protection Penney had when he started in business was his own meager capital—$500 in cash of his own, and $1,500 he borrowed from a bank in Hamilton, Missouri. To survive, he had to turn his energies and his thinking into doing the real things that make a store. He studied the needs of his customers and he trained men to be merchants. Although the company has grown large, it clings to those fundamentals. It continues to create savings for its customers through economies in its own operations—by "doing without," as Sams says, "the extras which others have considered necessary."

It was no accident that Penney located his first store in a small town. He chose Kemmerer over Ogden because "Ogden was too big." Today, 80 per cent of Penney stores are located in cities and towns having 25,000 inhabitants or less, and 90 per cent are located in cities and towns of 50,000 inhabitants and less. That is no accident either.

Wanting to be neighbors with its customers, the Penney company seeks the friendliness and the respectability of the smaller communities. It is interested in the preservation of the smaller cities and towns because it finds in them, as Penney said years ago, "its kind of people."

Up through the twenties when population was shifting to the large cities, there were those within the company who wondered whether Penney and Sams were not making a mistake by concentrating their stores where they did. Company records show that Penney and Sams never could be persuaded that the population trend would not reverse itself.

In 1902 when Penney was in Kemmerer, there were only about 200 miles of hard-surface roads in the entire country, and no paved highways at all. Today there are more than 1,300,000 miles of hard-surface roads, nearly 300,000 miles of paved streets and highways, and more than 1,000,000 miles of improved roads. Penney and Sams saw that these roads and highways over which people were leaving the smaller communities would become the same thoroughfares over which they would return.

It was their conviction that, having once lived where they had homes, lawns, and gardens and fresh air and safety for children playing, people would return to the smaller communities—"provided," Penney and Sams agreed, "that as merchants we can demonstrate there are no trading advantages in the large cities and that, with our managers active in community affairs, we can help build schools and hospitals and other civic institutions so that the only things the large cities will have that smaller cities lack will be crowds and confusion."

As the Penney company studied the problems of shifting population, other chains came along to help. As a result, it is likely that the greatest single contribution to the preservation of the trading centers, and the smaller communities in general, has been made, and is being made, by the chain stores.

Here are some paragraphs from a company survey to find out what was happening in Iowa in a merchandising way:

"Iowa is about three hundred miles from east to west and two hundred miles from north to south. In the state are hundreds of small and medium-sized towns. To the west of the center of the state is Des Moines, the capital. On the western boundary is Council Bluffs with Omaha just across the river in Nebraska and Sioux City to the north. East of Des Moines are Waterloo and Cedar Rapids and on the eastern boundary are Dubuque and Davenport. These are the largest cities in the state. There is no spot in the state from which a person cannot drive to one of these eight trading centers in two or three hours. Against the competition of these eight cities are scores of towns with merchants trying to make their livings.

"This is a typical story of a smaller community. It is the story of Atlantic, a town of about five thousand population. Atlantic is about sixty miles from Council Bluffs and eighty miles from Des Moines, with good highways to both cities.

"Woolworth was the first chain to open there. When the local merchants found out that a chain store was coming to Chestnut Street, the main street in Atlantic, they tried to stop it. Woolworth opened anyway. The merchants tried to convince their customers that they should not patronize a chain store. The merchants ostracized the Woolworth manager, refusing him membership in the chamber of commerce and the service clubs.

"The Woolworth store did not close. It became the busiest store in town and attracted so much other business to the town that when Safeway and Penney opened in the town they were welcomed by the merchants. As one merchant told us, 'Chain stores brought Atlantic back to life.' Before the chains came, few farmers traded in Atlantic. They used the good roads and their automobiles and drove to Council Bluffs or Des Moines. In those towns they found fresh merchandise at prices they were willing to pay. They found attractive, clean modern stores with alert salespeople.

"There are about a dozen chain stores in Atlantic now. When they came they began advertising in the local newspaper. Other merchants who had considered advertising 'a waste of money' followed suit. Every local enterprise—even competitive stores—benefited from the customers the chains *brought* to town, and the customers the chains *kept* in town. Real-estate values went up in the business and residential districts. Atlantic came back to life. People found it a better place in which to live and trade and spend their money."

"But," some may say, "what is being talked about here is the commercial life of the smaller communities—not the cultural life."

How could the cultural exist without the commercial? How could a community, even a community of esthetics, live without a store? That was one of the things that was driving people from the smaller communities. There weren't enough stores—not enough stores where people could get the things they needed at prices they were willing to pay; and too many stores where people were told what they should buy and how much they should pay.

On the cultural side, there are no Metropolitan Opera Houses and no Field Museums in the smaller communities; but, as in the large cities, there are automobiles to take people where they want to go, radio to bring them what they want to hear—and television will bring them what they want to see. And not to be slighted among their advantages is less promise of sensations and surprises.

In them, there is no hesitation about going to church. In the fresh air of these smaller communities, unworthy competition finds the going harder. In them, the Penney company finds the virility that is America.

TWENTY-ONE

Search Is for Creative Minds

FREQUENTLY LETTERS come to the Penney company inviting it to locate stores in particular communities. They come from chambers of commerce, from independent merchants, from landlords, and from local newspapers. Occasionally there is a round-robin letter from people who live in a community.

"Much as we would like to do otherwise," said President Hughes, "the company can give favorable replies to but few of these requests. In the first place, the store has to have a manager. That means we have to have available a man who is sufficiently trained and, at the same time, a man who wants the new job more than the one he has.

"These requirements do not always go together. Sometimes a man we believe is qualified to manage prefers to remain where he is. If so, his wish controls the decision. Then, too, even though we have a manager available we must have enough quality merchandise on hand or in sight to meet the store's responsibility in the new community. In the recent years there has been a great shortage in quality merchandise."

There are, of course, other considerations that enter into the opening of a store—considerations such as the size of the town, the trading area, the availability of personnel for store training, the transportation facilities, the probable future of the town, and its general character. Most of these details are in the records of the Penney company. Long since, the real estate department of the company surveyed practically every community in the United States and assembled pertinent data.

However, when a new store is contemplated, another survey is made of the selected community. In addition to checking information already in the records, company representatives examine the employment standards of the town, study the type of employment, the type of merchandise in the stores, calculate neighborhood pedestrian and vehicular traffic, interview people interested in various activities in community life, visit the factories, the stores, and the suburban areas. In other words, these company representatives reorient themselves in every phase of community life.

In the spring of 1948 the company opened in Cincinnati what is one of the finest department stores of the country. Both because this was new territory and because it was planning a large store, it is interesting to see how the company went about announcing the event. In a series of daily newspaper advertisements, the location of the new store was prominently displayed, accompanied by the following copy:

WHAT IS PENNEY'S?

PENNEY'S. The largest department store in the world . . . housed under more than 1,600 roofs . . . devoted to serving American families who live simply, but well.

Every department store has its own characteristics. These are ours:

Notwithstanding the beautiful modern setting in which we shall soon invite you to shop, our first consideration is modest prices. Ours is not a store for the luxury trade; you'll look in vain for mink and diamonds! Penney's is a store for people who want quality . . . expressed in solid value.

Our prices are cash and carry—that's one reason they're low. Our customers pay cash because charge accounts mean extra expense which would have to be included in our prices. What you pay for here is *undiluted merchandise value!*

Our customers carry their purchases home. Delivery is a heavy expense, too, which would have to be added into the price of every item. *What you pay for here is undiluted merchandise value!*

Our customers do their shopping in person; mail and telephone orders are often unsatisfactory to the customers, and always expensive to handle. *What you pay for here is undiluted merchandise value!*

It is Penney policy to rule out every possible element of cost that would add to the price of what you buy. This policy has built over 1,600 Penney stores, coast to coast. We believe it will appeal to the thrifty people of Cincinnati, too.

Regularly for several weeks in advance of the opening, the advertising copy impressed upon the people of Cincinnati the location of Penney's store, identifying Penney's as being the "largest department store in the world," expressing its personality of serving "the average family with the things it needs. . . ."

Nothing is added to the price of merchandise to cover the expense of such services as charge accounts, time payment plans, deliveries, mail orders.

Everything we sell is sold for cash.

Our buying experience commands respect and consideration in any market where we buy. No other organization, we believe, can buy better for less.

And no other can move merchandise from factory to user more economically, with less expense added on the way.

All this means savings for our customers.

If you like this way of doing business you will like Penney's.

Penney people are, first of all, J. C. Penney himself, the small-town storekeeper who started in business with $500, saved little by little. His first store, in Kemmerer, Wyoming, was the seed of the plant which is flowering in Penney's-Cincinnati.

The men he attracted to the Penney business learned to be merchants from the ground up. They learned how to please customers by taking an interest in them and their needs. That may not sound like the big business way to build over 1,600 stores, but that's the way Penney's grew, just the same.

From Fort Kent, Maine, on the Canada border, to Calexico,

California, on the Mexican line—from Bellingham, Washington, to West Palm Beach, Florida, you can go into any Penney store and find the Penney kind of friendly people. In Victor, Colorado, in Seattle, Denver, Columbus—in over 1,600 stores—the same welcome, the same helpfulness. The man who sells you a suit, the girl who tells you about Penney blankets or sells you a paper of pins—all have the Penney idea of friendliness and good service.

We have found such men and women in every community—eager to join forces with Penney's. They like merchandise—they like people—they like the business of bringing them together in the Penney way.

The men and women who will serve you in this store will be Cincinnati people of the same sort.

It is not a mere whim that leads us to name our Penney people 'associates,' rather than 'employees.' We do not think of them as working for us, but with us. Penney's offers each associate a place with its own dignity . . . the stockboy who does a good job is as important to the business of serving customers as the buyer who provides quality merchandise for them.

It is not mere chance that gives Penney stores everywhere their distinctive quality of warm friendliness, to which yearly thousands of voluntary letters attest. We choose our associates with care. We look for qualities that make it easy and natural for them to serve customers well—qualities of enthusiasm, patience, understanding.

And association with a Penney store means much to those who are accepted:

First and elementary—adequate pay for service rendered. Nothing means greater economy to a business than people who are well rewarded for working in it. Besides substantial basic rates of pay, Penney associates' incomes are swelled by cash bonuses for creative selling.

Penney associates receive generous discounts on their purchases. They are protected by sick and death benefits. They can build up old-age security through the Thrift and Profit-Sharing Plan, to which the company makes substantial contributions. Penney people get paid vacations.

And from the moment a person becomes a Penney associate, he or she has set foot on the ladder of *Opportunity Unlimited*.

It is such things that make life a pleasant and challenging experience for Penney associates—and make Penney stores so pleasant and satisfactory to shop in.

Another Penney policy, that of having no advertised sales, was explained this way:

Nobody can afford to sell an item worth a dollar for less than a dollar—if it's really a dollar value. That's why you'll never see, in Penney advertising, such claims as '$1 value for 79¢.'

Extravagant statements sound like 'something-for-nothing', but we've found that dependably low prices, every day, are better for merchant and customer alike.

We believe the real worth of a piece of merchandise is the lowest price it can be sold for—any day and every day. Therefore, our prices are always as low as we can make them!

We do not believe in urging people to buy what they do not need, nor more than they need. That's why we do not advertise SALES. That's why every day is a good day to shop at Penney's.

Our advertising is the simple, straightforward news of what you'll find in our store—things that are new, interesting, seasonable.

People who want the best they can buy within their incomes, will do well to study Penney advertising.

And finally, in salute to other Cincinnati merchants, this versification:

> So many a city never knows
> A store as nice as Shillito's—
> We hear its fame reverberate
>
> All over, and beyond, this state!
> So we at Penney's now propose
> A hearty toast to Shillito's!
>
> We wouldn't for the world prorogue
> Our compliments to neighbor Pogue!
> Where crowds foregather, well-content
> With what they've bought for what they've spent.
>
> Perennial we call the vogue
> For things that bear the label 'Pogue!'

And now we bow in the direction
Of Rollman's; held in warm affection
By Cinci shoppers near and far
No wonder you're so popular!

We greet you, Rollman's, call you friend
Long may the Rollman star ascend.

May we address this billet-doux
To Messrs Mabley and Carew?
And all their friendly personnel,
(We've met you and we think you're swell!)

Success continue to accrue
To neighbors Mabley and Carew!

Of compliments we send a pair
To stores McAlpin and The Fair;
It's lack of space, not admiration,
That doubles up this salutation!

McAlpin, Fair, our fondest greeting
We're looking forward to our meeting!

Next may we venture to bestow
A welcoming Bravissimo
On new arrivals Bond and Sears;
We wish you many fruitful years!

On Thursday next, we'll be here, too,
We hope you'll come to our debut!

Encore! Encore! Each shop and store
Whose name we couldn't mention
Again for want of ample space
And not for good intention.

So neighbor merchants, every one,
Let's serve our town in unison!

Decisions as to the opening of new stores are made, of course, by the board of directors, but sometimes there are complications. A few years ago when the lease of one of the larger stores approached expiration, the manager recommended a new location. Negotiations were started and concluded with the occupant of a selected building. Under the terms of the agreement the Penney company agreed to assume the unexpired year of the other company's lease and, in addition, signed a lease for a much longer period.

A few weeks before the move was to take place, the Penney company was notified that officials of the other company had changed their minds and intended remaining where they were for the duration of their lease. Meanwhile the property occupied by the Penney company had been rented to a new tenant.

The local store manager notified the central office, and after some discussion the company decided against dispossessing the squatter tenant. Hearing this decision the store manager posed two questions, "Do I go out of business and lose my people, or do I break up the store into units, locate these units in different parts of town, and keep my people?"

"What do you want to do?" he was asked.

"I want to stay in business."

"Can you get the necessary locations?"

"I have already picked out some."

"Are they good locations?"

"One is. The rest are terrible."

"How many will you need?"

"Five. I'll turn four of them into specialty shops and use the other for all the merchandise that is left over."

"This, then, will be your main store?"

"That's right."

"Is it the best location?"

"No. The worst!"

There was a pause at the New York end of the telephone line, then this question: "How do you think you will come out, profitwise?"

"I don't know. Probably I will lose some money, but I will be in business and I will be able to keep my people."

The problem was discussed by the Penney directors; the following day the store manager was told to use his own judgment. He established four specialty shops, three of them in poor locations. A long-vacant store on the outer rim of the shopping district was made over into the "main store." At the end of the year, his books showed not a loss but a profit. Moreover, when the Penney company moved out, the landlords of all five buildings were able to lease their properties at higher rents because of the increased traffic the Penney stores had brought to the different neighborhoods.

The central office is not only responsible for advertising and leasing but also for buying, for financing, for warehousing, general planning, for over-all policies, and for supervision. There are thirty-odd district managers who serve as a liaison group between the central office and the more than 1,600 stores.

These district managers grew into a department in the same way as the other departments in the company. Originally, the central office was very small, with simple functions—to help in buying merchandise and in establishing simple accounting practices for the stores. As the company grew, these functions expanded and with them came a real-estate department to help find building locations, a sales department to help in selling, an advertising department to help in advertising and promotion, a personnel department to help in the employment and training of men, a treasurer's department to handle banking and insurance, a secretary's department to handle the multiplicity of tax problems, and a traffic department to move the merchandise, as well as other departments. The purpose of all these departments is to service the stores and to help the store managers.

At first, although not in all cases, the company tried unsuccessfully to use men as district managers who had not been managers themselves. Today all district managers are Penney-trained merchants. They receive fixed salaries but, like everyone else, depend upon profit sharing. It is to their immediate interest to help managers to improve themselves as merchants, because the more the stores make, the more the managers make, and the more the company makes, the more the district and zone managers make.

In no sense, are the district managers "under-cover" men for the central office. They make reports on stores in their territories that serve as information material for the home office. However, a copy of each report must be left with the store manager and, whenever possible, must be gone over in detail with the store manager before it is forwarded. There have been times when district managers have torn up reports in preference to mailing them, saying to store managers, "Let's sit down together on my next time around and see if we cannot make out a good report."

In other words, the real job of a district manager is to bring information and guidance from the central office to the store manager and to bring to the central office information they gather from the stores; but, more than that, to pollenize all stores in their territories with whatever useful information they gather while visiting them.

"Any one of our district managers can tell you," said President Hughes, "that even in the smallest store, or even in the store having trouble, there is something that will help the largest and most successful store, if the district manager is alert enough to discover it.

"Some of the very excellent selling programs, some of the most important merchandise items and some of the most common sense personnel approaches have been found in small towns and in the small units of the company. The district manager likes to find these things because they give him a chance to help the local manager with ideas that have been proved workable."

Although operating directly under the central office, district managers live in the territories they supervise. Being residents, they know these areas from inside and reflect this same regional point of view. On paper this may not sound as important as it actually is. This decentralization policy is the strength of the company just as decentralization in government is the strength of the United States.

To expedite deliveries of merchandise to the retail counters, there are warehouse facilities in New York, in Statesville, North Carolina, and in St. Louis, Missouri. In addition to the main buying office in New York, there are buying offices in Chicago, St. Louis, Los Angeles, Dallas, and London, England.

Throughout this book emphasis has been placed on enlightened minds in business. The majority of American business organizations are operated by such minds. It is true that within this majority there are some organizations that are further along the way than the others; progress in business, as in everything, is always the work of the few.

Business organizations become great, and remain great, for exactly the same reason as nations. One reason is character and the other is the creative mind within them. Character prevents dissolution, and creative minds provide the necessary fuel which feeds them.

Students of social and economic history often comment on

what they call the "three cycles" in the history of families and of business institutions: "The cycle of building or growth, the cycle of preservation or conservation and the cycle of dissipation or decay." From this identification has come the familiar reference to family histories as running the gamut of "three generations from overalls to riches to overalls."

According to the students, the history of many business institutions begins with pioneers who blaze the way, lay the foundations, and rear successful structures. That period usually covers the active business lives of the pioneers—thirty to forty years. The second generation is interested in preservation and adds little to the strength of the organization. By the third generation, the business has ceased to grow; it falters and slips into bankruptcy or into other hands.

Put another way, the pioneers were builders. To be builders they had to be creative. Trying to preserve, the second generation rejected adventure so that the third generation has nothing left except brick and mortar, machines, and perhaps some money. By themselves, brick and mortar, machines and money are never enough to keep possession of a business. They are never enough because across the street, or in the next block, there are business minds that are creative.

In the Penney company the search has always been for the creative mind.

Instead of thinking of their employees in the mass, the company policy is to think of them as individuals. This is only a continuation of the original policy, established by Penney, of making partners of those who proved themselves qualified.

Not long ago the manager of one of the largest stores was hospitalized with a sudden, serious illness. The store personnel held a meeting. It was busiest season of the year. After the meeting word was sent to the manager that he was to confine himself to the single job of cooperating with the doctors; that the personnel had pledged itself to having the biggest month in the store's history—if he would just stay in the hospital and take care of himself.

From his hospital bed the manager watched the daily sales figures. When the month was ended, it was not only the biggest sales month but it was so large that it carried the store into the greatest yearly business in its history.

In Columbus, Nebraska, in 1943, a Penney manager celebrated his twentieth year as a member of the organization. Hearing about it, Edgar Howard, the editor of the Columbus Daily Telegram, signed this editorial:

"I take it for granted that at his christening service he was given the name of Peter, but today nobody hails him by any other name than Pete. Twenty years ago he came to Columbus as a humble employe of one of the greatest organizations of its type in the United States—the Penney stores corporation. Quickly his worth was recognized by that organization, and within three years he was made manager of the Penney interests, and today still retains that distinction. Not only did the Penney organization discover a prize when it found Pete Lakers, but Columbus has found in him one of its best assets. He has been through the years and still is first among all equals in promoting every civic interest in his home city. Columbus is, and well should be, proud of Pete Lakers. Yesterday he celebrated his twentieth birthday with the Penney store in Columbus, and I am wishing for him many more anniversaries of the day when he honored Columbus and profited his employer here."

There are a great many such incidents in the records. So long as they occur, the "cycle of building or growth" will be the history of the J. C. Penney Company.

Serving the Public Intelligently

W HEN PENNEY sent Sams to Cumberland in 1908 to operate his newly acquired store, no political fly cop went to Kemmerer to tell him:

"You can't do that, Mr. Penney. One store is enough for you. If we let you have two stores, pretty soon you will want four stores, then eight, then sixteen. That sort of ambition, if pursued, would wreck the economy of the state—yes, even the economy of the entire nation. You don't seem to realize, Mr. Penney, that we have no more frontiers and, consequently, too many stores already. Besides, the mining company has a store in Cumberland and competition is a very bad thing. Competition, Mr. Penney, is the root and stem of all social injustices."

That political lullaby was yet to be sung to the American people. Its first notes began to be heard in 1925 when laws imposing special taxes on chain stores were defeated in two state legislatures. In 1926 a similar unsuccessful effort was made in another state.

In 1927, special tax legislation against chain stores was passed by the legislatures of Georgia, Maryland, and North Carolina. Since then discriminatory taxes have been imposed in fifteen additional states. Many municipalities have followed the lead of the states; and beyond these state and municipal taxes, there is the Congressional Robinson-Patman Act with its various amendments.

All this legislation was started when believers in the strategy of getting rid of competitors by fair means or foul turned to politics. In the early twenties, a number of wholesalers (who were losing profits because, for the most part, chain stores were buying directly from manufacturers) hired professional agitators—and paid them well.

Using independent merchants as a front, by 1929 these mercenaries of the wholesalers had organized anti-chain store groups in 400 cities and towns. By the liberal use of advertising-dollars, they employed newspapers and radio stations to frighten a good many independent merchants into believing they were "doomed by the chain store menace" and a good many people into believing "chain stores were the spawns of Wall Street." Always on the alert for packaged votes, a good many politicians joined in the clamor.

In the thirties the agitation spread into Congress and on June 19, 1936, the Robinson-Patman Act became law. It reads that it is "unlawful for a seller to discriminate in price between different purchasers of like grade and quality, or for a customer knowingly to induce or receive such discrimination where the effect may substantially be to lessen competition or tend to create a monopoly in any line of commerce, or to injure, destroy or prevent competition with the buyer or seller, or with the customer of either of them."

However involved the Act seems to sound, its real purpose appears to have been to establish certain types of wholesalers in a permanently secure position so far as profits are concerned, and to cripple the chain store.

As the thirties progressed, previous scruples against repressive legislation were tossed aside. Wanting the American people to believe that all prosperity flows from campaign speeches, politicians branded business men as "enemies of social progress" and publicly stated their intentions to restrict and punish. So far as chain stores were concerned, Wright

Patman, congressman from Texarkana, Texas, and co-author of the Robinson-Patman Act, went beyond the intention to restrict and punish, and proposed putting chain store merchants out of business.

In 1938 he introduced a bill (H. R. 9464) into the House of Representatives. In "The Chain Store Tells Its Story," John P. Nichols examined this bill, and wrote:

"The author [Patman] proposed to meet the alleged menace of the chain store by imposing a graduated Federal excise tax on chain store companies, commencing from $50 annually per store on chains operating from 10 to 15 outlets, and progressing to a maximum of $1,000 per store for each unit in a chain conducting in excess of 500 stores. And it didn't stop there.

"According to the provisions of the bill, the foregoing graduated license tax automatically multiplied according to the number of states in which an affected chain store company operated stores. In other words, if a company operated 500 or more stores in, say 10 or so states, including the District of Columbia, then besides all the many other Federal, state, and local taxes for which that company was annually obligated, the Patman bill would additionally have taxed that company $1,000 per each of its stores multiplied by the number of states in which the company conducted store operations including, for good measure, the District of Columbia.

"For the first two years, only a small fraction of the special Federal tax would have been levied on companies in order to give them an opportunity to wind up their affairs, to write their obituaries, and to prevent a sudden wholesale loss of jobs among hundreds of thousands of their employees."

So far as the Penney company was concerned, a yearly Federal tax of $64,000,000 would have been levied. This tax would have wiped out its profits, several times over, on a volume business of $304,539,325.64 in 1940 (the year the bill was brought up for final vote) just as it would have eliminated a shoe company doing business directly with customers through the operation of its own stores in many of the states. The yearly Federal tax (1940) against this shoe company would have been $17,000,000 as against a total volume business of $36,000,000.

The bill failed to pass because the American people knew their ABC's as applied to household needs. They flooded Congress with protests.

The political attacks on chain stores have continued. Perhaps that is to be expected, considering the apparent desire of some politicians to rule instead of represent. But matters of high concern to the American people should not be degraded to the level of politics. Such matters as cost of living, for example, are above politics and beyond partisanship.

The fundamental of production and of distribution is to bring to the consumer the things he buys at the lowest possible price. As has been demonstrated many times in the recent years, production is no longer a serious problem in this country. But distribution remains a problem, and, while it so remains, automobiles as well as pins will cost more than they should. It has been well established by Federal agencies that chain stores sell equal merchandise for less money. If this means anything it means savings for many people. It also means that chain stores are further along the road to solving the problem of distribution than are most other businesses.

Contrary to what is so often heard, it is not because chain stores buy in such large quantities that they are able to sell for lower prices. Primarily, it is because chain store merchants are better merchants.

"The chain store, exactly as the independent store," says Sams, "depends for its success upon the observance of a few basic principles. In order of their importance, *in our company*, they are: (1) scientific training of the entire personnel; (2) knowing the merchandise needs of the community; (3) intelligent buying; (4) rapid turnover; (5) elimination of all unnecessary operating expenses; and (6) favorable location."

Because Sams and the other Penney executives considered personnel training the first basic principle, only about four of every hundred applicants are accepted for jobs. It costs a great deal of money to train people to be merchants. By satisfying itself as to aptitudes and integrity in advance, the company eliminates a great deal of unnecessary expense.

Once hired, an employee of the Penney company is expected to work in accordance with the spirit of the organization. His immediate instructor is his manager; his schoolroom and classmates are the store and the store personnel. First he is given a thorough grounding in the operation of the store, and after receiving this groundwork he takes other courses: the study of the town in which he works, its people, its merchandising demands, its industries, its efforts at civic betterment. All the while he is moving through these courses, he gets other training in such things as merchandising, salesmanship, personnel work, and advertising. All this training is to one end—to make him a merchant so he may serve the public intelligently.

Speaking frankly, the politician or anyone else who willy-nilly opposes a chain store operation, is the enemy of every good independent merchant. He is the enemy of every consumer. Many surveys have been made across the years to determine the qualifications of retailers. These surveys show that, percentagewise, just as many retailers failed in business before there were chain stores as since; and that even today 70 per cent of all retailers do no more than eke out an existence, and most of them end up in bankruptcy.

As a result, everybody loses. The bankrupt loses his money; employees lose their jobs; suppliers lose their money; property owners and consumers lose; and the community itself loses taxes needed to support all the services it renders its inhabitants.

To accuse chain stores of driving independent merchants out of business is to say it was Joe Louis, Gene Tunney, or Jack Dempsey or any other heavyweight champion prize fighter who kept a tenth-rate pug from becoming the world's champion; or to argue that Plato, Sophocles, or Homer kept some other Greek scribbler from becoming a great author.

These borderline and bankrupt retailers are driven out of business by no one except themselves. Ill-trained, or with no training for the task involved, they invest their savings in a small store, not knowing there is more to storekeeping than stocking shelves, installing a cash register, and opening the front door. The personal loss is tragic enough, but it is worse for politicians and self-seekers generally to delude these unfortunate would-be merchants and to use them to delude and use the public.

The fact is that no good merchant has anything to fear from a chain store. The presence of a chain store in his immediate neighborhood will attract business to the store of the good independent merchant. It does so for the simple reason that it brings more customers into the trading area.

What these pseudo reformers do not understand about business is that no large company such as Penney's can possibly exist without a myriad of small businesses to support it. Every day that a Penney man works, he provides work for at least six other people. The same thing is true of any large business. It is impossible to divide business into two segments—large business and small business. They depend so much on each other that they cannot exist independently. Wipe out the large companies and—immediately!— 75 per cent of all small companies will cease operations.

Here are a few of the other familiar arguments against chain stores, with their answers:

1. Chain stores sell merchandise too cheap. (Is that bad for the customer?)

2. Chain stores depress real estate values. (The opposite is true. Chain stores increase real estate values, as every independent survey shows.)

3. Chain stores drain money away from the town. (How can that be, if they sell for less? The independent merchant buys in the same markets as does the chain store. The fact is, as every independent survey shows, the chains leave more money in the town.)

4. Chain stores pay less local taxes. (No local tax agency will agree. Local tax records show that chain stores pay more in taxes than do independent merchants.)

5. Chain stores do not contribute to local charities. (Independent surveys show contributions equal the independent merchants.)

6. Chain stores are owned by Wall Street financial interests. (About one-third of all chain stores are locally owned. The remainder are publicly owned.)

But all this aside, whether chain stores sell for less or whether they sell for more; whether they are owned by Wall Street or whether they are owned by the same people who operate them; whether they pay their fair share of taxes or whether they don't—whether they do all the things they are accused of doing or whether they don't, the one fact remains that these complaints have nothing whatever to do with the right of the chain stores to do business in a community.

The fundamental is: no government, Federal, state, or local, has any right to pass a law levying taxes in different amounts for the same privilege—the privilege of operating a store.

The knowledge that discriminatory tax legislation against chain stores has only been upheld as constitutional by the narrowest of margins in the Supreme Court of the United States does not change that fundamental. For a time, it may make it inoperative, but only for a time. Having our particular form of government, we have our periods of depression in the caliber of men selected for public office. We always get over them; that is our great advantage over the rest of the world.

As honorary chairman, J. C. Penney opened this book by writing the introduction; as chairman, Earl Corder Sams closes it:

What I have to say here is said, not as an individual, but as the humble spokesman for those who have found their opportunity in chain store work; for those whose livelihoods depend on their business relationships with chain stores; for those who live in communities where there are chain stores; and for the great mass of American consumers who by their patronage have built the chain stores.

If I should become what may appear to be a little overly earnest in this presentation, I hope you will forgive me because always, when I deal with matters that are as close to me as this question is, it is difficult for me to refrain from the display of a little feeling.

If I use some personal facts or the story of my own company, the purpose is not at all one of self-advertising or self-justification—it is solely to give facts as I know them and not conclusions drawn from hearsay. Also, while I naturally feel that the J. C. Penney Company is one of the finest retail organizations in the world, my observation is that its principles and its story in varying degrees are the principles and the story of most successful chain store companies.

In 1907 I was operating, with the backing of some friends, a store in my small native town of Simpson, Kansas. I was an independent merchant. The store was equipped with fine fixtures. We bought our merchandise where we pleased or could, usually through jobbers. However, I couldn't see any real opportunity ahead. A livelihood—yes, perhaps—but not much more. In looking around for a bigger opportunity, an employment agency told me about a man named J. C. Penney who had a store in a little coal camp at Kemmerer, Wyoming, and who had a vision of something beyond a single store.

After some correspondence I left Kansas and joined Mr. Penney. Was I attracted by salary? No, that wasn't any more than I was getting. Was I attracted by a job? No, I had a rather imposing one as head of my own store. Was I attracted by Mr. Penney's buying power and his financial resources? No, actually at that time they weren't much greater than my own.

What did attract me? About the same things that have attracted thousands and tens of thousands of other young men, through the intervening years, to the Penney company and to the other chains that have grown like our own. These attractions were:

1. The opportunity to work with and to learn from a man who was doing a good job and who was a successful merchant. Chain stores have no monopoly on merchandise, or methods, or brains. What they do offer a young man is the chance to gain a practical education in storekeeping. They are the finest possible school for the boy who can't pay for an extended college education. Mr. Penney knew how to run a store. That's why I was eager to work for him.

2. The opportunity to share in what I helped to create. The Penney company has grown to its present size largely be-

cause it has given store managers, and later general office associates, the chance to be an actual part of the company. That's why Mr. Penney is frequently called "The Man With A Thousand Partners." In those earlier days Mr. Penney sold men who had proved themselves in his store an interest in the stores they opened and managed. He took their notes for their interest and let them pay for them out of earnings. That plan had to be changed in form in later years because of the size of the company. Nevertheless, the principle has been kept, and is maintained.

Today our managers do not have to put money into the business but every store manager receives, in addition to a livable salary, a percentage of the earnings of his store. This percentage in large part is one-third and in only a few of the largest stores is it less than one-sixth. The majority of these managers make more from their earnings' participation than from their salaries. The same is true of those in the central office and who are in positions of responsibility. The maximum yearly salary for any man in our company is $10,000. For the balance of their earnings, even our top executives are dependent on the results they help to create.

Men in the Penney company are working primarily for themselves. If you want to know what they think of their personal opportunities, ask them. I went to work for Mr. Penney because he offered me an increased opportunity.

3. The third thing that attracted me to Mr. Penney was the vision he had of more than one store—maybe a dozen, maybe even fifty which might be opened through the years and which would work together. The mortality among small retailers is heavy. It was even heavier in 1907 than it is today. The chief reason for retail failure, according to every analysis I have made, or have seen, is incompetency or lack of knowledge.

The greatest single asset of a chain store is not its buying power, its financial resources, or its size. The chief asset is the pooling of experience, the elimination of error, the establishment of successful methods, and the higher standards of personal accomplishment that come from comparison with others who are successful.

Many merchants actually fail and many more never accomplish what they might because, like myself back in Simpson, Kansas, they lack knowledge, or they do not have access to the things others have learned, or because they are too easily satisfied for lack of comparison standards.

The story of the average chain store—whether a corporate chain or a voluntary chain—is like the story of Robinson Crusoe. While alone, he couldn't do much. When he got a man Friday, he accomplished a great deal. The chain store brings together many "man Fridays" who pool their efforts for the greater success of each and to the benefit of all with whom they deal. I went to work for Mr. Penney because he gave me better tools with which to work.

I would like to tell you more about the degree of independence that the Penney opportunity or the chain store opportunity makes available for the individual. All this talk about stifling initiative and making machines out of men amuses and irritates me because it is so contrary to the truth. What a successful chain store and what my own company tries to do is to relieve the store manager of the financial worries, of the heavy buying expense, and of the doing of many things that can be done better cooperatively, thus leaving him free to do the creative job of storekeeping.

To save the store manager time and to enable him to know how his business is going, we furnish him with simple accounting forms and records that he keeps to tell him what he needs to know. To make his job more productive, we furnish him with advertising and sales promotional material, but he works out the actual advertisements with his local newspapers. To be sure his merchandise is right, we scour the markets for the best sources and test in our central laboratory what we buy.

But he selects the actual merchandise stock for his own store in the kinds, quantities, and qualities he needs. He actually does the buying job, but neither he nor his customers have to worry about the intrinsic value. We give him training help for his associates, but he does the great bulk of the employment work and training. In other words, tools are furnished him, but he determines their use. He is a merchant in his own right.

My observation is that our managers and most chain store managers work harder and are more aggressive than many competitors. The picture is frequently presented that they do this because someone is cracking a whip over them. My years of working and my own experience tell me another story. The ambitious chain store manager works because he gets a substantial part of what he produces and he has the vision of something worth working for.

He knows his chances for success are good because of what other men have done and are doing with the same setup. He knows that his opportunity is not limited to one store. From the small store he may move to a larger. From a large store he may move into a district managership or into a position of general company responsibility. Whatever his particular ability or ambition, he knows there is freedom of opportunity for him.

Where do men at the top in the chains come from? There are some thirty-five district managers in the Penney company; each started as a clerk or in a stock room. Through effort and training, each became a successful store manager and then a district manager. We have eleven directors in the Penney company. Each has made his way to the directorship by start-

ing in the ranks and growing with the company.* Their suc-
cessors will come from the same source—country boys or
youngsters from Hamilton, Missouri; Simpson, Kansas; or
Monmouth, Illinois. Right now, young men throughout our
company are fitting themselves for bigger responsibilities and
are working hard for them because they know the opportunity
actually exists.

They realize that the road to enlarged opportunity is found
in effort and accomplishment, not in family ties or in relation-

* From its beginnings all directors in the Penney Company have come up
through the company. A complete list follows:

Name	Date employed by company	Term of office — Elected in annual meeting of	Resigned
J. C. Penney	1902	1913	
E. C. Sams	1907	1913	
E. J. Neighbors	1907	1913	1918
D. H. Mudd	1906	1913	1926
J. I. H. Herbert	1911	1913	
Geo. H. Bushnell ..	1911	1916	1947
C. E. Dimmitt	1912	1916	1926
J. M. McDonald ...	1905	1916	1930
G. G. Hoag	1909	1916	1926
Wilk Hyer	1910	1918	
F. R. Payne	1915	1920	1926
A. F. Lieurance	1911	1920	1922
D. G. McDonald ...	1913	1922	1930
G. G. White	1915	1926	1928
R. H. Ott	1911	1926	1933
L. V. Day	1912	1926	1945
G. H. Crocker	1920	1926	1945 (deceased)
L. A. Bahner	1914	1928	1932
W. A. Reynolds	1924	1930	1947
E. A. Ross	1916	1930	
C. E. Dimmitt	1912	1932	1934
A. W. Hughes	1920	1933	
F. W. Binzen	1926	1935	
F. J. Bantz	1922	1945	
J. F. Brown	1921	1945	
H. H. Schwamb	1923	1947	
G. E. Mack	1921	1947	

ship to some individual or family. They create their opportunity. They are not born to it.

To summarize this question of opportunity in a brief way, here is the picture as we see it in our company. The chain store system offers to the young man who wants to be a merchant an education in merchandising, the resources needed for success, and the opportunity to go as far as he will. I still treasure the letter Mr. Penney wrote me in 1907 in which he told me, "You can have all the rope you want if you are competent."

That policy remains, unchanged.

Just as the chain store has created freedom of opportunity for young merchants, it has also created employment opportunities of a desirable type for more than a million employees. There isn't space to cover this in detail. In the Penney company, for the rank and file of our associates below the management level the wages are as good or better than competitors pay. Since good salespeople can usually find jobs and since we want to employ and keep the best obtainable, competition with other merchants demands that our wages be right.

In addition, the company provides paid vacations, free sick benefit allowances, free death protection equal to a year's pay to the limit of $2,500, a bonus for unusual production, a savings or thrift plan to which the company contributes—*and job security.*

I know of no independent store corresponding in size to the average Penney store that has all these benefits. Certainly the small department store does not have. These provisions were not established from a philanthropic or soothing-syrup viewpoint. They are part of a plan of sharing with those who produce, what is produced. They are based on the realization that our success depends on the happiness and the welfare of every worth-while associate.

On the basis of all I know, it is my sober judgment that our associates, both in the management group and throughout the company, are making more of their lives and have more to look forward to than they would if they were operating their own stores, or working for the average so-called independent merchant.

TWENTY-THREE

No Favors from Government

C HAIRMAN SAMS continues speaking:
From the standpoint of the Penney company, we have tried for what you might term purely selfish reasons to pack the consumer's dollar as full of value as possible.

To this end we have tried to operate our business without adding the frills for which our average customer does not ask, which our average customer does not want, and for which our average customer cannot afford to pay. In that first store of Mr. Penney's, neither wrapping paper nor cardboard boxes nor cord were wasted. We did without many things in order to sell goods for less. We did not have big buying power or big resources, but we were determined to cut the spread between producer and consumer.

That first store in Kemmerer opened in the face of practically a local monopoly of a company-owned store. The mining company issued scrip; the company store sold on credit and accepted scrip; and outside competitors were decidedly not welcome. Mr. Penney made a success of that store by bucking that local monopoly with values so much better that customers were willing to pay cash, to carry home their purchases, and to make that store the seed for the present company.

Our company has continued to find other means of cutting the margin between producer and consumer, in a way Mr. Penney could not do. We buy direct from the most efficient manufacturers we can find. We buy in quantities that make possible savings in quantity production. We regularly buy staple merchandise in large quantities during dull seasons and thus stabilize employment. We help manufacturers devise ways of making better merchandise—and better ways for making good merchandise. We operate regional buying offices and regional warehouses so we may keep in closer touch with markets and deliver merchandise to stores on short notice.

I have always been amazed at the job Woolworth and the other variety stores have done in bringing thousands of necessities, or even luxury items, within the buying power of our entire population. There is no more fascinating example of American genius in production and distribution than the counters of the five-and-ten-cent stores. To appreciate this, we need only spend a short time in a community without one of them.

In our own company we haven't had quite the same range of merchandise with which to work; but, in our own way, we have tried to standardize merchandise and to simplify its distribution so that more and more people might buy better merchandise for less money.

I could talk all day about chain store savings for consumers; about the effect of chain store prices on keeping down the level of all retail prices through competition; about the job the chains have done in fashioning the one great contribution to distribution in this century—direct quantity distribution to match quantity production.

Particularly would I like to stress the value of the far-flung national operation of interstate chains in their savings to consumers. The larger chains set the pace in establishing new merchandise values for communities remote from the markets. The larger chains blaze the trail in bringing wanted items within the buying power of the ordinary pocketbook. If all larger chains were wiped out, isn't it probable that the abler merchants would concentrate their operations in the heavily populated, wealthier states, where the possibilities are greatest?

This action would inevitably take away from the less populous and less wealthy states the full benefit of the direct distribution system. It would be another blow at the purchasing power of the communities which need most of the advantages and savings large-scale distribution offers. It would be a heavy indirect tax on the purchasing power of the smaller income consumers.

Millions of Mrs. Consumers know that chain store operation makes possible better living for those families which need to watch what they spend. What do you think Mrs. Consumer's reaction would be if she were told that the Penney company was going to be destroyed in order that a jobber in Salt Lake City or Ogden might get his cut on the merchandise that was sold in Kemmerer?

What would she think of price-fixing measures which are intended to stamp out the efficiency of large-scale distribution from which she and millions like her have benefited?

What would she think of a bill intended to reestablish the higher prices that existed before chain store operations began?

Through all the years of prosperity, of depression, of business revival, the chain store has been a constant and effective means to those ends without government subsidy and without special favors.

Many of the larger manufacturers depend on our orders for staple merchandise to keep their mill organizations together during the year and to cut down seasonal unemployment. The resulting economies don't help only chain stores; they benefit every retailer handling merchandise from those mills. Many small manufacturers have built productive businesses by specializing in certain types of standardized merchandise for the chains.

Their entire success and the livelihood of their employees is tied in with the mass distribution that chains give. Some of my best friends of long standing are manufacturers with whom the Penney company has dealt practically from its beginning. If time permitted, I would like to emphasize the mutuality of interest which has characterized our relationship.

Especially am I thinking of the blow that would strike all the Main Streets throughout the country if chain stores were legislated out of business. The Penney company owns few buildings and practically all our stores are in rented buildings. Most of our new locations in the last fifteen or twenty years have been opened because an owner or his broker came to us and said:

"We have a store building for rent. Our experience has not been profitable and we are anxious to rent to the Penney company because we know the rent will be paid and the location will improve in value. We are willing to spend some money in fitting the property for your occupancy because we feel it is the safest investment we can make."

By and large this same process has been going on along all the Main Streets throughout this country. If chain store leases were destroyed by law, what would happen to these investors and to the other investors or to the insurance companies who hold the mortgages?

May I state one point very clearly. Our company is not opposed to any necessary taxes which are not discriminatory and which apply equally to our competitors and to ourselves. We ask no special favors. We are opposed to discriminatory taxes intended to raise prices and to take money from our customers in order to subsidize our competitors.

It has been said that chain stores don't pay their full share of taxes. It is a matter of record that chain stores pay more taxes in proportion to their business than do most of their competitors. There are several reasons for this. Any state or Federal tax auditor knows that in dealing with a corporate chain he has access to carefully kept certified figures. How many of our smaller competitors even keep such figures? Our own tax department has been told many times by tax auditors that, in the case of certain taxes such as personal property or sales taxes, it was impossible to check the figures of competitors alongside our stores.

If anyone in a local community is going to get an advantage in a low assessment, it will not be a chain store. The advantage, if any, would be with the local merchant, because the human equation enters even the realm of taxes and the local merchant naturally gets the break. I know this from experience.

In the isolated comparisons I have seen published by anti-chain store propagandists, where a specific Penney store was accused of paying inadequate taxes, there was a joker in the figures. In most cases this joker was that the taxes paid by our store were compared with those of a local store which owned the building and included real estate taxes in the comparison.

We rent our buildings. In renting them to us, the landlord figures the rent to include his real-estate taxes. Usually he tells us what these taxes are and we accept them as a partial justification for the rent. Of course, in the tax rolls the Penney company does not appear as the taxpayer on the real estate, although it actually pays the taxes, as the landlord well knows.

I would like to emphasize that Penney men are essentially small-town merchants. We have a few stores in large cities, but the bulk of the Penney stores are in small or medium-sized centers. If our company knows anything about merchandising and customers, it knows them from the small-town angle rather than the metropolitan.

A chain store leaves more money in a community and adds more to the purchasing power of the community generally than does a competitive independent merchant.

The four largest operating expenses in retailing are, in the usual order of their importance, salaries, rent, advertising, and taxes. The chain store pays its salaries to local people; the chain store pays its rent locally; the chain store does its advertising locally; the chain store pays its local taxes locally. In these four respects the chain differs in no particular from any other merchant.

Now, let us consider the largest single item of expenditure, the cost of the merchandise itself. When a merchant buys silk hose, or men's clothing, or children's shoes, he does not buy them in Lansing, Michigan. He buys them from a jobbing house in some large city or from a manufacturer in another state. Of necessity he must send the bulk of his daily cash receipts out of Lansing to pay for the merchandise he sells.

The chain store manager does the same thing with two important differences. He sends less money out of town because his bills for merchandise are not swollen by the additional amounts that the jobber charges the local merchant to cover the jobber's costs and profits. This saving, through direct distribution, is much greater than the small profit that goes to the stockholder.

Secondly, the chain store, because of the better values given, takes less of every customer's dollar. The chain leaves several extra cents out of every dollar in each of his customer's pockets to spend locally. These dollars continue to work at home in Lansing. They increase Lansing's volume of retail business and its importance as a trading center.

If the national chains were wiped out it would remove the

most substantial bulwark which these smaller trading centers have against the pull of the big cities. It has been said of chain stores that they were ruining the smaller communities. Chain stores did not do that; the automobile and good roads naturally caused people to turn to larger cities to do their trading.

No law, no human mandate can breathe life back into the very small trading center which formerly supported a couple of general stores. Those stores existed because without automobiles or good roads the customer could not get to the city. Because of horse and buggy transportation and because of mud roads, the customer bought what the general store offered at its own price, or he ordered by mail.

However, the chain store has served as a check on the drying up of towns and small cities. It has done this by bringing to these smaller centers the same values, the same reliable merchandise, the same prices, the same styles, and the same modern stores that were available in the bigger cities. And the customers know it.

This particular effect of the chain store picture has never been given the recognition to which it is entitled. In our office we have a file of letters and petitions asking us to open stores in towns. I want to cite a couple of specific cases to make my point clear.

The owner of a vacant store property in an Iowa town was seeking a tenant. In a rather unusual manner he sent letters to the 124 leading professional and businessmen of his community. Two paragraphs of his letter read as follows:

"I need your advice. The building which I own is vacant and we are seeking desirable occupancy. We have already discouraged some inquiries because we thought them no good for the town—nonessential.

"By desirable we mean something permanent and something the town needs for creating more and better business for the town as a whole. Something you think will be profitable to the owner and profitable to the community."

The first we of the Penney company knew about it was when the owner wrote us and sent us answers to his circular letter. These answers urged him to get a Penney store in the location. Then he added, "You might be interested to know that 70 per cent of the replies mentioned a J. C. Penney store in the same manner as these two replies enclosed."

Why did 70 per cent of the businessmen in this town ask for a Penney store? Why do the general offices of the Penney company get frequent requests from chambers of commerce and from service clubs asking us to locate a store in their town?

It isn't because they have something to sell to the Penney company. It is because they recognize that a Penney store in a community makes it a better community in which to live. They recognize that customers will trade in a town where there are representative chain stores because the customers know their money will buy as much as it will in the big city several hours drive away. Newspapermen tell us that a Penney store helps the paper because other stores advertise in the local paper when Penney does. Real-estate men say that when a Penney store opens up with an improved building or when we improve an existing store, the other local stores step up their appearance.

The presence of a good chain store in a county seat makes that town a better trading center for every merchant. Smart independents don't try to keep out chain store competitors. They try to locate next door to them. Some of our choicest locations are leases made with us by the leading department store owners in a town because they want a Penney store alongside them to keep trade in the town and to attract trade from the farmers.

A group of chain stores in a town means money to the doctor and dentist because these stores keep customers at home. They mean money to the local railroad man, the local truck man, the local property owner. They mean money for the local movie house because the family doesn't make a day and an evening of it in the neighboring city. They help every enterprise, even the competing merchant, because they produce traffic in the town and keep dollars from rolling down the highway to some big city.

Several years ago the Penney store in Sauk Center, Minnesota, was destroyed by fire. Practically all the merchants of Sauk Center and many of the residents of the town petitioned the Adjutant General of the state of Minnesota to let the Penney company use the armory as a temporary home. This petition was signed, so I am told, because the people of the town wanted the conveniences and advantages of the Penney store and regarded it as a community asset.

The Adjutant General granted the petition, and the Penney store remained in the armory until a new building was erected.

This social influence of the chain store has never been given the credit to which it is entitled. My impression is that most socially-minded people live in the small cities and towns and want to check the heavy pull toward the crowded cities. The chains are a potent influence to this end. Perhaps the editor of the Marshall, Texas, newspaper put it in a brief way when he wrote his congressman a number of years ago:

"I think you will do the whole country an irreparable damage when you drive the chain stores out of business . . . or drive them entirely out of the small towns and into the larger cities. The small towns of your district are having a hard enough time now trying to keep from drying up in favor of the larger cities nearby; and . . . this bill (the Patman Bill) is certain to be the death of all the chains or at least of those in towns from the size of Marshall, Paris, and Texarkana on down.

"A good many far-sighted and more aggressive independent merchants had rather be in the same block with or next to a big chain store than anywhere else in town. This is because they realize that these stores attract shoppers. Now put them all in Dallas or Shreveport and see where our business goes."

This statement of mine has been lengthy, although I would like to have elaborated in even greater detail the points on which I have touched, and many others. I have been speaking for the freedom of opportunity which the chain store system affords; for the consumers and for the American standards of living; for the workers in the chain stores and those whose interests are tied with these chains; for the communities whose existence the chain fosters.

As a conclusion I would like to refer to a letter that came unsolicited to Mr. Penney's desk. It is one of hundreds that come to him in similar vein. The writer of the letter told her story in a better way than I, or anyone else, could hope to put it. It follows:

"I remember so happily our meeting and little chat of a few years ago on that occasion of your latest visit here and I trust you will remember me.

"You may remember from my professional card that I left in the store for you that I was connected with the school system in the capacity of Visiting Teacher. I am still in that position and through it I have had occasion recently to be in your store here and have an urge to write you about it.

"A group of men placed at the disposal of the four Visiting Teachers a sum of money to be expended for indigent school children. Our recommendations are passed upon by a committee and orders written for the clothing items which we select with the children at the store. Last year was the beginning of this worthy work. The committee in charge, being new in the work, experimented somewhat and directed us to three different stores with our various cases, trying to distribute their patronage. Evidently, after they had studied the results they decided that Penney's had given the greatest values, for this winter our orders took us almost entirely there.

"Personally, I was delighted; for I had found it so much easier to take care of this phase in our work at your store than at either of the other two stores selected.

"While we all found it a rather big task to buy clothing for as many children as we had on our lists, we also found it a pleasure to deal with as pleasant, courteous, efficient, and accommodating staff as we found your employees to be. The young men served us with a manner that left us feeling that it was their personal pleasure to do it. Whether they have been trained to such pleasing service or whether you simply found the right men for their right places, I wish to congratulate you. Surely, they and their kind are the secret of your many successful stores.

"Your manager I did not get to know personally, but my co-workers did and they are as enthusiastic about him as I am about the men in charge of the different departments. The girls who helped us with the school girls' clothing were as nice as the young men. They all entered into the spirit of the thing with a zeal that was gratifying so that is why I felt I should like to tell you without any prompting from anyone how four Visiting Teachers, who deal with great numbers of people all the time, appreciate just what they found in your store."

That letter is an unstudied picture of chain stores—of values for those who need them, of opportunity-minded young men, of happy, pleasant salespeople, and of satisfactory dealing.

It is common knowledge, of course, that in recent years a constant stream of vicious and destructive tax proposals has been aimed at chain stores by competitive elements who would like, in that way, to create a subsidy from the public for the benefit of their own private businesses.

Freed from the time-consuming harassment of that sort of thing, it is not too much to hope that chain stores may do a still better job in the maintenance of our American standards of living. At this time when we of America, in common with the whole world, face a tremendous economic task to maintain even the present level of our national stability, it would be not less than folly to risk the destruction, or even the slightest impairment, of so valuable an agency as the chain store.

In the matter of production, the United States, as everyone knows, leads the world. In the matter of distribution at lower costs to the consuming public, the chain stores, as everyone *should* know, lead *all* others.

In the introduction to "Main Street Merchant," Mr. Penney speaks of the industrial growth of the United States since 1902 when he opened our first store in Kemmerer, Wyoming:

". . . We have grown unbelievably great in production and in industry. . . . It is doubtful, however, if our spiritual growth has kept pace with our material development, for there is abroad in the land a notion that society, or government, should do for us what, individually, we lack the moral stamina to do for ourselves."

Those among us whose active lives go back beyond thirty years have seen this lack of moral stamina appear not only among our people but in our affairs of government.

We have seen municipal and state governments surrender to the Federal government powers they should have kept for themselves.

We have seen freedom and liberty extinguished in more than twenty nations.

Twice in less than thirty years we have fought terrible wars to save these precious possessions for ourselves and for others; and, once again, as I write, all remaining civilization is threatened by a few men in the Kremlin whose goal is not peace and good will for mankind but tyranny and slavery for the world.

We have learned in this country that local self-government is the only government that will avoid the disasters that come with the despotism of communism or dictatorship in any form.

Because our strength as a nation lies in local self-government, so does the strength of our Company depend primarily upon local self-government in individual stores in more than one thousand six hundred cities, in the individual management within those stores, and in the caliber of the people who find in this company "an ideal strongly believed in and pursued with a single mind."

In keeping the company this way not only do we best serve our customers but, also, we best serve the thousands of Penney associates who, every day of their lives, challenge the custom of letting others do for them what they should do for themselves.

Index

DATE DUE

2/5/70			
MAR 3 1984			
GAYLORD			PRINTED IN U.S.A.